Why Oh RYE?

Bohemia Bartenders Mysteries
Book Seven

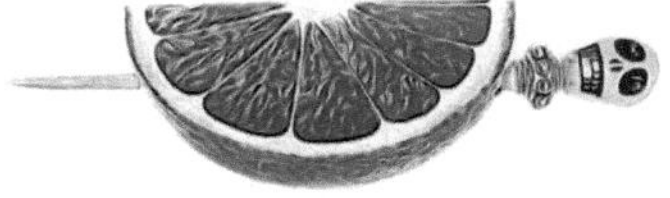

LUCY LAKESTONE

Velvet Petal Press
Florida

Cover design: Sky Diary Productions

First edition

Paperback ISBN: 978-1-943134-47-2

Velvet Petal Press, P.O. Box 922, Cocoa, Florida 32923

Learn more about the author at LucyLakestone.com

About the Book

Bunnies, bonnets and bedlam in New Orleans…

Are the rhyming threats of a crafty con man a good reason to return to New Orleans? Maybe not, but mixologist Pepper Revelle wants to neutralize her nemesis. She hopes she'll have time for cocktails and Easter parades with her friends, too—as well as the next step in her romance with fellow bartender Neil.

But they don't count on finding a body in their hotel room, the machinations of her vexing ex Mr. Mixy, and drama with her quirky family. To clear her name and settle the score, Pepper must crack the case—and figure out if her increasingly dangerous enemy engineered the murder or if another killer is involved.

As they face a farting ghost, an unexpected gig, spooky surprises and the wacky charms of the French Quarter on Easter weekend, can Pepper and Neil unravel the mystery before they're flamed like a lemon peel in a Vieux Carré?

Why Oh Rye? is the seventh book in the Bohemia Bartenders Mysteries, funny whodunits with a dash of romance set in a convivial collective of cocktail lovers, eccentrics and mixologists. These quasi-cozy culinary comedies contain a hint of heat, a splash of cursing and shots of laughter, served over hand-carved ice.

*For Cathy T.
Pen pals are forever.*

Chapter One

You can tell a lot about a woman by what she carries in her purse: a sharp cocktail knife. The printout of our New Orleans hotel reservation. A case for my cat's-eye glasses. Lipstick. Dog treats. A tin of black jelly beans. And a death threat written in two lousy poems, folded and enclosed in pink and yellow plastic Easter eggs.

Yeah, it was a big messenger bag to have room for all of my stuff *and* two rotten eggs from my nemesis. His vague threat included doing something terrible to my parents on Easter. But since he'd already tried to kill me once, I figured death was implied.

I had plenty of reasons to be nervous about returning to my hometown of New Orleans. My nemesis was one. But topping the list was the handsome guy with the trim, dark beard in the driver's seat next to me.

Neil, leader of the Bohemia Bartenders and author of a popular cocktail book, shouldered his big, black SUV into the narrow, bumpy streets of the French Quarter. Its sidewalks teemed with tourists and locals, cooks having a smoke, musicians playing in front of open instrument cases, and the occasional party of bridesmaids prowling in their hunting gear of sashes and tiaras. As a soft April dusk set in, the lights came on, injecting a neon glow into the dense cityscape.

My aunt sat one row back with our dog Astra, a sweet Cavapoo, who barked as she spied a fluffy little dog dyed in purple and green for the holiday. The other three Bohemia Bartenders had already arrived, along with a few other friends who'd chosen to fly. But Neil wanted his car handy, since we didn't know where this weekend would take us.

"This isn't how I wanted to come back to New Orleans," I said.

"It'll be all right, Pepper." Neil reached over and squeezed my hand.

I warmed at his touch and smiled at him. "I hope so."

"We'll have fun," Aunt Celestine said. "Should be perfect weather for the parades."

She'd been weirdly cheerful about this trip, despite the threat to me and my mother—her sister. But she didn't take much crap from anyone. A retired NASA engineer in her fifties, she wrote science-based books about plants and healing. We each lived in half of a duplex back home in Bohemia Beach, where we shared the backyard and the dog.

She'd been my substitute mom and best friend for years after my parents shipped me to Florida in the wake of Hurricane Katrina and never invited me back. She'd even helped me buy my bar. I didn't want anything to happen to her *or* my parents.

Or Neil.

He seemed tense, though he was unusually casual today. We both wore jeans. His T-shirt advertised his bar in Bohemia, The Junction Box. My top was cute and black with a V-neck, and my caramel hair was up.

I wondered if his mind was racing the way mine was. This was a big night for us. We'd finally get to share a room.

He'd moved slower than a soused sloth when it came to our

relationship. Oh, his kisses had reached the hot lava stage. Our friendship had grown into something more over the past year. But would we finally seal the deal given the shadow that loomed over us?

I was determined we would, even if it was the last thing I ever did. Though I'd try to make sure it *wasn't* the last thing I ever did.

"So we're all staying at Hydrangea House, right?" I asked Neil. Our planner extraordinaire, Millie, had booked the rooms.

"No, unfortunately. Some of our friends are, but a lot of places were booked since it's a holiday weekend. Millie found rooms in a hotel next door for Barclay, Luke and Melody. The Fantome. It's supposed to be haunted, but they don't mind. They're just happy we only have one gig this weekend."

Wait—*what?* "We have a gig?"

Neil hesitated. "Remember I said someone pinged me about us working an Easter party?"

"Omigod. I'm sorry. Did I blank? I've had a lot on my mind. I must've missed it."

"Well ... I didn't talk about it much. I had to, um, clear up some details."

My tummy did a flip. This evasiveness was not like Neil *at all*. "What's up?"

"Uh, it's an Easter party on Sunday in the Garden District."

I glanced at my aunt, who shrugged. Then I turned back to Neil. "Out with it."

He cleared his throat. "The host of the party wanted a celebrity bartender."

"So they hired you? That's awesome," I told him.

"Not exactly." He braked at a crossroads to let a herd of dudes in matching *May Contain Alcohol* T-shirts walk by.

I got a really bad feeling. "They hired you—us—or not?"

"They hired the celebrity bartender, who hired us."

It took me a second. "Whoa, no."

And as we pulled up under the hotel's porte cochere, there he was, walking into the lobby with a loaded luggage cart: Mr. Mixy.

I opened my mouth and closed it again, trying to process this feeling. It was like someone had stolen the blue cheese out of my stuffed olive.

Not just anyone. Neil.

I couldn't remember ever being mad at Neil. Not *really* mad. The sensation was new and uncomfortable.

But I couldn't believe he'd agreed to work for my ex-boyfriend Mr. Mixy. *And* didn't tell me. The big-bearded mixologist kept showing up to torment me after several years of peace, in which I'd tried to forget I ever had such terrible judgment.

This was the price I paid for joining the Bohemia Bartenders and going out into the world more, mingling with wonderful cocktailians. Our gigs put me into the path of the not-so-wonderful Stephan Sully, as he was known before he found an audience with his cocktail videos online. Now Mr. Mixy starred in a cocktail-themed reality TV show that did annoyingly well in the ratings.

Talk about a mood-killer.

"You didn't."

"It was the perfect solution to fund this trip," Neil said.

"But you gave this trip to me for Christmas!"

"Yes, of course. And I plan to spoil you. Wait till you see the suite. I mean the job was a way to make it easier for the other bartenders to come along, so they don't have to pay their own way. Luke is trying to pay off his car, and Barclay and Melody have put everything into opening their new bar."

A valet guy hovered briefly outside the closed driver's side window, then stepped away when it was clear no one was in a hurry to move.

"I'll just take Astra out." Aunt Celestine exited the car with our dog and closed the door, letting us have a moment.

My head spun. Luke was Neil's direct employee at The Junction Box. Barclay and Melody had recently quit their bartender jobs to open a beach bar together, though they were still getting it ready; Neil was one of their investors. With all that going on, they'd agreed to keep working with the Bohemia Bartenders for our craft cocktail gigs, which made me happy.

"I'm up for anything that will help our friends," I told Neil. "But did it have to be Mr. Mixy? And we have a lot of other things to think about this weekend."

Like consummating this—I mean, like stopping Beau.

"It's just one party. And maybe Beau will think we're here to work, not play his game, and will leave you alone." Neil's tone suggested he wasn't convinced by this argument, either.

"Beau's twisted invitation was for Easter weekend. He knows if we're here, we're here because of him. And he's not going to forget it."

Neil sighed. "You know I'm not comfortable with you going after him. He wants to get to you, Pepper. Why don't you let the police find him?"

"I called the cops, but they weren't exactly responsive. They sent me to some guy who's simmering the Beau case on the back burner." Detective Colby had sounded skeptical and frustrated by his fruitless search for the con man, who'd tried to pass himself off as my long-lost brother in an attempt to swindle my parents out of a newfound fortune.

"Since Beau has disappeared," I told Neil, "and my parents have been less than helpful, the police haven't had much to go on. But the detective said we could talk once I got into town —*if* I learned anything else. He was not impressed by Beau's poetry."

"You're in danger," Neil said.

"He's targeting my parents," I replied, even though I knew that wasn't the whole story.

"He sent the poems to you. I'm worried he thinks he has unfinished business with you."

"You mean because he didn't kill me in Kentucky?"

"Not for lack of trying."

I shuddered. If it weren't for Neil and my half brother, Royce, I'd be nothing but a memory. "I have to do this. You know that, right? I have to protect my parents, even if we haven't been on the best of terms. Maybe if this detective is helpful, we can get Beau locked up and I can breathe again." I paused. "But that's not really what we're arguing about, is it?"

"I'm not arguing."

I shot him a skeptical look. "Maybe you didn't bring up Mr. Mixy because you didn't *want* to argue with me."

He seemed surprised. "I—I think you may be right. I haven't had much experience with this sort of thing. You know. Relationships. And I didn't want to make you unhappy."

"Neil, you're really good at managing things. But you can't manage *us*. And I want you to know you can always talk to me, even if you think it's going to make me unhappy." I took a breath. "Is there more to this gig than helping out our friends? Did you schedule it thinking I would just forget about Beau?"

Neil stared out the front window and tapped the steering

wheel with his fingers. After a moment, he looked back at me. "I care about you, Pepper. I'll do anything I can to support you. And to protect you." He reached out to grasp my hand again and stroked my knuckles with his thumb. "And yes, I guess I thought if I could distract you with work and a beautiful hotel and some nice meals and cocktails—"

"You can still do that," I said, brightening.

"Good." His smile was wry as he released my hand. "I did mention an Easter gig to you, but you were preoccupied, and once I realized just how awful it would be to tell you we'd be working for Mr. Mixy, I kept finding reasons not to remind you about the job. Including not wanting to make you unhappy. But that's no excuse."

"Oh, Neil. You know why I dumped him, right? Other than the cheating and the fact he turned out to be a horrible person? It was because he was such a liar. And what you're talking about is dangerously close to lying."

Neil looked stricken. "I'm so sorry. I pride myself on telling the truth. Somehow I convinced myself that delaying the truth wasn't as bad as lying. I feel terrible."

"You should." I gave him some side-eye, but I softened it with a smile.

He gave me a tentative smile back. "Can you forgive me?"

"Only because you were looking out for me and the other bartenders. Because you always look out for everyone."

"If you don't want to do the gig, that's fine. You go enjoy yourself, and we'll do it."

"Don't be silly. Of course I'll do the gig with you. Just don't spring any more delightful surprises on me," I said. "Tell me what you're thinking, OK? You can be unreadable sometimes."

"I'm an open book."

I raised an eyebrow at him.

"Except for this," he said.

"See, that wasn't so bad."

"What?"

"Our first real argument as a couple. It's a landmark moment."

He chuckled, looking relieved. "Are we OK?"

"We're OK. Just keep Mr. Mixy away from me as much as possible."

"Done. And thank you for understanding. I'm not used to feeling so muddled."

I wasn't used to feeling so muddled, either. I'd felt a lot for this guy over the past year. It started as infatuation. Now my heart was invested. His little prevarication about Mr. Mixy had hurt. But Neil's desire to spoil me, to protect me—my heart thumped faster to hear him talk like that.

Maybe I just needed to get into that pretty suite Neil promised and see what came next. Or who. Ahem.

A few minutes later, two bellhops rolled carts loaded with our stuff toward the elevators while Neil checked us in at the desk. Aunt Celestine brought Astra in and shot me a questioning look that I returned with a reassuring nod. Then she grabbed a key card from Neil for her room and vanished into an elevator with the dog, the bellhops and their cargo.

I wandered around the lush lobby. Very promising. I was starting to feel happy again when an elevator dinged and Mr. Mixy walked out.

I ducked behind a potted palm, but it was too late.

"Pepper!" he called, striding right over to me, his big black beard bouncing like a poodle running an agility course. His dark hair on top had grown out some, curling a bit. He looked like a Neanderthal hipster in a black leather jacket, button-up orange shirt and *almost* matching plaid pants. "You're here! I'm so glad I could help you out."

"What?"

"Oh, Fairman told me about your secret mission to New Orleans, and since I needed a crew for my celebrity appearance, I talked to Neil about creating a cover for you."

At the volume he was speaking, our "secret mission" was anything but. And why did Mark Fairman, our hunky, well-heeled distiller friend from London, have to tell Mr. Mixy? The last thing I wanted was Mr. Mixy's brand of "help."

Neil stepped away from the counter. His brow creased as he saw Mr. Mixy talking to me. "Pepper?" he called.

"Looks like I have to go, Stephan. See you later." I side-stepped the beard, grabbed Neil by the arm and headed for the elevators. One opened at my press of the button.

"But Pepper—we're going to have a drink later, right?" Mr. Mixy's plaintive voice followed us into the elevator.

I glowered at Neil as the door closed.

"I'm sorry?" Neil sounded pained.

I let him off the hook and laughed. "You are in so much trouble."

An anxious smile crossed his lips.

I tried to forget my furry ex as we took possession of our fifth-floor suite, our luggage in a pile near the door, the grinning bellhop leaving with a fat tip.

We stood in an elegant living room whose windows offered a glimpse of the Mississippi River. The decor blended modern comfort and nineteenth-century style, very New Orleans, with plump pastel furniture and antique-looking lamps.

The wallpaper's pink roses were lovely. Even lovelier was the grand bouquet of showy flowers that sat on a round, marble-topped, claw-footed table flanked by two ornate Queen Anne chairs.

On the table, a silver tray held two rocks glasses, a silver ice bucket glistening with condensation, a nice bottle of rye whiskey, Peychaud's Bitters, a jar of sugar cubes, a couple of lemons, and a small spray bottle I guessed held absinthe.

"Aw, are you going to make Sazeracs?" I dropped my messenger bag on the floor and walked over to Neil, who still seemed worried. I slipped my arms around his waist and beamed up at him.

He visibly relaxed and pulled me close. He ran a finger along my cheek. Then he leaned in for a warm kiss that made me want more. "Will this do?"

"It's perfect. But are we going to sleep on the couch?"

He laughed and released me. His voice was rough as he gestured to the double doors. "I think the bedroom's in there."

"We should take a look, then, hmm?" Our friction forgotten, all I could think about now was where the magic would happen.

He nodded, his gray eyes smoky. I grabbed him by the hand and pulled him toward the double doors, and we each grasped a handle and pulled. Then we stepped inside.

A big canopy bed loomed in the dim light. Canopy beds were so romantic. This was really happening!

I turned to Neil as he reached to the wall and flipped on a light. I was about to pull him in for another kiss when his eyes widened. He stared over my shoulder toward the bed, and a chill shot through me.

I spun around. And then I screamed.

Chapter Two

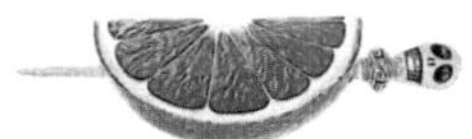

"What is that?" I screeched.

I probably should have said "Who is that," but deep inside I knew the who had become a what. A person lay in the bed, atop the covers, without the slightest movement, breath or reaction. Oh, yeah—and a knife stuck out of his chest.

Neil released me with a slight touch that told me to stay where I was as he stepped forward and leaned closer. "Better call 9-1-1."

"On it." I sounded cooler than I felt. I went to the phone by the bed, hit the emergency number, quickly gave our hotel, room number and situation, and hung up. A moment later, the phone rang again, and I answered with a touch of fear, given who had lured us to New Orleans this weekend. "Hello?"

"This is the front desk. We see you've called 9-1-1. We're going to send up a manager. Are you all right?"

If "all right" meant alive but freaking out, then ... "Um, yes, but the guy we found in the bed isn't. Pretty sure he's dead."

"I'm sorry to hear that. Don't touch anything. We suggest you step out of the bedroom and wait."

"OK." I hung up, still shaky. "I guess the hotel got an alert. They're sending up a manager. They want us to step out."

"This place is going to be overrun in a few minutes," Neil

said, but he lingered at the foot of the bed. "Looks like he was stabbed to death."

"Um, yes. Unless he was poisoned or something first."

"Right." He looked over at me. "Sorry for stating the obvious. I'm a little—"

"Shaken up? Tell me about it." My mind spun with thoughts of who could have done this and why. The scariest of these scenarios was that Beau had done it because I was here. Not that it was all about me.

I circled around to where Neil stood, clutched his arm and looked over the body. The man was in his late twenties, maybe. He had longish black hair with a wave to it, and his mouth and eyes were open, his face drained of color. Blood had soaked through his white ruffled shirt, and over that he wore a dark green velvet frock coat and black trousers.

"No shoes," I said. "Oh, wait. I see boots on the other side of the bed. What's that other thing on the floor?"

Neil stepped toward the pile of black fabric and examined it without touching it. "Maybe a cape?"

"Weird. Does he think he's Batman? Otherwise, it's the wrong season for those socks." They were gray with little black bats on them.

"Vampire cosplay?" Neil asked as the sound of sirens encroached on the silence.

"There's some kind of cosplay going on, unless he usually dresses like Oscar Wilde. And that knife or dagger or whatever is pretty fancy." I looked away. This was a little too real. "Let's get out of here."

"Good idea." He put an arm around my shoulders and led me out of the bedroom. We left the doors open. All I could think was that our fingerprints were already on the door handles and the phone. Not the knife, though.

"Did Beau do this?" I asked as we entered the sitting room.

"Good question."

But we couldn't discuss it further, as a knock came at the door. When I opened it, I was surprised to see Aunt Celestine and our dog.

"Did I hear you scream?" Leave it to my aunt to recognize my scream from two rooms away.

Astra pulled at the leash to get to me, and I picked her up. "Yes. I'm OK. But you probably don't want to be here." The next moment, the sound of an elevator ding and a crowd tramping down the hallway heralded an army of emergency personnel, starting with an ambulance crew. Not that they could do much good. We directed them to the bedroom.

As more people poured in, I hugged the wall with Astra and Neil and my aunt and told her what we saw.

She gave me a hug. "Maybe I'd better take Astra back to my room."

"Please do. I'll update you soon." I handed over the dog, whose tail wagged at the increasing commotion.

My aunt had to tell a police officer who she was and where she was going as she headed out. Also crowding the room that had seemed so large when we arrived were a couple of uniformed police, black-clad women on the crime-scene crew, a hotel staffer with a name tag, and then, I figured, a couple of detectives. They just had that look.

One was a pale, husky guy with a silvering brown crew cut, a rumpled white shirt, sport jacket, patterned tie and brown pants. With him was a portly fellow with an umber complexion, a suit, bow tie and glasses. They had a discussion and went into the bedroom. Then the scruffier one emerged and came to us.

"Which of you is Pepper Revelle?" he asked in a two-pack-a-day voice.

"That's me. I made the call."

"So we meet at last. I'm Sean Colby. Detective. We spoke on the phone."

My eyebrows lifted. "It's you! How did you end up here?"

"I heard your name on the dispatch and made sure I was volunteered. Homicide's not usually my bailiwick, but Beau Moritz is a special case. First, tell me what happened. And then we'll talk about whether this is linked to your little friend."

I let the "friend" comment slide. "Beau Moritz?"

"His real name. You didn't know? He has a lot of names." He whipped his phone out of a jacket pocket, tapped a few times and showed me a picture of Beau—a mug shot. It was startling to see him again, though he was noticeably younger in the photo—maybe in his twenties—than the last time I saw him. Now he was around forty, though he had an ageless quality. Even in the mug shot, he was mischievously attractive, with a square jaw, dark blond short hair, pale blue eyes and light freckles. He looked like someone you wanted to know. Until you didn't.

"I don't know much, apparently," I replied to Colby. "We just got here. This is Neil. What else can you tell us about Beau?"

Colby scrolled down to a list. "He's from Texas. He had a couple of arrests there for minor crimes. Did less than a year for writing hot checks before he got clever. Hence the mug shot. And I have a list of scams I suspect him of running. But I need more evidence. And I need to find him. My primary concern right now is that you found a body in your hotel room that may or may not be linked to Beau Moritz, since it's now linked to you."

Through the next several minutes, we told Detective Colby how we found the body and answered his questions. His colleague drifted through and asked a few more, and then we were alone with Colby again. Well, not alone. The room was still full of people. It was getting late. We'd spent all day in the car. I was hungry, cranky and worried. And I had no idea where to go next, because there was no way we were staying in this room.

"Do you think Moritz—uh, Beau did this?" the detective asked me.

I shrugged. "I was going to ask you the same thing."

"I haven't been able to pin any murders on him yet, but given he almost killed you, he's capable. Do you think he's sending you a message?"

"I don't know. The only messages I've had so far are bad poems in plastic Easter eggs."

The detective reviewed his notes, then looked at Neil. "He ever contact you?"

"Never," Neil said.

Detective Colby turned back to me. "A little nervous, are you?"

I tried to keep my face stoic, but my voice gave me away. "As much as you might expect."

"So you're on edge? Worried about running into Beau?"

"Yes. But I mean I want to run into Beau, or rather find a way to keep him from doing something to my parents. I was hoping you'd help with that."

Sean Colby ignored my remark. "So if you found someone waiting in your room, you might've attacked first, asked questions later?"

"What?" I stared at him.

"No," Neil intervened. "We went into the dark bedroom and found the man there when we turned on the lights. We didn't kill anyone."

The detective almost seemed amused as he regarded Neil. "Protective, are you?"

"He's not protecting me!" I cried. "It happened just like he said."

"Uh-huh. We'll be fingerprinting you both."

"The police already have mine," I said.

"Oh, really?" Colby narrowed his eyes at me. "This should be good."

"I didn't commit a crime. There was some trouble last year when we came to New Orleans."

"Uh-huh." The detective rolled on as if he hadn't just accused me of murder. "Did Beau ever say anything to you about ghost tours or a guy named Ed or Edgar?"

"No. Is that who's in there?" I asked. "What does he have to do with ghost tours?"

"He's a tour guide," the detective said. "Goes by Edgar Poeville. Real name's Ed Potts. Kind of a character around here. Ran Ghostville Tours. Pretty well known. One of his stops is the place next door."

"The Fantome hotel?" Neil asked.

"Yep," Colby answered. "All right. Even if you didn't kill him—"

"We don't even know him!" I interrupted.

He smiled and shook his head. "Don't be surprised if my colleague wants to ask you some more questions later. Also, don't do anything stupid, like trying to track Beau down."

"We think he's going to try to get to my parents this weekend, based on the poems," I said. "Can you give them any protection?"

"I already tried," he said. "They were having none of it."

Argh. My parents were clueless, stubborn or both. "I'll talk to them again."

"You're in town for a few days?"

"We leave Tuesday morning," Neil said.

"Fine."

"May I have your card?" Neil asked. "We can call or text if we see Beau."

"Just no sexting. HR hates that," the detective said dryly as he handed a business card to Neil. "Welcome to New Orleans."

He left to head into the bedroom, and the woman who'd been hovering nearby came over to us.

She had radiant brown skin and wore a crisp skirt and blouse and a sympathetic look. "I'm Maybelle Jones, the manager of this hotel. I'm told it will take several hours for the police to finish their work. I'd love to move you to another room, but I'm afraid there isn't one available."

"Nothing?" Neil asked. I felt worse for him than for me. He'd gone to all the trouble of reserving this pretty room and ordering the flowers and Sazerac setup.

"I'm afraid not. We will of course refund your money and, in addition, offer you a comp room when one becomes available."

"Not this one. Not ever," I said.

"Of course." But I could tell she was thinking about when she could get her suite back and fill it again with paying customers.

"We could try next door," Neil said.

"I called Mr. Joshi—he's the owner of the Fantome—and he said they don't have anything either," Maybelle said. "I've done a little looking. We might be able to get you into one of the convention hotels across town ...”

"Oh, Neil." I didn't mean to whine. But this sucked.

He put an arm around my shoulders and addressed Maybelle. "When will you have an opening here again?"

"Monday night. In fact, I should have a suite available on the eighth floor then. That's the top. It's very nice. I can reserve it for you if you like. No charge."

"Yes, please," Neil said. "We'll see if we can find an alternative in the meantime."

"I understand." Maybelle looked relieved. "Let us know if we can move your luggage to the lobby for you."

"I have a thought," I said as she walked away. "Royce is staying here, right?" I hadn't had a chance to talk to my half brother yet, but I knew he wasn't planning to stay with his parents. In fact, he'd left his Kentucky distillery for the weekend just to tell my mother *he* was the baby she gave up when she was a rebellious teen, before she found religion and founded a church with my father.

Neil nodded. "Yes, he is. So are Mark and Diana."

"Each in their own room," I noted. Though I had hopes of matchmaking Mark Fairman with his brilliant botanist-on-retainer after their sparks over Christmas, I didn't think they'd taken that step yet. "Maybe one of them is in a suite and can put one of us up? Worst case, my aunt has a king, I think. There might be a couch. I can stay with her. Or I could call Melody ..."

"Those rooms are small at the Fantome." His tone was mournful. "I'm sorry, Pepper. This wasn't what I planned."

"You didn't plan a murder? How careless of you."

He chuckled then and wrapped me up in a hug. I felt better when he released me a few moments later.

"I'll call Aunt Celestine first," I said.

Ten minutes later, we had a plan. Mark Fairman, who never did anything halfway, had booked a suite with two bedrooms for himself and put Diana Silva in her own double room with two beds. I'd stay with her, and Neil would room with Mark.

Meanwhile, the bartenders had been out drinking while they waited to hear from us, and they agreed to meet us for dinner in the restaurant in their hotel. A couple more phone calls, and Royce and our rum-collector friend who lived in New Orleans, Conan Cray, were on board as well.

Maybelle had vanished, but Neil called the front desk and asked them to move our bags to our respective rooms a couple of floors up. Then he let a crime-scene tech scan his finger-prints as I grabbed my messenger bag from another officer. She'd dumped it out and taken her time cataloguing the copious contents before throwing everything back in.

I surveyed the continuing chaos in the room, listened to a rain shower pattering against the windows, and rubbed my brow. I not only had to head off Beau; I had to solve a murder. Had he left us the terrifying gift in the next room? Even if he hadn't, Neil and I could both be suspects.

I picked up the flowers and looked at Neil, who was heading back to me. "Can you pack the Sazerac stuff in your bar bag?" I asked him. "I think we're going to need it."

Chapter Three

My list of favorite bars to revisit in New Orleans was long, but I had no problem with meeting our friends at Fantome. From what I'd read, the hotel's owners had spiffed up the place, and the bar-restaurant there had improved over the past few years. Besides, I always liked trying new-to-me places.

Tonight, I wasn't picky, as long as I could get a drink. And since I wasn't rooming with Neil—alas—I didn't have access to the rye.

I'd calmed down a bit, and Diana was happy to welcome me into her spacious room, where I freshened up and donned a daisy-dotted light green dress that cheered me and complemented my lichen-colored eyes. I put my hair up and wore my geek glasses, dangling flower earrings and my good-luck gator-tooth bracelet. I'd worn it since my last visit here, when a voodoo priestess gave it to me—while cajoling Neil to make a donation.

Diana sported a modified version of the usual adventure outfit she wore when traveling the world in search of botanicals for Mark's gin: khaki pants, a white blouse, a pretty scarf and subtle silver jewelry. In her thirties—a decade I would join on my next birthday—she had short, dark hair and intelligent brown eyes and rarely wore makeup, though her amber skin glowed anyway. I'd gotten to know the English botanist better over the holidays after some trouble in the swamp at home in Florida, and I found her warm to her friends, cool with strangers and impatient with stupidity.

Via texts, we told the guys we'd meet them at the Fantome. I gave Diana the details of what happened as we walked over from Hydrangea House through the lively evening crowds. The showers had stopped, but the streets were wet. The pavement reflected the neon of the bars across the street while smelling of rain and faintly of booze.

"So our hotel room is a crime scene," I concluded the story.

"How ghastly!" Diana said in her crisp accent.

"At least it wasn't someone we knew."

"Indeed." Diana looked troubled for a moment. "You have enough to worry about."

"I know. I wish we had a better plan to deal with Beau. The best thing seems to be to make sure my parents are on guard, maybe under protection, but they've blown off the only detective who cares. Still, maybe he'll try again now that we found a body in our room."

"One would hope," she said.

Fantome might not be as luxurious as Hydrangea House, but it had a lot more New Orleans charm. Balconies—or, technically, galleries, since posts supported them—encircled the second and third floors of the corner building, trimmed with intricate cast-iron railings. Black shutters accented the red brick, and hanging baskets of ferns and flowers added a touch of romance.

As we approached, the tourists in front of us stopped in their tracks to whip out their phones and photograph its iconic facade.

To get to the bar-restaurant, we had to go through the lobby. Black and white tiles formed a checkered pattern on the floor, and black marble and brass accented the front desk.

The lobby smelled a little funny, in spite of a heavy fake floral scent that should've masked anything. Maybe the funk was just the miasma creeping in from the street. My supernose tended to pick up odors no one else could detect, and I almost preferred a little stink to a cloud of cloying chemicals.

We headed through the glass doors into the modestly busy restaurant, which adjoined a pretty courtyard I could see through the windows. It smelled better than the lobby, too—of whiskey and something delicious cooking in the kitchen. The bar gleamed with rich, dark wood and more black marble. The shelves of the subtly lit back bar behind the two bartenders were stocked with a robust selection of premium liquors, along with the usual lowbrow stuff for casual tourist drinkers.

My aunt leaned against the bar, sipping a glass of wine, her silver-touched red curls fluffing around her shoulders.

I smiled. "How's Astra?"

"Asleep after a good dinner," she said, then turned to hug Diana, a fellow plant nerd. "It's great to see you."

"Especially in an alligator-free zone," Diana replied.

"Not necessarily," I said. "Depends how far out from New Orleans you go."

"Lovely ladies," said the male bartender, sidling up to us. He had wavy black hair, deep brown eyes and a come-hither grin. "What can I get you? Wine? Cocktail?" *Or me?* was implied.

"This is Jai. He's very helpful," Aunt Celestine said in a dry tone.

"Thank you, pretty lady," he said. He must call everyone lady, and ladies were thin on the ground in New Orleans.

"I'll have a Sazerac, please," I said.

"A gin and tonic for me," Diana added.

"Coming right up." He called out to the young woman working her butt off serving other customers at the end of the bar. "Sazerac, Avani!"

Avani, maybe in her early twenties with lustrous brown eyes and long hair that fell over her shoulders in mahogany waves, gave him a withering look. She finished her current order, then set about making my drink as he worked on the gin and tonic.

"My little sister," Jai said. "She likes to keep busy. She's also better at this than I am."

I chuckled. At least he was honest. "You're not really a bartender?"

"I'm tending bar, aren't I?" He gave Diana the G&T and headed down the bar to greet another pretty lady.

"He told me their father owns this hotel," my aunt said. "How are you?"

"I'm OK. Better now." I accepted the cocktail from Avani, paid for it in cash with a good tip, then took a sip. "This is really nice," I told her. "Your brother implied you're the real bartender around here."

Avani smiled. "I'm more of a hotel manager than a bartender, but you have to know how to do everything."

"So your dad isn't the manager?" I asked.

"Owner and manager, but he travels a lot to his other properties, so Jai and I are in charge most of the time." She glanced at her brother, who was flirting hard with his latest customer. "I'm almost finished school for hotel management. We're trying to take this place to the next level."

"Well, these are a good way to start." I lifted my glass to her in a silent toast.

"Thanks. Enjoy. I have to go take care of manager things. My father's heading out of town tomorrow afternoon and has a to-do list for me." She turned and vanished through a door behind the bar.

I turned to my aunt. "This Sazerac definitely makes my day better."

Aunt Celestine chuckled and gave me a sympathetic look that suggested she understood everything, from the trauma of finding the body right down to my disappointment at being separated from Neil.

And then the man himself appeared, entering the bar with Mark Fairman.

"Hot Pepper!" Mark called out in that delicious, deep, slightly gruff English voice, leaning in to buss my cheek. The redheaded distiller was as sexy as ever in an open-collar light green dress shirt and brown trousers. "Diana, darling." He kissed her cheek, too, and I could swear he lingered for a microsecond. *Hmm.*

Neil came to me, now dressed more like his usual mixologist self, complete with vest and bow tie. He looked me over with a smile and kissed me lightly on the lips. Behind his back, Mark winked at me. He was so naughty. Was he trying to provoke my boyfriend? My boyfriend—the way things were going—I might never share a bed with?

Or if I did, would I always imagine a corpse dressed like a nineteenth-century vampire stealing our blankets? Yuck!

One crisis at a time, Pepper. At least you're not in jail.

The rest of our crowd tumbled in. I hugged Royce, my half brother with the same color eyes as mine and hair a shade more brown than my caramel. I'd already told him what was going on when we made our phone calls earlier.

"How're you doing?" he asked.

"I'll survive. I hope." I grinned at him. "I'm glad you're here."

"So am I, I think." His smile held a hint of irony. "We'll see how it goes with your mom. What we both need is a nice whiskey."

"This is pretty good." I offered up the rocks glass with the Sazerac, and he took a sip, lifted his eyebrows in appreciation and gave it back to me.

Barclay and Luke arrived, each wearing aloha shirts—Barclay's had a black background and green palm fronds that brought out the color of his amber-flecked green eyes and complemented his light-brown complexion. Luke wore a light blue shirt printed with scattered white hibiscus. Slender, he had longish, gold-streaked brown hair and brown eyes, along with pale pretty-boy features that we teased him were right out of a teen vampire movie.

While Barclay's arms displayed tattoos of a dragon and Korean characters, Luke's showed monkeys and parrots and tropical foliage.

Melody, one of my best friends at home, made the most of her entrance in a short, skin-tight white dress, her blond hair piled high, her blue eyes lined with dramatic makeup. Her lack of sleeves meant her tattoos of flowers and musical notes were on full display on her arms.

She rushed right over to me and gave me a hug, then held me at arm's length and scanned my face. "What happened?"

"Give us a second and I'll tell you. It's good to see you."

"I *know.*" She released me, put one hand on her hip and waved the other up and down to show off her look. Everyone within earshot laughed, but Luke turned pink. He was still crushing on her.

He'd better hurry up. Melody was making big changes in

her life. She'd partnered with Barclay to open that bar in Bohemia Beach. While Barclay already had a sweetheart—Gina, my business partner Jorge's youngest sister—I wouldn't be surprised if finding a guy more serious than her usual fare might be next on Melody's list.

"How's the hotel?" I asked her.

Melody shrugged. "It's nice. A little creaky. Small rooms. They say it's haunted. I mean, it's in all the marketing materials. Apparently they even renamed the hotel to double down on the ghost mystique."

"Paranormal tourism?" I suggested. I wasn't sure I believed in ghosts, but I'd seen some weird stuff in NOLA, like the voodoo priestess who looked into my soul during our last visit. I had a feeling she was the same woman who'd told Royce that he was destined to meet me, if not in so many words.

Conan Cray walked in, clad in a cream-colored linen suit, his flyaway white hair contained by a straw hat. Our elder statesman smiled and shook hands all around, his pale blue eyes crinkling.

"Kayanne Pepper," he said, using my given name. I loved hearing his drawl; he was originally from Savannah and still had the accent. "I understand you're here for a purpose. I do hope some drinking will be involved."

"Mr. Cray." I hugged him. "After what happened earlier, drinking is absolutely essential. Why don't we get a table so we can fill you in?"

Neil talked to the hostess, who got us seated at a long table, and we ordered more drinks from a friendly waiter.

"Is that an extra chair?" I asked Neil after I ordered another Sazerac and he requested a Vieux Carré.

"No. I'm expecting one more."

I looked at him curiously, and then the doors opened again

and a familiar man with deep brown skin and a big smile entered. He carried a motorcycle helmet but wore a porkpie hat, leather jacket, white T-shirt and dark jeans. He waved at Neil and sat on the other side of him. Then he looked at me.

"Oh my God," I said. "Tuba Guy."

He chuckled. "Kirby. Kirby Banks. Nice to see you again."

"You gave me his card after our last visit, remember?" Neil said to me after shaking Kirby's hand. "He's working on a cocktail app for me."

"Oh, yeah." I looked at Kirby. "You're a jack of all trades, if I remember correctly." He was the guy who not only played jazz tuba at agonizingly late hours outside the Hotel Lebeau but drove a rideshare, built furniture and wrote software.

Kirby nodded. "I know a lot of people, and I know how to get around. Neil thought I might be able to help you out, so he hired me on an as-needed basis for the weekend."

"Well, I really appreciate it," I said sincerely. "I appreciate both of you. Just don't play the tuba outside our hotel."

He laughed again. "I'm too busy now to be there every night, but I still like Royal Street."

"Good." That was halfway across the Quarter.

"You could always come hear my band instead."

"Now that sounds good."

As everyone settled in with their drinks, chatting, a new person entered.

Backlit, the man loomed ominously, a shadow presence. And like the proverbial needle screeching to a halt on a record, the chatter stopped.

Chapter Four

The shadow man came into the light and stopped to stare at me.

"Pepper, weren't you going to invite me to dinner?" Mr. Mixy's voice held a tremulous pathos that was almost convincing.

I let out a breath now that I knew it wasn't Beau. "Does he have a tracker on me?" I whispered to Neil.

"Mixy!" Barclay called. "Come sit by us." He nudged Luke, who got up and dragged over a chair for the big-bearded mixologist.

Thank you, I mouthed to Barclay.

"I'm afraid that's my fault," Mark murmured from his seat across from me. Mr. Mixy looked our way longingly and sat at the other end of the table. "I ran into him in the lobby and spilled the beans about dinner."

"You're dangerously sociable," Diana admonished him.

"It's part of my charm," Mark countered.

Diana seemed amused. I'd gotten over Mark's flirty charms. Mostly. But man, that voice—and that accent! I supposed Diana was immune to the accent, since it wasn't really exotic to her. As for his muscles—I saw her sneak a glance or two at him when he wasn't looking.

After we ordered dinner, Neil clinked his glass, the sort of thing he usually did before a toast. But that wasn't how he started. "I'd like to explain why we were so late this evening."

"Whoa-ho-ho! Boom chicka-wow-wow!" Barclay and Luke began until I froze them with an icy glare. They looked sheepish and shut up.

Neil allowed himself a half smile. "It's because we had to talk to the police. We found a body in our hotel bed. A *dead* body," he added to head off any more hoots.

Those who weren't in the know exclaimed at the news, and it was a minute before Neil and I could tell them what we saw. All of them knew about my fears of Beau and why we'd chosen Easter to come to New Orleans, so naturally the first questions were about him.

"Did Beau do it?" Melody asked with more than a little trepidation in her voice. She'd succumbed to his wiles in Kentucky before we knew what a bad egg he was.

"We don't know," I said. "The cops don't know either. They have no idea where he is."

"How did someone leave a body in your room without anyone noticing?" Cray asked.

"A very good question," I said. "They had to have access. And to get him through the room without leaving a trail of blood—well, he was probably killed there."

"In the bed," Barclay mused. "That suggests a lot of things."

He had a point. Was Edgar Poeville having a romantic assignation? Or was he meeting someone there for another reason?

"And you say he's a ghost tour operator? What's his deal?" Luke asked.

"We have to figure out all of those things," I said. "If we don't, I'm worried we're going to be arrested for his murder."

"I'm not too worried about that," said Neil, whose imagination wasn't as dark as mine, "but I'd like us to figure out if Beau did this. Maybe he's trying to send us another message."

"Do you have the messages from before?" Royce asked. "Maybe you can read them to us again."

"I have them." I pulled the eggs out of my purse.

"Why do you have eggs?" Mr. Mixy said.

"Shhh," Barclay told him. "Watch and learn."

So I read them Beau's two poems, which I'd received separately in small boxes over the holidays.

> *In her trusting little mind,*
> *Mama's eggs are scrambled.*
> *Who's to say just who she'll find*
> *in NOLA while I ramble?*
> *Brothers come and brothers go*
> *but mother, she'll stay true*
> *to the man she knows as Beau.*
> *The yolk will be on you.*

"So he's saying your mom thinks Beau is her son," Royce said. "I need to talk to her as soon as possible to tell her otherwise."

"And I need to talk to her too," I said. "Tomorrow, we'll go together. Here's the other poem."

> *Did you like my little song,*
> *the Ballad of Beau Reed?*
> *If you think I'll do no wrong,*
> *consider this a seed.*
> *Your fear will grow as you realize*
> *I have them in my sights.*

In spite of you, I'll win my prize
as Easter turns to night.

"He's a terrible poet," Cray said.

"But he clearly possesses a rhyming dictionary," Mark added.

I smiled as the others laughed. "It's effective enough. It sounds to me like he plans to finish his con of my parents by Easter night."

"It's the 'fear' part I don't like," Neil said.

"Me either. We'll do this carefully." I took a comforting sip of my Sazerac, savoring the lovely rye and the hint of absinthe. "First we'll figure out if we can run interference with my parents. And I want to see if we can find the return address that was on the packages, though Google Maps doesn't seem to think it exists."

"We should start with your parents first," Neil said as our dishes started to arrive. "If we can get them to accept police protection, maybe we can relax."

And maybe Astra will learn to fly.

I looked at Neil. "Even if they're safe, we still have a murder to solve."

"They have police for that, too."

"Police who think we're good suspects."

"Which ghost tour was it?" Kirby interrupted.

"Ghostville Tours. Detective Colby said the man went by the name Edgar Poeville."

Kirby's eyes widened slightly. "I know that guy. Seen him around doing his tour with a woman in a cape. Want me to call and see if she'll talk to you?"

"Oh, wow, that would be great," I said. "Maybe mid-morning? We need to see my parents first thing tomorrow."

"No problem." Kirby lifted his drink to us, then got involved in a conversation with Cray on his other side.

As the others talked among themselves, Neil lowered his voice. "I said I'll help you, Pepper, and I will. But I can't let you walk into anything dangerous."

I just eyed him and sipped my drink. That ship had already sailed, right into our hotel bedroom. We had to take the fight to Beau. I just didn't know how.

"I'M PRETTY SURE this is going to suck," I told Royce, Neil and Aunt Celestine in advance of our foray to see my parents the next morning.

We stood outside the front doors of our hotel, waiting for the valet to bring the car around, scarfing the beignets and coffee I'd picked up at a bakery around the corner. Cafe du Monde was great, but there were other eateries that made the melt-in-your-mouth fried dough treats and didn't have a line that stretched to Baton Rouge.

Astra, attached to my aunt on a leash, barked in agreement. Actually, she probably barked for beignets. I offered her a bite, and she got powdered sugar all over her nose. My aunt gave me a dirty look.

"I'm kind of relieved to finally talk to your folks," Royce said. "It might suck, but at least the truth will be out there."

"Don't get your hopes up," I cautioned him. "They live insulated lives. It's going to be bad enough that we're throwing all this stuff about Beau at them."

"Nothing they haven't heard before," Neil said. "The Beau stuff, anyway."

"We just have to convince them to take protection and

cooperate with the police," my aunt said. "It's not like I can leave Astra with them as a guard dog."

Astra barked again, clearly offended.

"There's the car." Neil tipped the valet, and we all piled into the SUV. "What's the address again?"

I gave him the Lakeview address of my parents' house, and he typed it into his phone so it displayed on the navigation screen.

Hurricane Katrina and a failed canal levee had devastated the pretty Lakeview neighborhood. The roads still buckled in places from the apocalyptic flooding. But it had recovered nicely, as evidenced by my parents' newish two-story brick house. We were rescued off the roof of the old, smaller house by boat, all those years ago.

The white cottage next to them was all spiffed up and for sale. On the other side, kids played in a well-manicured lawn in front of a stately home with pale green siding and gallery porches. This neighborhood was pretty sweet—except for the canal a stone's throw away whose water level flowed above street level even on a dry day, held in place by the levee and wishful thinking.

Aunt Celestine eyed the spring flowers, sculpted shrubs and quirky statuary that flanked the front stoop of my parents' house. "Wow."

"I forgot you haven't been here," I said as Neil parked on the street. On our rare visits in the past, my parents met us out somewhere for dinner, if they could get away from the church or weren't traveling in Central America doing mission work.

"Evangeline is not going to like us just popping in," Celestine said.

"It's an emergency," I answered.

"And even if it weren't, I need to talk to them," Royce

added.

"Everybody ready?" Neil asked.

We headed down the sidewalk toward the few steps that led to the green front door. I held Astra by the leash but was so preoccupied I didn't have a chance to stop her from peeing on the praying garden gnome.

"Astra!" I hissed, pulling her back.

"Let's hope they aren't looking at the video doorbell." Royce pressed the ringer.

The doorbell was new since I was here last. If they were looking at the video feed, they'd see a mostly well-behaved band. In addition to my cat's-eye glasses, a dark red lipstick, subtle jewelry and my good-luck bracelet, I wore blue jeans and a simple black blouse. I fastened one more button in the name of discretion. Neil had on dark jeans, a white button-up shirt, a vest and a skinny tie; Royce, a simple light green polo shirt, tan sport jacket and khakis. Aunt Celestine was comfy in a flowing boho dress.

Astra was naked except for her harness, the hussy. I had no idea how my parents felt about dogs. They never had one in the house.

I was relieved when my father answered the door. He was easier to talk to than my mother.

"Kayanne? Oh my goodness, Celestine? And I recognize you, young man. Neil, wasn't it?" Wow, my dad had a good memory after meeting Neil a year ago. He eyed Royce a bit suspiciously but let us all in. He even reached down to pet Astra.

Kevin Revelle was slight of build—no doubt I got my short genes from him—and seemed a bit more hunched every time I saw him. He was older than my mother by several years, and the difference was starting to show. He wore glasses—real glasses, not like mine, which were more for looks and keeping citrus out of my eyes.

"What on earth are you doing in New Orleans?" he asked as we crowded into the living room. "Do you have another convention?"

"No, Dad. We came to see you and Mom."

"Well. Well, then." He seemed at a loss. "Evangeline!"

"Who was that at the door?" My mother emerged from what I supposed was the kitchen, given she wore an apron over her polyester pants and blouse. She froze as she recognized at least some of us.

She hadn't changed much in a year. She was still more polished than she was when I was a kid, with precision makeup and dyed-black hair.

"Evangeline," Aunt Celestine said warmly, stepping forward and hugging her sister. "What a lovely house you have." Though my aunt raised an eyebrow at the holy manger snow globe collection.

My folks still had photos from their mission work here and there. My eye caught a wink from a new adornment on the wall, a gaudy bejeweled cross that hung next to the larger, more rustic one I'd seen last year. Another souvenir from their missions, maybe. Or a half-price sale at Rhinestone Emporium.

It took my mother a second to respond to her sister with a tenuous embrace. Then she untied her apron, rolled it up and set it on a credenza. "A visit. How nice," she said with little inflection. "Won't you all sit down?"

"I'll get some iced tea." My father scurried through the door she'd come out of.

We found seats around the well-furnished but mostly beige living room. Aunt Celestine chose an antique rocking chair.

Royce landed on the couch next to where I sat, near my mother in her comfy chair. Astra, sensing tension, curled up at my feet, apparently invisible to my mother. Neil stayed in the background, choosing a hard wooden chair at a pretty little antique desk against one wall.

I gestured to him. "That's Neil—he was with me last year when we stopped by?—and this is Royce." It wasn't the time yet to add "your son," so I said, "We met on a job in Kentucky."

"How interesting. Are you a coal miner?" my mother asked him.

Royce snuffled, muting a chuckle. "No, ma'am. I run a distillery and cooperage."

"Oh, I see. So you're in the same business as Kayanne here." Her voice was not approving.

"You might say that."

My father returned with a tray and set it on the wooden coffee table. We each took a glass of tea as he sat in a chair next to my mother.

"It's very good. Thank you," Neil said after a sip.

Holy crap, this was awkward. I wasn't patient enough to wait for more small talk. "Mom, Dad, we need to talk to you about a couple of things."

My father and mother exchanged a glance before looking back at me. "This is fortuitous," my mother said, "because there's something we need to discuss with you." She took a deep breath. "Remember you mentioned that young man Beau after some kind of misunderstanding last fall?"

"You mean when he tried to kill me?"

To my astonishment, she blew right past that, sipped her tea and set it on a coaster on the coffee table. Maybe she didn't hear me. "Well, I was a wayward young woman once upon a time, lured by the sins of the city, and I had a child out of wedlock. I put him up for adoption." When she didn't get the reaction she clearly expected—was she hoping to convey some sort of lesson to me?—she stuttered. "B-Beau, well—he's my son."

"No, he's not. Beau told me the same thing when I met him, but he's a liar." I could have been more diplomatic, but we had a lot of ground to cover, and I had to get through to her. "I'm sorry, but he's an extremely dangerous criminal, and he really did try to kill me in Kentucky. The police told you that, didn't they? Are you still in touch with him? He sent me notes threatening you."

My father's pained expression shifted to one of shock. "You knew about your mother's son, didn't you, Kayanne? How did you know?"

I looked at Royce.

He didn't hesitate, but he spoke gently. "Ma'am, I did a DNA search through one of those services, and I found out something interesting. *I'm* your son."

Her breathing sped up, and sweat broke out on her face. "That's not possible. Beau—Beau—he's—"

"A con man," I said.

"I have some paperwork here on the test results if you'd like to see it." Royce pulled an envelope from his jacket and offered it to her. When my mother didn't take it, my father did.

"What did you say your name was again?" my mother asked my half brother, her gray-green eyes widening as she looked closely at his face.

"Royce." He paused. "Royce Doucet."

My mother's eyes rolled back. She crumpled and slid right off the chair to the floor.

Chapter Five

"Evangeline!" My father's tea glass rattled and sloshed as he plunked it hard on the coffee table and knelt next to my unconscious mother. Celestine jumped up, Royce and I moved in to help, and Astra rushed over to lick her hand. By the time Neil made the few steps over to us, we had lifted my slender mother back into her chair. Her eyes fluttered open a moment later.

"I'm so sorry to give you a shock." Anxiety laced Royce's voice. "Do we need to call 9-1-1?"

The very idea seemed to jolt my mother back into control, though it took a second. "How foolish of me. Of course not. I'm fine."

We waited a minute to be sure as she sat up straight and rubbed her temple. As we settled back into our places, she took a few deep breaths, and my father rubbed her back.

"Are you sure you're all right?" he asked her.

I pressed her tea glass into her hand. "Drink. It's nonalcoholic, I promise."

She looked at me and *almost* smiled at my joke. There was no booze in this house.

After a deep sip, she set the iced tea back onto the table. We all watched her closely as she took a few more breaths. Her posture straightened. She folded her hands in her lap and turned back to Royce and scanned his features for another uncomfortable minute.

"You look like him," she said.

Royce raised his eyebrows. "My father?"

"Yes. But what I don't understand is, how can you also share his name? Though I knew him as RJ, of course."

"So you believe me?" Royce looked from her to my dad.

"How can I not? I see it now, right before my eyes. Kevin, what do those papers say?"

My shaken father picked up the envelope from the floor, where he'd dropped it when she fainted. He slid out the papers, unfolded them and scanned the first page, then the second.

"You took one of these tests?" he asked her.

"I did, some time ago."

"You didn't ask Beau to?"

"I trusted him," my mother said simply.

My father seemed to have aged a decade in the last few minutes. "These papers seem to verify what this young man is saying."

I smiled a little at "young man." Royce was in his early forties. It had been that long ago when my mother had her short-lived fling with fun. I wished I could go back in time and meet her then, understand what made her a wild child in the first place, however briefly. Her parents were long gone, and I remembered them only as old-fashioned and severe—the way she was when I was growing up.

"To answer your question," Royce said, "my father—RJ, as you knew him—used his family's influence to bend the system and adopt me. With his new wife."

My mother blanched. "He never told me. We haven't spoken since before you were born."

Royce gave her a sympathetic look. "He never told me anything either. My mother—my adoptive mother, that is—she eventually told me I was adopted and encouraged me to take the DNA test, even though my father wouldn't take one and didn't know I knew. So his parents also got a test without his knowledge. And here we are."

My mother nodded slowly. "He was older than me, of course, but I was too selfish and enamored of sin to care. I found out I was pregnant about the same time I found out he was getting married. I told him I was done with him. Giving you up was my penance. And then I found the righteous path."

That was one way to look at it, but I cringed. Of course, I couldn't judge her. She was a kid at the time. Still, Royce was lucky to end up with parents who cared about him, even if they kept secrets and, as Royce told me, his father gave him a hard time about being gay. There probably weren't enough smelling salts in New Orleans to drop that bomb on my mother this morning.

"I'm very glad to meet you," Royce said. I was so proud of him. He was such a gentleman. I hoped my mother would come to care for him as I had.

She nodded like a queen, perhaps not trusting herself to say more. Still processing, I thought.

Maybe it was time to shift topics. "Mom? We have to talk about Beau. The notes he sent me said he was planning something and mentioned Easter specifically. He mentioned getting the 'prize.' You didn't give him any money, did you?"

My mother seemed numb. She rocked slightly in her spot on the comfy chair, staring at her iced tea as if it might boil over.

My father spoke. "He said he was going to invest it."

Uh-oh. "You gave him money? How much?"

"We promised a million dollars, not quite half of what our dear parishioner left us," my father said. "We were looking for ways to invest the money, and Beau was so helpful with different ideas. He said he'd triple it with a real estate deal he was working on. He was also working through his legal troubles, of course, so he had to do it quietly, but he's such a nice boy ..." His voice trailed off in confusion as his old image of Beau clashed with the one we'd painted for him.

"What kind of real estate deal?" Royce asked.

"It's very exciting." My mother perked up. "There's a new theme park planned for outside of New Orleans, and anyone who buys property around it will see the values skyrocket. Beau has copies of the plans. We signed something, so we're not supposed to say who's behind it—we have insider information—but it's a *major* company."

My father held up his hands on his head in the shape of mouse ears and wiggled his eyebrows.

Holy crapnoodles. The Mouse?

But of course it wasn't The Mouse. It wasn't anyone. "He's making it all up," I told them.

"Almost certainly," Neil said. "I read a book about something like this once. Same thing happened in Texas. The scammer told his marks about plans for a major theme park outside of Dallas. He bilked investors out of tens of millions of dollars over several years."

My parents looked at Neil like he'd just pooped in their flower garden. Which I was sure he'd never do. Astra, not so much.

"But he had drawings of hotel plans. Copies of e-mails. Park layouts," my mother said.

"Remember, he also said he was your son? And he tried to

kill me?" I was a little frustrated this detail kept sliding off their consciousness like butter on a griddle. Which made me think of pancakes. *Focus, Pepper.* "So you gave him a million dollars?"

"We haven't given it to him yet," my father said. "We're supposed to wire it to his company later today. He was very specific about the time. Twelve thirty. Something about getting a percentage off one of the real estate deals."

I blew out a breath of relief, but I was still perplexed. "Well, the deal is obviously a crock. So why did he pick twelve thirty?"

"It's Friday," Royce said. We turned our attention to him. "I've learned a little bit about this from my father, since one of his businesses is banking. Wire transfers usually don't happen over the weekends because outgoing funds have to be approved at the bank. If a scammer gets money sent just before the cutoff time—3 p.m. is pretty typical—then transfers it to another account, there's no way to even think about getting it back. There's a whole weekend for the trail to go cold. Not that it's easy to stop a wire transfer anyway."

"Isn't Good Friday a bank holiday, though?" I asked.

"Our bank is open until one," my mother said.

"That must be why he said twelve thirty, to make sure it went through," Royce said. "He probably made sure your bank would approve a transfer sent today, since a lot of banks are closed in Louisiana on Good Friday. But in most states, this isn't a bank holiday, so he may have an account with one of the big national banks or an overseas account or both. Once he gets the money, he can easily transfer it again, and then it's gone forever."

I looked at my parents. "Why didn't he just look over your shoulder and make sure you sent the money to him?"

"Maybe he didn't want to come on too strong," Neil suggested.

"There've been police coming and going in the neighborhood," my mother said. "This detective kept stopping by. If what you say is true and they want to talk to Beau, maybe he thought it wiser not to visit. We haven't seen Beau for weeks."

"But this is good," Aunt Celestine said. "You haven't sent the money. Problem solved."

"Is it, though? Beau tried to kill me." No harm in reminding them one more time. "Is he just going to walk away?"

Neil leaned forward, his elbows on his knees, his hands clasped together. "He's definitely going to ask about it. Maybe we could let him think the money was sent just after the deadline, so the bank didn't process it. So he'll have to wait until Monday to get it."

"That might put him off long enough to get him," I said.

"Get him?" My mother looked horrified.

I nodded. "Arrest him. You know, arrest the guy who tried to scam you out of a million dollars and *tried to kill me?*"

"You always were prone to exaggeration," my mother said.

I lifted my hands in the air and looked to my aunt, who snorted.

"He might be scamming other investors, too," Neil pointed out.

"So we tell Detective Colby what's going on," I said. "And if Beau tries to contact you, Mom, tell him you couldn't get the money sent in time. Tell him you had computer problems."

"I don't like the idea of lying, but he'd believe that," my father said. "He knows I hate that horrible computer. It doesn't work for me half the time. And the links just keep getting longer and longer. My notebook is full of them."

"The links?" I looked at him blankly.

"My favorite websites. I hate having to write them down."

Royce covered up a laugh with a cough. Having my guileless, techno-clueless parents hoodwink Beau wasn't going to be easy.

"You're OK with having the detective put some protection on you for a few days?" I asked.

"We'll be awfully busy with Easter," my mother said, not really answering the question. "In fact, we have a service this afternoon. We have to get going."

"Yes," my father said to me. "I suppose we don't have a choice now, do we?"

"Not a good one, no," my aunt said as Neil looked at his phone.

"Maybe we can see you again tomorrow?" Royce suggested to my mother—his mother. "See how it went?"

"That should be all right," she said. "Please call first."

Zing. Whatever. If managing us helped my mother feel more in control, so be it.

"Call us if you need anything, OK?" I offered anyway.

A minute later, we were out the door, and I nudged Astra just in time so she didn't poo in the flower garden. I used a bag to pick up her present and dropped it in a trash can sitting on the curb.

"That went OK?" Royce posed it as a question after we'd climbed back in the SUV.

I lifted one shoulder. "I thought Mom took your news pretty well."

"Other than the fainting," Celestine said dryly.

We laughed.

I tried to be positive, though I had a feeling this wasn't over. "We headed off Beau's scam. That's got to be good."

"We'll see," Neil replied, starting the engine. Why did he have to be so realistic all the time?

"I hate to ask," Royce said as Neil pulled away from the curb, "but can you drop me at my parents' house? It's in the Garden District. I think it's best I talk to my father now, since Mrs. Revelle knows the truth. I want to go there first, just in case she gets a wild hair to call him."

"Highly unlikely," I said. "That would mean revisiting a time she's written off as her narrowly averted path to hell."

"But *I* came out of it," Royce joked.

I chuckled. "And I'm really glad of that."

"No problem," Neil said after looking at his retro watch. "We should have just enough time to drop you off."

"Meaning what?" I asked.

"I heard from Kirby. The ghost tours aren't taking any time off to mourn Edgar Poeville. He booked us on the ten thirty tour in the Quarter."

"I hope 'us' means you and Pepper," my aunt said. "Astra and I are going shopping."

Chapter Six

We dropped off Royce at his parents' ostentatiously large and elegant house in the Garden District without attempting to join him. Maybe another day. I was really curious about his father for obvious reasons, but the conversation Royce was about to have would be hard enough without him introducing his cocktail-crazy half sister.

As Neil drove us toward our hotel, I called Detective Colby and explained the situation.

"He's running a real estate scam?" The detective sounded skeptical. "How can he do that while he's on the run?"

"Maybe he's only running it on my parents. Either way, I think they believe us now, and they're fine with the police watching out for them for a couple of days."

"Hmph. I'll have to see if I can get somebody now. With all the parades and everything this weekend, we're spread thin. And it sounds like you headed him off."

"I don't know if Beau is just going to forget this all happened," I told him. "He's still trying to get a million dollars out of them. Please do what you can. They're going to their church this afternoon."

"I'll touch base with them and see what I can do. I'd like to nail the guy. If he's running a scam that big, the district attorney and the FBI might be interested too."

"Excellent." We could use all the help we could get.

The detective's tone became less congenial. "So you're leaving this alone, right? My colleague is very interested in you and your boyfriend for the Poeville, er, Potts murder. Don't make it worse for yourselves."

Oh, crap. "We're innocent! We'll let you know if we find out anything."

"What are you talking about? Don't try to 'find out anything.' I read the file on the last time you were here. You're lucky you're not a melted splat of marshmallow on the tarmac. Stay out of trouble, Ms. Revelle."

I ignored his warning and tried to sound chipper. "Thanks for your help!" I snuck a glance at Neil to gauge how concerned he was as I ended the call.

He caught me looking. "What was that all about?"

"He's going to try to get someone to watch my parents, but I'm worried he's not taking us very seriously. Except maybe as murder suspects."

"Surely not."

"His colleague is looking at us, or so Detective Colby claims. I hope we get something out of this ghost tour."

Neil frowned, and I turned to my phone to learn more about the tour.

A few minutes later, we reached Hydrangea House and stopped under the overhang out front. Aunt Celestine disappeared with Astra, the valet disappeared with the car, and after I looked around to make sure Mr. Mixy wasn't following us, we hoofed it to St. Louis Cathedral for the start of the tour.

"Don't you think it's strange they're still doing tours after their leader died?" I said to Neil. We hovered on the edge of a group of about a dozen tourists gathered outside the towering, magnificent church, which gleamed white in the midday light. My stomach growled. I offered him a black jelly bean from the tin I kept in my bag and took one for myself.

He popped the candy in his mouth and chewed. "It's strange, but everything about this is strange."

"True. The website for the tour said there were multiple guides, but Edgar Poeville seemed to be the centerpiece of all their marketing. In all the photos, he wore a getup like the one he had on yesterday."

"Do women like that sort of thing?"

I laughed. "Depends on the woman. And the situation. But after yesterday, I'm pretty sure an outfit like that will never do anything for me ever again."

The woman who approached the group now might feel otherwise about velvet frock coats. Waifish with purple streaks in her shoulder-length black hair, she wore tall black lace-up boots, tight black pants, a purple blouse, a brocade navy-and-black vest and a blue-satin-lined black cape. Multiple ear piercings and a nose ring sparkled in the sun. Goth meets nineteenth-century poet.

"Welcome to Ghostville Tours, my friends! Are you here for the Express Ghost Tour?" She took in our nods. "I'm Lady Sierra, and I'll be guiding you to some of the most haunted spots in the French Quarter this morning. For those of you expecting Edgar Poeville, who was supposed to lead this tour, I have sad news. Edgar himself may soon be on our tour in a completely different way. He was murdered yesterday at Hydrangea House."

She looked suitably sad as the tourists gasped. I blinked, shocked that she would not only callously drop this fact but that she'd graduated Edgar to the status of ghostly attraction.

"Now let me just confirm your tickets," she said.

I leaned closer to Neil as she went around and checked everyone's name off a list on her phone.

"Is it just me, or has she taken the weirdness up a notch? We need to talk to her," I whispered.

"Afterward. And yes, this is all weird."

Then again, so was New Orleans.

The exhausting "express" walking tour sped us through one haunt after another: Priests and a clockmaker at the church. Voodoo practitioners at Congo Square in Louis Armstrong Park. Victims of fires and murder, a pious nun and a vengeful madam haunting rooms at hotels throughout the Quarter. And a horrible woman who tortured slaves at LaLaurie Mansion, now posh apartments. Basically, anywhere you slept in the Quarter, you shared space with a ghost, if Lady Sierra was right.

The last stop was right next to Hydrangea House, where Sierra took a long moment of silence to stare up at our hotel. After she'd given us all the creeps, she took a few steps toward Fantome, taking a spot on the sidewalk that another tour had just vacated. As we gathered around, I spotted a mustachioed man in a suit and tie step out of Fantome, cross his arms and glare at Lady Sierra as she launched into her spiel.

"The Fantome is well-known for being haunted," she said, gesturing to the graceful corner building with its fancy filigree icing. "A jilted opera singer fell to her death from a third-floor balcony, and guests report hearing her singing Verdi late at night. On the second floor, a wounded soldier is sometimes seen limping down the hallways, probably a legacy of when this was a makeshift hospital that cared for wounded Confederate troops during the Civil War, many of whom died horribly. And of course, there's the famous farting ghost."

I snorted a laugh, Neil smiled, and several in the group chuckled. The man standing outside the hotel shifted his stance, his mustache twitched, and his thick, dark eyebrows merged over his hostile stare.

"Legend has it that a writer used to live in a room in this hotel. It was called something else then. The novel he spent years writing was spurned by every publisher he contacted. So he took to drinking himself into oblivion in the Fantome's bar. Finally, he went on an epic binge and ate everything on the restaurant's menu one day back in 1919. He drank three bottles of rye whiskey as well. And then he choked on an oyster. As he perished, he emitted the worst-smelling cloud of noxious gas ever recorded in New Orleans."

"How was it recorded?" someone asked.

"Another drunk writer wrote about it, of course, in the *New Orleans Bee,*" she said, and everyone chuckled. "Even now, you can smell the Fantome farts when the writer is stirred into haunting the guests. They say he appears whenever you order a rye cocktail."

"Enough!" shouted the man standing in front of the hotel. "Begone with you!"

"Facts are facts!" Lady Sierra shouted back at him, then shrugged at us with a smile.

Farts? Facts? Who knew what was true? One thing was clear. This man did not appreciate the legend of the Fantome farts. Could he be the owner, Jai and Avani's father? I wanted to find out.

But we had to attend to Lady Sierra. She wrapped up her tour, asked people to review the company online and graciously accepted tips and condolences for the late Edgar Poeville.

We had to wait for an avid groupie with raccoon eyeliner

and a skull T-shirt to grill her about the farting ghost. Lady Sierra finally suggested he sign up for their haunted bar tour. As he walked off, Neil gave our guide a very nice tip in cash and thanked her for the tour.

"My pleasure." She looked at him with a lot more interest than she gave the ghost groupie.

"We're very sorry for your loss," I said. "We're staying in Hydrangea House, and—the police have asked us a lot of questions."

"You and me both," she said. "Did you see what happened?"

I shook my head. "We didn't see any act of violence. Do you have any theories?"

"I heard he got a knife in the chest. Probably that dagger he always carried in his boot."

I blinked. "Oh! He was killed by his own weapon?"

"I wouldn't be surprised. It was no secret he had it. He was always flashing it around, twirling it for the tourists."

Yikes. "Who would want to kill him?"

"Everybody," Sierra said. "Including that guy who told us to shoo. He owns the Fantome. Doesn't he realize how much business the farting ghost brings in? All his ads now are about the ghosts in his hotel, but he's disowned Carl completely."

"Who's Carl?" Neil asked.

"The farting ghost! At least, that's what we call him." Her impish smile thinned. "Called him. Me and Edgar."

I gave her a sympathetic smile. "Hey, can we buy you a coffee or a drink? I'd love to know more about Edgar."

"I don't have time. I have to reset for a tour at two."

"Please?" My urgency must have belied my gentle curiosity, because she narrowed her eyes at me.

"Why are you asking all these questions?"

"I'm sorry," Neil said. "The truth is, we found his body in our room. The police say we're suspects. We'd just like to know a little more about what happened."

"You're suspects?" Lady Sierra's eyes lit up. "That's pretty cool. Look, I'll give you five minutes. You can buy me a cold drink at the cafe around the corner."

Chapter Seven

It turned out the cafe was the same one where I'd snagged the beignets this morning. It was less crowded now, and we got a seat right away as Neil went to the counter to get our drinks.

"So did they arrest you?" Lady Sierra said.

I shook my head. "Not yet."

"You saw the body, right? What did he look like?"

Ghoulish much? "He was just lying there in his costume in the bed, on his back, with the knife sticking out of his chest."

Instead of being horrified, she chuckled. "Not a costume. He dressed like that all the time. I only do it for the tours."

"When did you find out about Edgar?" I asked.

"Late last night." She looked up at Neil, who set the root beer she'd requested in front of her. He got the same thing for all of us. The old-school glass bottles said, *Drink Barq's It's Good.*

The sweet, cold soda felt good going down my parched throat. "The cops must have come to you pretty late."

"They did," she said, "but I lived with him, so I guess they went to his home first."

I tried not to show how surprised I was. She didn't seem all that upset. "So you guys weren't friends? You just worked together?"

"Oh, we used to sleep together, but that fizzled soon enough. We were roomies and mostly stayed out of each other's way except for the business. He was grooming me to have a bigger role. I did all the website stuff and the paperwork, and I was listed as one of the officers of the corporation, but he was always the guy everyone associated with the tour. The star. And he spent a fortune on promo to make sure everyone knew it." She made a face. "I'm going to make a go of it myself. Maybe hire somebody to help. Now that Edgar's not around to drain the coffers, it should be easier."

Did she realize she'd just admitted to a motive for murder?

"Is your real name Sierra?" I asked.

"Sierra Felt. That 'lady' stuff is just for the tours, you know? Like the costume. Edgar always did look good in a frock coat." She sighed, wistful.

I suppressed the urge to glance at Neil as I recalled his question about whether women dug the vampire look. He didn't jump in, so I kept going. "What did you mean about Edgar draining the coffers?"

"Oh, besides the vanity advertising, he always had some business enterprise or other. That's what he called it. Mostly, I think he was buying and selling, if you know what I mean."

"I don't want to guess."

Sierra ran a hand through her black and purple hair. "He was always hanging out with losers like Alfie Boudreaux and Jai Joshi. Partying. Selling pills, too, I think. I saw him with stuff once or twice, though I never asked. I didn't really want to know. I'm not making much, and I didn't want him to kick me out. At first I thought that's why the police came to the apartment, to talk to him about the drugs. But they just told me what happened, asked a few questions and left."

Wow. "Does Jai work at the Fantome?"

"That's the guy."

"What about Alfie? What does he look like, and where can we find him?"

"Frat boy type, though I think he washed out of school. He sometimes works at this cheesy souvenir shop on the next block. You know, sunglasses and postcards and crappy masks and that kind of thing. It's easy to spot. There's usually a mannequin outside the door wearing a miniskirt and a ton of beads that just cover her tits." Sierra rolled her eyes.

"Sounds classy," I said.

"Don't you know it. Look, I have to get going. I hope the cops don't arrest you. Thanks for the tip and the drink." And then she was gone.

I knocked back the rest of my root beer and looked at Neil.

"She was chatty," he said.

I smiled grimly. "Yeah. And not broken up at all. Her relationship with Edgar would probably be called 'complicated' on social media. Either Sierra's totally innocent and not worried about implicating herself or a sociopath who's cunning enough to cast suspicion on those other guys."

"I suppose we should talk to them."

"After lunch," I said. "I'm starving. Think any of our friends are around?"

"Let's find out." Neil got out his phone and sent a couple of texts—one pinged my phone, since it went to the bartender group chat. I texted my aunt, too.

"Good idea, meeting at Hydrangea House," I told Neil. "If anyone can make it, we can go from there."

We got a couple of pings back as we walked through a freshening breeze to our hotel. It sounded like most of our crew had slept in after staying out late last night.

"Mark says he and Diana will join us as well. They were up early to go to the World War II museum and are just heading back now," Neil said.

"Cool." We stepped into the plush lobby of Hydrangea House. "What about Kirby?"

"He's busy running his empire, but he said he'd be available whenever we needed him. Cray's occupied at home."

"Counting his bottles of rum, probably." I tried texting Royce and didn't get a reply. "Aunt Celestine is coming, but no word from Royce. Maybe he's still visiting his parents."

"At least they didn't throw him out."

"It's not like it's his fault his dad was so secretive. His mom wouldn't let him go anyway. She's been anxious for Royce and his dad to talk things through."

"Ms. Revelle?" came a voice from the direction of the desk. It was Maybelle, the manager. "You got a package."

I halted in my tracks. Neil and I looked at each other with trepidation. Then we both walked up to her.

The box she handed me was slightly bigger than the ones I'd received over the winter holidays. Maybe it wasn't from Beau.

"How did this arrive?" I asked Maybelle.

"A cute little boy brought it in. Said he was a messenger. Then he asked me where the nearest candy store was." Her smile faltered as she took in our faces. "Is something wrong?"

"I hope not." I cradled the package, and Neil followed me to a grouping of cushy lobby chairs. I dropped my bag on the floor, hanging on to the box, and he sat next to me on a love seat that faced a coffee table. I leaned my head against his shoulder for a second. I needed the support.

"You want me to open it?" he asked.

I lifted my head and looked at him. "No way. What if it's from a secret admirer?"

A corner of his mouth twitched. "If only. Your admirers are anything but secret."

I laughed. Then I looked at the box. Brown cardboard, clear packing tape, no return address. "So Beau could've paid that kid in cash to drop this off."

"And the kid went candy-shopping. Makes sense. But it might not be from Beau."

"I'm not going to shake it." I held it to my ear. Did bombs tick in real life? This box was silent. "Should I open it outside?"

"Your call. I'm not leaving you."

"Thanks." I kissed him on the cheek. Then I dug my cocktail knife out of my bag and used it to slit the packing tape so the box would open easily.

"Whatcha got?" came Luke's voice. He and Barclay had appeared, with Melody right behind them.

"Hi, guys. I got a package."

Their cheer sagged into looks of concern.

"It's not from *him,* is it?" Melody asked.

"I don't know yet." I put my knife away and waited as Aunt Celestine got off the elevator with a small rabbit on a leash.

Wait—that wasn't a rabbit.

"You bought Astra bunny ears?" I exclaimed.

My dog sported a pair of tall, pink-lined white ears in addition to her own floppy real ones, not to mention a tiered skirt of sequined tulle ruffles in purple, green and pink.

"Isn't she cute?" my aunt asked. Usually pragmatic, Celestine got carried away when she had a chance to dress up our dog.

"Let me guess. You found a dog store?"

"An *amazing* dog store. I stocked up."

I stifled a groan as Astra came over to me and put her paws on my knees. I scratched behind her real ears as she sniffed the parcel, then looked at me curiously.

"I don't know what it is either, girl." I eased her to the floor, and my aunt pulled Astra back once she realized what I held. "Are we ready to find out?"

I lifted the end flaps of the box.

Chapter Eight

"Ugh! It's horrible!" I exclaimed as I popped open the flaps of the mysterious box.

"What is it?" Melody asked breathlessly as Neil tensed at my side.

"Easter grass! I hate this stuff!" I pulled out a handful of iridescent strands as Barclay laughed and everyone else visibly relaxed.

"Is there anything *besides* Easter grass?" Neil withdrew his arm from my shoulders, sat on the edge of the love seat and watched me closely, ready for action.

"Just a minute. I think there's something." I dug through the froth of plastic grass and touched a smooth and flexible surface. "It might be a bag? I think there's something in it." I pulled out the object as gently as I could and set it upright on the coffee table.

We all just stared at it for a second.

"A chocolate rabbit?" Aunt Celestine asked with skepticism. She sat and held Astra-Bunny so the dog wouldn't jump on the candy critter.

"As you see," I said. The milk-chocolate bunny, about nine inches tall and wrapped in a clear plastic bag taped shut at the top, had a deep pink bow tied around its neck.

"Any messages?" Neil asked. He took the box from me and dumped the rest of the Easter grass on the table. He and Barclay spread it out and checked the box again but didn't find anything else.

"Maybe the rabbit *is* the message," Luke said.

"So," I said, "basically, 'Eat me'?"

They chuckled just as Mark and Diana walked up to us, windblown and rosy from their walk.

"What's all this?" Mark asked.

Diana took in the scene. "I see a box. We don't like those, do we?"

"Correct," I said. "So far this one just has a chocolate rabbit and a bunch of Easter grass."

"And it's not ticking?" Mark asked.

"No. I already checked."

"Well, then." He plopped into one of the comfy chairs. "Should we eat it?"

"No way," I said.

"It looks positively demonic," Diana added. "Perhaps it's possessed."

She had a point.

"Seems to me most of the rabbits I got in my Easter basket were hollow," Neil said. Aw, I got a sudden image of Neil as a little boy tearing into his Easter candy. It was hard to square that picture with the staid Neil of now. I'd have to ask his parents if they had any old photo albums I could look at, if I ever met them, that is.

"I remember hollow rabbits, too," Luke said. "I always bit their heads off."

"Typical vampire move, Twilight," Barclay ribbed him, using the nickname that never failed to annoy his friend.

"Luke's right." Melody's declaration made Luke smile.

No one seemed ready to state the obvious. "So I guess we break it open and see if anything's inside?" At their nods, I leaned forward, pulled the tape off the clear bag's flap and extracted the rabbit. I didn't want to smash it, given I didn't know what might be in there.

"Wait!" Mr. Mixy's shout stopped me cold. He'd just entered the lobby from the street and ran over to us. "Let me have that."

He snatched the rabbit out of my hand and bit the ears clean off as we shouted "Nooo!"

I leaped back as the rest of the head popped off the rabbit's body and fell to the table, along with the ribbon.

I turned to Mr. Mixy. "Have you lost your mind?"

"Well, I figured you weren't going to eat it since you were just standing there holding it."

"Correct. We think this came from my stalker," I told him. Not mentioning that Mr. Mixy was my other stalker.

"Oh?" He looked at the beheaded body in his hand as he kept chewing. "It tastes pretty good."

I stood and grabbed the rest of the rabbit from him. "We're trying to figure out what it means."

"I don't know why you're so upset," my ex said. "Everybody knows you eat the head first, starting with the ears."

Luke crossed his arms and nodded knowingly.

"Not if they might be, I don't know, poisoned," I told Mr. Mixy.

He swallowed audibly. "Geez. That's not very nice."

"*I* didn't poison it." Though if I'd known Mr. Mixy was going to eat it ... *No, Pepper. Take the high road.*

"So what's inside? Anything?" Melody asked.

I sat again next to Neil and looked carefully inside the rabbit's body, turning it so the light hit its innards.

Then I leaned forward and struck the chocolate against the surface of the table, making everyone jump. The rabbit shattered, revealing a folded piece of paper among the debris.

"Not again," Barclay said.

My thoughts exactly. I picked up the paper and unfolded it. "Looks like another poem."

"The only man in America without a phone," Neil said.

I read it aloud.

> *Little Pepper, I'm impressed.*
> *You really make an entrance.*
> *Did you kill your foppish guest*
> *to get dear Beau's attention?*
>
> *You may think you've got it made,*
> *but I hold all the bunnies.*
> *When I finally get paid*
> *you'll see it's very funny.*
>
> *I don't like a double cross*
> *Unless I do the crossing.*
> *You can't stop your parents' loss.*
> *Your life away you're tossing.*

"I see he still has his rhyming dictionary," Mark said. "That last line's a stinker."

"Right? It sounds like Yoda talking," Luke added.

Neil wasn't amused. "He's explicitly threatening Pepper's life."

I took a deep breath and tried to be rational. "I think he's just messing with me. He probably saw the news about the body and couldn't resist."

"The news stories I saw didn't mention our names," Neil said. "How did he know we found the body?"

"He clearly knows we're staying here. That would have been easy enough for a slick guy like him to find out by calling around with a convincing story. Maybe he made a follow-up call when he found out what happened and put two and two together." I grimaced. "Or he killed Edgar and left the body in our room."

Diana sat forward. "What's odd is that he sounds surprised about the body."

"True," I said. "He asks if I killed him. Which I didn't, of course. But he's a professional liar, so I don't think we can take any of this as truth."

Mr. Mixy licked his fingers and eyed the rest of the chocolate pieces on the table. A couple of brown crumbs were melting in his beard. "Maybe I should be your bodyguard, Pepper."

"No," Neil and I said at the same time.

"I had that vision when I was in Florida," the big-bearded one said. "I'm pretty sure one of my purposes in life is to be a guiding light for Pepper. That's one reason I hired you to make drinks at the Easter party."

"Oh, dear lord," I said as Neil uttered, "Holy hell."

"I don't need your guiding light, Stephan," I told him.

"But I'm a celebrity!" Mr. Mixy seemed shocked that I turned down his largesse.

Aunt Celestine ignored him. "What worries me is that Beau seems to think he holds all the cards."

"'All the bunnies,'" I quoted.

She frowned. "I refuse to say 'all the bunnies.'"

"You just did," Luke said. Barclay elbowed him. "Ow. What? She did!"

"When he talks about your parents' loss, do you think he means the money?" Neil's voice got quiet. "Or—the loss of you?"

"I think he's full of Easter grass," I said. "We're ahead of the game. He can't know about our visit to my parents this morning."

"Unless they told him," Neil replied. "Or he had another way of finding out."

"What, like hacking the video doorbell?" I scoffed. Then I realized he might have done just that. Or been watching the house. Or ... but no, he also had to arrange the delivery of the chocolate bunny. But he could have done that while we were on the ghost tour.

I looked up to see everyone staring at me.

"What are you thinking, Hot Pepper?" Mark asked.

"Trying to figure out Beau's timeline. Whether he's watching us and how. And the bunny." I stared at the pieces on the table and the fuchsia ribbon. "He put this together somehow. Look. Is that glue? Those are probably neck pieces." I pointed out the weird residue on some of the chocolate, then looked at Neil. "The ribbon hid the seam. He might've touched the ribbon."

His eyes widened slightly. "Or the bag. Or the piece Mr. Mixy ate."

I looked at Stephan. "Let's cut him open."

Mr. Mixy held a hand over his belly. "What? Why?"

"Fingerprints." I smiled. "Beau probably isn't that dumb, but it's worth a try, isn't it? I'll call Detective Colby."

A few minutes later, after much complaining about bad

poems and Beau and me, the detective agreed to have his lab do a rush analysis for fingerprints.

"I don't think it'll do much good," he said over the phone, "but if I can match the prints to other crimes by your little friend, maybe it'll be worth it. I'll swing by to pick it up. Put it all in a clean bag and leave it at the front desk. And don't pick it up without gloves on!"

"OK," I said. "Uh, we might've already touched some of it. As did the messenger and the hotel staff. And Mr. Mixy bit its ears off."

"I love this case," the detective said sarcastically.

"Well, great! We're going to lunch," I told him and hung up while he was still grumbling. With the help of the front desk and a nice cleaning lady, I used gloves to pack the pieces and the poem in a clean bag. While I was at it, I put the two eggs I'd received at Christmas with a note in a second bag and left it all for the detective.

An hour later, a shrimp po'boy and another caffeinated root beer had done a lot for my mood and my stomach, as had the comfort of being with my friends in a lovely courtyard restaurant surrounded by walls of old brick and dotted with flowering trees.

Astra had quietly shed her bunny ears on the walk over, to my relief, at least until my aunt told me she'd bought a spare pair. The dog still resembled a cheerleader's pom-pom, but she was plenty happy sitting under our table, especially since Mr. Mixy kept dropping bits of shredded pork from his barbecue sandwich. So far, it didn't seem like the chocolate rabbit had been poisoned. Oh, well.

"Why do you think Beau hates me so much?" I asked as we relaxed after the meal, waiting on our desserts. Or at least

Diana and I waited on our desserts. I was glad I had one partner in crime.

Mark tipped his Sazerac in my direction. "Because you made him look like a fool."

"By surviving Kentucky? It's only because of Neil and Royce that I did."

"I think it's because he's worried you'll spoil his plans for fleecing your parents," Neil said, "even though he sort of invited you to try to stop him. I don't get why he's so cocky."

"Maybe he doesn't know we know about his scheme?" I suggested.

"Maybe he has something else up his sleeve." Neil sounded worried, and I tried not to let his pessimism get to me.

The server, a woman who looked too thin to have sampled the restaurant's desserts, brought Diana and I each a wicked-looking bread pudding that prompted Luke and Melody to order one to share. At the first warm, sweet, gooey bite, I closed my eyes and sighed. Why couldn't Neil and I just have a fun weekend in New Orleans eating, drinking and having wild monkey sex? My eyes flew open and I looked around. I hoped no one could read my mind. Except maybe Neil.

He looked too preoccupied by other things to think about wild monkey sex or whatever kind of sex Neil had. *Gah!* I had to stop tormenting myself. The bread pudding was an inadequate substitute, but it would have to do.

Luke and Melody got theirs quickly, took a bite and exchanged moony glances. Maybe dessert was what we needed to get those two together. I glanced over at Diana, who held out a forkful of the bread pudding to Mark. He closed his lips around it, savored his bite and moaned. Now *that* sounded like foreplay.

My phone rang deep inside my bag, and I had to interrupt my impure thoughts and dig around until I found it.

The caller ID showed the New Orleans Police Department. "This is Pepper."

"Ms. Revelle? This is Jane Russell in the crime lab. Detective Colby said to call you and tell you Beau Moritz's fingerprints weren't on the materials you left for us. But yours were, and we got a hit on a couple of others."

Chapter Nine

"Whose prints were on the chocolate bunny besides mine?" I asked the police expert.

"I'm not authorized to tell you that."

"Aw, come on, Jane. This guy is trying to fleece an old pastor and his wife—my parents—out of a million dollars someone left to their church. Can you give me a break?"

There was a pause before Jane said, "Some jerk conned my parents out of ten thousand dollars. If we could find him, I'd volunteer to shoot him in the face. So I'll tell you if you don't tell Colby."

"No problem."

"The first one was a Stephan Sully. Arrested for public drunkenness in California."

Mr. Mixy, arrested? "Oh, really? We know who that is. He's with us." Though it pained me to say it. "Who's the other one?"

"Jezebel Harlow, forty-five." Jane spelled it out for me. "Arrested once on a pot possession charge. A couple of traffic tickets. Lives in the Bywater."

I'd retrieved a pen from my bag and wrote the name on a napkin. "Anything else?"

"No. Be careful. I hear this Moritz is a hazard."

"Thanks." I ended the call. I kept forgetting Beau's last

name wasn't Reed. At least we had something to go on. I searched for Jezebel Harlow on my phone and found a home address and a website that touted her as the expert owner of an antiques, art and gift shop in the Bywater.

The chatter at the table died down when I looked up.

"What do you have?" Barclay asked.

"Fingerprints on the ribbon. And a name to go with them. Neil and I need to check her out once we talk to another guy here in the Quarter who partied with the man who died in our hotel room."

"What can we do?" Mark asked.

I looked at Neil, then at everyone else. "Can you all talk to the owners of hotels and other spots deemed haunted and see if they had any problems with Edgar Poeville's tours? Apparently he and his cohort Sierra ticked off Mr. Joshi, who owns the Fantome. See if anyone else was angry enough to kill him?"

My friends were enthusiastic about joining the hunt and started looking up sites on their phone. All except my aunt, who said she and Astra needed a nap, and Mr. Mixy.

"I want to go with you," he told me.

"I don't want you to go with us. Besides, it might be dangerous." I really didn't think going to an antiques store would be that dangerous, but I didn't want him along.

"Pepper, I need to go with you. I'll be your good luck charm."

He was more like a barnacle. I looked to Neil for help.

"You know what," Neil told me, "I think Stephan could be really helpful. Let's take him with us. I have a plan."

I couldn't believe it. Was Neil trying to torture me after letting Mr. Mixy hire us for his gig on Sunday?

We settled our bill, and everyone promised to touch base before dinner.

"I just learned something about you," I told Mr. Mixy as he followed Neil and I out to the street. "You have an arrest record."

"It's a lie," he said. "I never touched Randy's Donut."

Neil choked back a laugh while I tried to imagine what Stephan might've done to the iconic giant doughnut in L.A. I didn't plan to ask.

"So," Neil asked, "any idea where the souvenir shop is? The one where Alfie Boudreaux works?"

"Sierra said it was on the next block and to look for the mannequin with all the beads covering her bazongas."

"Oh, hey," Mr. Mixy said. "I know exactly where that is. She's pretty hot."

I rolled my eyes. "Lead the way."

"Who is this guy?" Mr. Mixy asked.

"The woman who ran the ghost tours with Edgar Poeville —the dead man—said Alfie used to party with Edgar and Jai, who works at the Fantome. We want to see if he knows anything. He works at the souvenir shop."

"Excellent," Mr. Mixy said. "I've been perfecting my interview technique for my book."

Whoa no. I'd almost forgotten the hybrid memoir/cocktail book he was writing, the one he claimed had Hollywood interest. I was exposed to his interview technique in Kentucky, when he manipulated all my answers to his questions so they were flattering to him.

"Here's what we want you to do," Neil said to Mr. Mixy in a conspiratorial tone as we spotted the blinged-out mannequin standing outside the shop door. "If we find him in there, casually walk by the shop and get a look at him, but don't go in. Then wait outside so he doesn't associate you with us. Later, when he leaves, follow him. We want to know everywhere he goes today."

"Right! Like a secret agent!" Mr. Mixy seemed enthused, and I was delighted. What a clever way to get rid of him.

As Mr. Mixy lingered on the sidewalk, Neil and I entered the store.

It was a typical low-end souvenir shop, narrow and long, stuffed with T-shirts, beads, masks, snow globes, disgusting gator heads, ornaments, feather boas, inauthentic voodoo dolls, sugar skulls, silly sunglasses, stickers, buttons and candy. It had a pretty good jelly bean selection, so I picked up a small bag of black ones and took it to the counter.

Was this Alfie? Blond with short-cropped hair, wide blue eyes and a roguish smile, he had the frat-boy looks Sierra had mentioned.

"Good afternoon," he said as he rang me up. "You like the black ones, huh? I hate licorice."

"I love it! But I'm an outlier."

"So am I," Neil added.

"That's why they make different flavors, I guess." Alfie took my ten-dollar bill.

I had to make sure it was Alfie. "Hey, do you know of any good ghost tours around here?"

A shadow crossed his face as he made change. "There was a great one, Ghostville Tours, but unfortunately the owner was murdered yesterday. We were friends, actually."

"I'm so sorry! How terrible." Especially terrible because he was murdered in our bed.

"Yeah, it sucks. Though I saw Edgar's gal pal out running tours this morning. You'd think she'd take a day of mourning or something, wouldn't you?"

"Maybe she's doing it as a tribute to him," I suggested.

"Ha! She's always wanted to run the company. Now's her chance."

"You don't like her?" I asked.

"She's a witch. Always nagging Edgar if he got in too late, that kind of thing. He liked to party, but he worked hard, too. Sometimes he did a little work for me."

My ears perked up. "Here at the store?"

His averted his gaze and straightened a display of souvenir pens on the countertop. "Not here. He used to help out tourists who needed a little lift, you know?" He gave us a shrewd look. "You guys need anything?"

From his tone, I didn't think he meant another souvenir.

"I prefer cocktails," Neil said in a friendly way that curbed Alfie's illicit sales pitch.

"Oh, yeah, I love those, too." Alfie was back to bland sales clerk.

"Did you know Edgar well?" I asked him.

"We used to meet up at the Fantome a lot, Edgar and me. We have a friend who works there."

Jai. "Who do you think might've killed him?"

"He wasn't good with money. Had a way of getting on the wrong side of people." Alfie's gaze darkened. "But I don't know."

It was clear the conversation was over. We thanked him and headed outside.

I looked around for Mr. Mixy and spotted him through the picture window of a bar across the street. He waved at us. Some spy. "There he is."

We stepped inside the dark bar. Mr. Mixy slouched in his bentwood chair at a tiny square table right up against the window, a beer in front of him.

"You saw Alfie?" Neil asked him.

"I'm on it. If he leaves, I'll go where he goes." He took a gulp of his beer, leaving traces of foam in his bushy 'stache.

"Great. Be careful," I told him.

Mr. Mixy gave us a cocksure smile. "He doesn't look like much trouble. Holler if you need me."

I gave Mr. Mixy a thumbs-up, grabbed Neil by the arm and practically dragged him toward our hotel. "You're pretty sneaky when you want to be."

Neil smiled. "Who knows? He might actually learn something."

"What did you think of Alfie?"

"I think he was trying to sell us drugs and that Edgar sold them, too," he said. "Sierra mentioned pills. If he was into drugs, the list of suspects goes way up, including Alfie."

"Yeah. If Beau didn't do it."

"Right."

"I'd like to check out that fictional address that was on Beau's packages while we're in the Bywater," I told Neil as we paused outside Hydrangea House.

Neil asked the valet to get his car. "How can we check out a fictional address?"

"Just look around a little. It was Dauphine Street, and the number didn't exist, but it was still that neighborhood by extension. Except the address was in the middle of the Industrial Canal, if the road extended that far."

"Maybe he has an underwater supervillain lair," Neil jested as his car arrived and we got in.

"I wouldn't put it past him. If he's not in a submarine, we can track him down."

Were we tracking Beau? Or was he laying the tracks for our train—chasing him at full steam—to slam into a brick wall?

Chapter Ten

The antiques store was nestled deep in the Bywater, a riverside neighborhood of funky galleries and murals, graffiti and grunge, quirky cafes and colorful little houses, and lots of art. To access the river here required extra effort; the steep, sweeping arch of a rusty pedestrian bridge allowed visitors to cross over the train tracks to the skinny Crescent Park next to the Mississippi.

We wound through narrow streets and found the small gravel parking lot of the antiques store, where a couple of other cars were parked. A tall sign by the road announced "The Remembered Past" in a hand-painted serif font, with a smaller line that said "Art, Gifts and Antiques." The sign seemed as weathered as the shop was bright, with its metal walls painted fire-engine red.

An overhang helped protect a few vivid modern paintings that hung outside. A jumble of antiques sat outside the door— a carousel horse, a comical pig statue, old farm equipment, and several cloudy medicine bottles in green glass atop what looked like a mid-century stereo cabinet.

A bell jingled as we entered. The brightly lit store was the size of a small warehouse and much less rustic than the outside implied. A couple of customers browsed serious small antiques in glass display cases; larger antiques were grouped in aisles in the back. Interesting art hung in an area with movable walls. Island displays showed off various upscale gifts, and another section featured greeting cards, pretty bags and wrapping paper with a table that might have been used for wrapping.

I walked in that direction with Neil on my heels. "Ribbon," I said. "Lots of it."

"The right color, too." He pointed to the rolls you could buy by the yard. They included a fuchsia that matched the chocolate bunny's necktie.

A woman in her late forties strolled over to us, wearing subtle eye makeup and red lipstick in a pretty shade I coveted. A red scarf pulled her long, light-brown hair away from her pink cheeks. She wore a white peasant blouse trimmed in red, black and yellow embroidery with flared black pants and sandals.

"Good afternoon." She smiled at us. "Did you need some help? I'm happy to cut lengths of ribbon for you."

"Yes." I hesitated. There was no use being coy. "We actually need help with more than that. We're looking for someone who we think bought some ribbon here. It was attached to a— a gift that was sent to me. We know who sent it. But we want to know if he was here."

The woman paled as I spoke. When I added, "Are you, by chance, Jezebel Harlow?" she put a hand on the table as if to steady herself.

"I am. How—who sent you the gift?"

"We know him as Beau Reed, but he goes by other names," Neil said.

"Beau," she whispered, her eyes widening. "Who are you?"

"Just somebody he met along the way," I replied. "I take it you know him?"

Her nostrils flared. "Why should I tell you anything? He said some people were after him. Are you trying to hurt him?"

"Ha. Sorry, but that's rich," I said. "Here's the deal. My name is Pepper, and this is Neil. Beau is not a good man. He's running a con on my parents, and he tried to kill me. He might have murdered someone else yesterday. If anyone is after him, it's the police. They found your fingerprints on the ribbon."

"Mine?" Her voice rose, and she looked around to see if the other customers had noticed. They were too involved with their shopping.

"They mentioned a minor drug charge," I said. "I guess that's how they have your prints?"

"Oh, Christ. That was so long ago. Smoke a little weed in the wrong place back in the day, and you end up in the system. Why on earth would they care about a bit of ribbon from my shop?"

"It was wrapped around a chocolate bunny with a death threat inside."

"You've got to be kidding."

"I don't think they suspect you or even care that much about the ribbon, but they might come calling since it's connected with Beau," I said. "Do you know where we can find Beau now?"

Jezebel looked us over, weighing my question. Weighing whether to tell us the truth, I thought.

"No, I never know where he is. I don't talk to him much. Once I did." Her low laugh held a trace of bitterness. "I met him at a bar where he was playing. He's so good, and I've always been a sucker for musicians. He wasn't into me for long, but sometimes he drops by when he needs something. Like the ribbon."

"When did you sell it to him?" Neil asked.

"I gave it to him about a week ago. I didn't ask what it was for."

"He didn't tell you anything? You must have talked about something," I said.

"We talked about nothing. We're good at that. He's good at it, almost made it an art. He flirts. He asks how I'm doing. He asks for something. He leaves." She sighed. "Sorry."

"So am I." I looked at Neil. "I guess that's that."

"Wait," Jezebel said as we started to walk away.

We turned to look at her.

"I'm pretty sure he still lives around here somewhere, in the Bywater, judging from his small talk about the neighborhood. It's stuff he might not know if he just dropped in from somewhere else. A coffee shop that closed for a few days when they had a flood. Problems at the abandoned naval base. A new gallery opening."

"OK, thanks," I said. "We'd appreciate it if you didn't tell him we came calling. And please be careful around him. He's dangerous."

A dreamy spark lit up her eyes for a moment, then was gone. She nodded, and we left.

"Do you think Jezebel still carries a torch for good ol' Beau?" I asked Neil as we climbed into the SUV.

He started up the car. "I do. And I don't like it."

"She might be on the phone to him right now."

"Not if he only communicates by poem." He pulled out of the space and headed for the street. "She's probably typing up something in iambic pentameter."

"Ha. She did give us some information. He might actually live around here. Let's drive around a little and see if anything jumps out at us."

"Like Beau with a chainsaw?" Neil suggested.

"Or a guitar."

"All right." He turned left. "It's an interesting neighborhood anyway. I like the murals."

"And I want to go down Dauphine Street. And maybe get a coffee."

"This is New Orleans. We should be drinking cocktails," Neil lamented as he stair-stepped through the one-way streets.

"Hey, that's my line. Hopefully tonight we can enjoy ourselves."

"Yeah, tomorrow Mr. Mixy wants us to meet the client."

"Oh, joy. Let's stop here." We were outside another red building, this one on Dauphine advertising coffee and pastries. Neil parked, and we popped in. He bought us a black coffee for him and a mocha for me. I resisted getting a second dessert. Or a third, if you counted the mocha.

Then we got back on the road, winding through the neighborhood until we circled back to Dauphine Street. Plenty of people were out enjoying the pleasant spring weather. But we hadn't seen anyone who looked like Beau.

"This feels like a fool's errand," I admitted.

"We'll play it out. Let's head down Dauphine toward the river and Beau's secret underwater base."

I giggled as we turned east, sipped my mocha and enjoyed myself. Maybe we were looking for a wicked man who wanted me dead, but with Neil, it was fun.

We passed an art garden and more brightly painted, densely built one-story houses on our way to where the canal met the Mississippi River. And then, at the last stop sign, an apocalyptic vision arose before us.

"What is this?" Neil asked.

"I almost forgot about this. It's the old naval base Jezebel mentioned."

"Looks like a zombie movie."

"I wouldn't want to go inside and find out."

Before us loomed the huge abandoned office buildings and parking garage of the complex the U.S. government signed over to the city several years ago. From the guard hut out front to every crosswalk and level of the structures, graffiti stood out in a rainbow of tall letters, recording the names of the artists. Many of the tags, painted on seemingly unreachable surfaces, suggested feats of skill and daring. On the six-story building close to us, a two-story cartoon rat with spiky hair, a pointy nose, a black heart and X'd-out eyes lifted his arms as if to cast a dark blessing over the wasteland.

This was no triumph of art. Pocked with broken windows, the buildings reeked of despair. Trash littered the pavement outside. This was not a tourist spot.

"Pepper, look." Neil pointed to a cute little bar that lay just outside the fallen kingdom of the navy base.

"Love the turquoise and purple paint on that! What are those sketches, cats? So adorable!"

"No, look at the guy who just came out of the bar!"

"Oh!" I refocused on the unremarkable man walking down the sidewalk. Perhaps deliberately unremarkable. Bent forward, head down and half hidden by a baseball cap, hands in jeans pockets, he seemed to cloak himself in invisibility. But now that I saw him, I really saw him.

"Oh my God," I said. "It's Beau."

Chapter Eleven

Neil eyed our quarry. "He's getting into a car."

"We have to follow him," I said as Beau eased the 1980s-era beige Plymouth Reliant out of its space and headed down Poland Avenue. The car was as invisible as Beau had been a moment ago on the street.

Neil turned to pursue.

"Not too close," I said.

"I know."

Beau turned onto Rampart Street, and we followed.

"I don't like this. Too open. He'll see us." I scrunched down a little in my seat.

Neil fell back a little more, and a car turned in front of us and just behind Beau. "Maybe that will help."

He let one more car get in front of us as we continued on Rampart. Beau seemed in no particular hurry.

"Do you think he's going to the Quarter?" I asked.

"I don't know, but we're passing through the fabled Storyville."

"The old red-light district. I've heard the stories."

"All gone now," Neil said, almost sadly. For such a strait-laced guy, he had an uncommon interest in seedy history.

"But we still have the Quarter. And it looks like he's not

heading there." High-rises loomed in front of us as we crossed Canal Street. "Now what?"

"Whatever he's doing, he's avoiding the highway." And so Neil continued on the surface streets, letting cars come between us so it wouldn't be so obvious we were following Beau.

"I'm surprised he hasn't noticed us," I said.

"Maybe he has. Or maybe he's so confident, he can't imagine we'd find him."

"He has a lot of balls to stick around New Orleans, knowing the cops are looking for him."

"But how hard are they really looking?" Neil asked.

As Beau went through a light, Neil turned right.

"What are you doing?" I sat up in panic.

"Hang on. I'm just letting him get a block or two away, and then I'll move back over."

I was literally on the edge of my seat until Neil maneuvered back onto Beau's trail, two cars separating us now.

"Maybe he doesn't know what your car looks like," I said.

"We don't know what he knows. That's the problem. But he can't see our Florida plates from here, so that's a good thing."

"Oh, yeah, the plates! I guess you can't let him see your butt."

"Definitely not."

I snickered at his tone as the houses got bigger and fancier. "We're getting into the Garden District."

The Garden District was my fantasy neighborhood, full of grand historic houses with neat little lawns and gnarled, spooky oak trees.

"There's Cray's house," Neil said as we passed a gray-green Victorian that looked more haunted than its neighbors. But again, it was New Orleans. There were more than enough ghosts to go around.

We'd lost our cover, and now only Beau drove ahead of us. Neil gave him lots of room. When Beau slipped into a space in front of a stately white house surrounded by a black cast-iron fence, Neil made a hard turn left.

"We'll shark it," he said to head off my protest. "I don't want to be obvious, though it may be too late for that."

He hastened to turn right, went up a long block, turned right again and parked in the shadow of an oak tree, just shy of the street where Beau had stopped. We could see the big house from here, with its pale green shutters and elegant columns delineating upstairs and downstairs porches and an elegant bumped-out front window, all framed by a couple of large, wizened oak trees whose branches encircled the mansion like arms.

The front door was just closing.

"Did he go inside?" I whispered. "Why am I whispering?"

Neil chuckled. "I don't know the answer to either of those questions. His car is still there, so maybe he went inside. Maybe I should text Detective Colby."

Part of me wanted to see what else we could find out on our own. "I suppose you're right," I acknowledged.

Neil texted the detective, and a moment later, his phone rang. Neil put the call on the car's speaker.

"Thanks for the address," Colby said. "Can't check it out now. On a robbery."

"But it's Beau!" I exclaimed. "We don't know how long he's going to be here."

"I want to talk to him, too, but truth is, we've found no physical evidence to tie him to the hotel murder, and even though I'm looking at him for a real estate scam, it's just not urgent enough to send out an officer right now. Unless he's actively committing a crime."

"Really, detective?" I sounded snippier than I meant to. "He tried to kill me."

"Not recently. Look, we're stretched thin, and I'm under enough heat for chasing your little friend around. The good news is, we have someone keeping an eye on your parents for the next couple of days. You got plates?"

I read off the number to the detective.

"I'll check it out. Don't do anything stupid." He rang off.

"At least they're watching my parents." The relief was tangible, and I let out a sigh. "Maybe I should go in there."

"*Pepper.* No."

"I know. You're right. But this is so aggravating."

"There." Neil leaned forward and peered out the windshield.

The front door of the house opened, and Beau stepped halfway out. So did a curvaceous platinum-blond woman, maybe around fifty, in a loose flowery blouse and white pants. Beau said a few words to her, smiling as he held her hand. She leaned forward and delayed his departure with a sultry kiss on the doorstep. Carrying a small bag, he left through the gate and got in his Plymouth.

"What a slut! Beau, I mean," I said as Neil guffawed.

Neil put his SUV in gear as Beau eased out of his space.

I put a hand on Neil's shoulder. "Wait."

"What?" Beau was already a block away.

"I think we should talk to that woman."

"But we'll lose Beau."

"Not necessarily," I said. "We think he's in the Bywater. We know what his car looks like. I gave the detective the plates."

"True," Neil acknowledged. "And I don't want you confronting him."

"Right now it's more important we find out what he's up to. Let's see what this woman knows. At the least, we could warn her about him."

"He does seem to leave a trail of bruised hearts in his wake."

"That's the truth. I pity Beau if he runs into Melody again," I said. "She'll crush him like a sugar cube for his hanky-panky in Kentucky."

Neil thought it over. "It would be nice to stop him from destroying someone else."

"This way we aren't giving Beau a chance to recognize us, either."

"You've convinced me. Let's see what we can find out." He put the car back in park.

I squeezed his shoulder, keeping him in place. "I think I should go alone."

"What? Not happening."

I unbuckled my seat belt. "You know exactly where I am should anything happen, which it won't. Do you think she's going to spill her guts to you? Not likely. This needs a woman's touch."

"A Pepper Revelle take-no-prisoners touch?"

I quirked my mouth at him. "I'll be gentle."

He gazed at me for a moment. Then he unfastened his seat belt, reached over and pulled me close for an intense kiss.

A moment later, he released me. I sighed and leaned back, my head spinning.

He spoke softly. "Call me if you need me. Or run out of the house screaming. OK?"

"Yes," I said hoarsely. "Or we could stay here and make out."

"Don't tempt me. If you're not out in thirty minutes, I'm coming in."

"You're so hot when you get all action hero on me."

He laughed. "I'm going to sit here and think about cold drinks."

I laughed, too, leaving my bag with Neil but taking my phone with me as I stepped out of the car. "Just in case she mugs me."

"Don't even joke about that." He looked after me with concern as I closed the door behind me.

I gave him a reassuring little wave and walked toward the gate in the forbidding cast-iron fence.

Chapter Twelve

I slipped through the unlocked gate of the elegant white mansion and made the short walk through the lushly planted yard. I stepped up onto the wide porch and rang the old-fashioned doorbell.

The doorbell didn't have a camera, but a quick look around revealed a lens in the corner of the porch ceiling aimed at the cheerful red front door. The porch held pots of ferns and flowers, along with a couple of freshly painted red rocking chairs.

After a moment, the woman herself answered. I was expecting a servant, for some reason. These Garden District houses really pulled me back in time.

"May I help you?" the woman asked politely. Her blue eyes weren't as friendly as her voice or as merry as her laugh lines might suggest.

"Ma'am, my name is Pepper Revelle. This is going to sound kind of strange, but I'd like to talk to you about the man who just left your house."

Her eyebrows lifted. "Are you watching my house?"

"Oh, no. We're watching Beau. At least, we know him as Beau."

"We?"

"My boyfriend and I." It still sounded strange to call Neil

my boyfriend, but I liked the idea. "It's kind of a long story. May I come in?"

She looked me over and must have decided I wasn't much of a threat, because she didn't send me packing. She also didn't invite me in. "Have a seat on one of the chairs here. I'll be right back."

She closed the door.

I glanced toward Neil in his car, half hidden around the corner down the street, and gave him a little shrug. I sat in one of the rocking chairs. This was probably better than going in anyway. Safer. Though I kind of wanted a peek inside.

The woman reappeared with a tray holding a glass pitcher of golden liquid, a small silver jar with a lid, a spoon, and two lowball glasses filled with ice. She set the tray on a small wicker table.

"Lemonade? That's very kind of you," I said.

"Oh, no, honey. Whiskey sour. It's that time of day, isn't it?"

"It's almost always that time of day, isn't it?" I returned.

She laughed. "Oh, I like you, Pepper. I'm Camelia Landry." She poured us each a drink, then lifted the lid of the silver jar, dipped in the spoon and scooped a cherry into each of our glasses. She handed one to me.

"Thank you." I accepted mine and took a sip, relaxing at the happy taste of rye whiskey, lemon juice and simple syrup in perfect harmony. "You know what you're doing."

"I've had a lot of practice." Camelia sat in her chair and sipped her cocktail.

"So have I. I'm a mixologist."

"Is that right? We should get along fine. But I expect what you've come to tell me is not happy news, is it? Are you involved with Beau?"

I almost choked on my drink. "Me? No! I have a boyfriend, remember?"

"Well, that doesn't stop some of us. There's so much of this world to taste. Don't you agree?" Camelia smiled at me and rocked in her chair.

"I've tasted a fair amount already." Yeesh. One sip of whiskey sour and Camelia and I were best girlfriends. Anyway, I wasn't that girl anymore, at least not since meeting Mr. Neil Rockaway.

She chuckled. "So what did you want to talk about?"

I gave her the abridged version: how Beau tried to pass himself off as my brother in an attempt to con my parents. How he almost killed me. How he was still sending me threatening notes.

As I spoke, her eyebrows came closer and closer together. "This doesn't sound like my Beau at all. He's such a nice man. He's my music teacher."

"And maybe a little more than your music teacher?"

She seemed unfazed by my observation. "Ah, I see you *were* watching my house, at least a few minutes ago. He has on occasion stayed for a cocktail after my music lesson. And stayed a little longer after that. He cares for me."

Whoa no. Another mark for the con artist. "Why was he here today?"

"Just picking up his payment for my lesson this week. He prefers cash, and I didn't have any on me the other day."

"He hasn't asked you for money for other things, has he?"

"Oh, now don't be so negative. I've helped him out once or twice with rent. On occasion, he's given me investment advice in return."

Now we were getting somewhere. I took another sip of my whiskey sour. "Real estate, by chance?"

She nodded at a butterfly flitting through her flowers. "An American Lady." She turned back to me. "I can't disclose what Beau might have said to me about that sort of investment in particular. I've signed a nondisclosure agreement."

"Well, if it involves a certain empire headed by a cartoon mouse, it's a scam."

Her face tightened slightly. She drained her drink and set her glass on the table. "My dear, I think we've talked enough. I'll take what you've told me under advisement. But I'm sure you're wrong."

Why was it when I told people that Beau tried to kill me, nobody believed me? If they'd been sealed inside the bourbon barrel with me, would they believe me then? People were way too good at ignoring things they didn't want to hear.

"I'm sorry to disturb you, but I felt I had a responsibility to tell you." I stood and set my glass on the table. "Thanks for the drink, and take care of yourself."

"I will. You, too." Her voice was cool and polite as she stood and waited for me to leave her porch.

I felt her eyes on me as I crossed the street and walked down to where Neil was parked just around the corner, not doubting she watched me get into the car.

"What happened?" Neil asked.

"Another true believer. Just drive."

He pulled away from the curb, and we both looked back toward the porch, where Camelia still stood. I waved. She didn't wave back. And then we were on our way back to the Quarter.

"Do you think Cray knows her?" I asked.

"Probably. He has a long memory, and he's lived here forever. Do you want to stop?"

"No need, really. We can ask him if we run into him later."

"So who is she?" Neil asked.

"I didn't get much past her name—Camelia Landry. I liked her, sort of, but she clammed right up when I suggested her pretty boy might be scamming her."

"What's Beau to her?"

"Music teacher, apparently."

"Hmph," Neil said.

"And investment advisor. And not above taking cash now and again and sampling the delights of his hostess."

"That sounds bad."

"She seems happy with the arrangement. So happy, she wouldn't hear any bad news about Beau. Said she'd signed a nondisclosure agreement, just like my folks."

"She might change her mind if Detective Colby comes calling," Neil noted.

"True." I watched the city roll by as we passed a trolley on St. Charles. "She served me a whiskey sour."

"Was it good?"

"Really nice, actually." I smiled at him. "Maybe we should have a happy hour meeting with our friends before heading out and enjoying the Quarter for a while."

"Excellent idea."

I picked up my phone again, ready to text everyone, and noticed the time. "Ugh."

"What?"

"It's five thirty. I should call my parents. Just in case."

"Also a good idea."

What if they'd given in and sent Beau his money? Apparently, he was really good at talking people into things. I called my father's cell, figuring it would be easier talking to him.

"Pepper?" Kevin Revelle answered.

"Hi, Dad. How did it go today?"

"We did like you suggested. We haven't tried to send any money. We got a call from Beau just a few minutes ago."

"You did?" I sat up straight. "What did he say?"

"He asked where the money was. We told him we'd had computer trouble but that we'd send it as soon as we could."

"What did he say then?"

"He got real quiet. Then he said it was OK and to make sure we sent the money as soon as possible. He told us we were going to miss that nice discount on one of the real estate parcels. He got me all worked up about that. It sounds like such a great investment. Are you sure he's a bad man, Pepper?"

Blah blah blah, he tried to kill me, blah blah blah.

I rolled my eyes. "Dad, I'm sure. Did he believe you?"

"Honestly, I'm not sure he did." My father sounded nervous. "He seemed very disappointed."

Oh, great. "Well, the important thing is that he didn't get the money. And the police have someone looking out for you. Have you seen an officer?"

"Oh, yes." My father brightened a bit. "Officer Glenn. He's parked outside the church right now. That's where we are. Your mother has already made him coffee."

"I'm glad to hear it. Be careful, OK? We'll touch base tomorrow."

"All right, Pepper. Take care."

I ended the call and looked at Neil. "They didn't send the money, thank Dionysus. Though I think they wanted to. Damn Beau."

"Don't they know he tried to kill you?"

"I know, right? At least you believe me."

"I helped get you out of the barrel." He reached over and squeezed my hand. We were getting back into the Quarter, on our way to Hydrangea House. "Let's not go through that again."

"Agreed. Now I'm going to text the fam. A quick one at Fantome and then the world is our oyster, OK?"

"Oysters sound good."

"But not the ones the farting ghost ate."

Neil smiled. "Right. And I need to get to Latitude 29 sometime this weekend."

"You'll get your Mai Tai this weekend even if it kills me."

He shot me a worried look.

I gave him an "I'm sorry" grin. "Just an expression. Nothing's going to kill me!"

Not yet, anyway.

Chapter Thirteen

I freshened up in the room I shared with Diana, though she wasn't there. I donned a fun frock with a body-hugging, scoop-neck black sleeveless top and a flared above-the-knee black skirt printed with white palm fronds. Cute black-and-white sneakers were next, since I expected more walking during our bar hop, plus silver jewelry, my eyeglasses and a rich red lipstick. I put my hair up and paused in front of the mirror.

I ran a finger along the leather cord, beads, and silver wire wrapped around the gator tooth on my bracelet. It was a necklace when Neil and I got it from the voodoo lady, but I liked it wrapped around my wrist. The more I wore it, the more superstitious I got, especially given all the bizarre stuff I'd survived in the past year. I hoped its magic was still potent.

Neil waited for me in the lobby, looking good in an aloha shirt, albeit a muted one of grays and blues. Luke and Barclay favored Hawaiian shirts, too, but they always looked like radioactive parrots next to Neil's color palette. And indeed, when we found them in the Fantome bar, they were dressed in their full tropical glory. Melody glowed in a long yellow dress with sprays of pink hibiscus that caressed her curves and flowed down to a handkerchief hem.

"You have some catching up to do," Melody said, holding up what looked like an Old-Fashioned.

"I can help with that." Jai was back behind the bar.

And that was good. We needed to ask him about his friendship with Edgar Poeville and see if he had any ideas about his death. Drinks first, though. I needed one after today's chase.

Jai's sister was working, too, making gin and tonics for Mark and Diana at the other end of the bar. They called out a greeting. A second later, Royce and Cray entered.

"Sazerac, please," I asked Jai. And like last time, he shouted for his sister to make it. I raised an eyebrow at him. "You don't make Sazeracs?"

"Sometimes. It's more fun to make her do it. How about you?"

Neil looked amused. "Do you make a Vieux Carré?"

"Since you asked so nicely, I do," Jai said, and got to work on the drink, another classic New Orleans rye cocktail. He even flamed the lemon twist.

"Can I have the check?" Neil asked. "We can only stay for one."

"Oh, that British guy's got you." He gestured down the bar toward Mark. *Nice!*

I waved at Aunt Celestine, who'd arrived without Astra, then accepted my Sazerac from Avani and took a sip. "Very nice, thank you."

Avani nodded, looking shy.

I eyed the reddish whiskey drink with its twist of lemon and delicate overtone of absinthe. "I always wondered why the most famous New Orleans drinks were made with rye."

Cray, who snagged a Hemingway Daiquiri from Avani, caught my question and answered it.

"The Sazerac likely owes at least some of its history to Mr. Peychaud, known for the bitters he made in the early nineteenth century. His product was available at the legendary Sazerac House, with which the cocktail became associated, hence the name."

"It wasn't always a rye cocktail, was it?" Neil asked him.

"The drink was made with brandy first, I believe, but rye has become the standard," Cray said. "The liquor landscape was quite different back when these cocktails were invented. Rye was also popular when Mr. Walter Bergeron created the Vieux Carré at the Hotel Monteleone before Prohibition.

"Rye is considered the original American whiskey, though between you and me, it started with German immigrants," Cray continued, happily sipping his rum cocktail. "George Washington even had a rye distillery. Before Prohibition, you were as likely to find rye as not in American cocktails. Even though Prohibition wasn't terribly well-enforced in New Orleans, the national ban on alcohol still damn near killed rye in this country. Smuggled Canadian whisky of poor quality masqueraded as rye, bringing down the standard for the drink. When the government subsidized corn after the second world war, it became even cheaper to make bourbon, and then vodka began its terrible rise to prominence."

Our friends, who'd gathered around to listen, laughed as Mark put a hand to his heart as if wounded. He was known for a lovely gin and a nice spiced rum, but his Fairyland Distillery also made vodka.

"This is the last time I pay this lot's bar bill," he said to our laughter.

"Thank you, Mark," I proclaimed for all of us, and he grinned.

"The craft cocktail movement is bringing rye back, and I'm

so glad." Cray smiled and held up his drink. "Though I still like my rum."

"Rye's getting as collectible as bourbon," Royce said. "So collectible we're starting to see shady flippers offering pricey counterfeits on the secondary market. When the taters can't buy any more of my bourbon, I figure they'll turn to rye, so I'm making more of it now."

"Aw, not all your collectors are taters," I teased him. Taters were considered overeager and not necessarily well-informed.

"I love collectors!" Royce backtracked. "Though they've almost priced my Penny Brilliant out of the market. Anyway, it's fun to play with rye. I like that it's different, interesting, a little peppery."

"Well, anything that's peppery has to be good," I said.

"Indeed, Pepper, indeed." Cray's eyes twinkled.

Jai cut in. "That's what the farting ghost drank. Lots of rye."

Avani, who'd drifted closer, gave him a dark look. "Stop it," she told her brother. "You know Dad hates that story."

"But it's a great story! Do you all know it?" he asked us.

"Neil and I heard about it on a Ghostville tour this morning," I said.

A shadow crossed Jai's face at the mention of Edgar Poeville's tour, but since he'd opened the subject, the others demanded the tale of the farting ghost, and he obliged.

I exchanged a look with Neil as the story ended.

He turned to the others. "Why don't we go out in the courtyard for a minute and enjoy the twilight?"

Our friends seemed to get the message. We wanted our conversation about the tours to be more private. But as everyone headed outside, where the golden hour was in full shimmer among the trees and flowers, I lingered at the bar.

"It's a shame what happened to Edgar Poeville," I said to Jai. "Sierra told me you knew him."

He rearranged glasses for a second, then picked up a rocks glass and polished it with a towel, avoiding my eyes. "We were good friends. He liked to drink here."

"I'm sorry. Did he have any enemies?"

He set down the glass and towel and looked up. "Why do you want to know?"

It was tricky, questioning suspects when you were a suspect yourself. "I'm afraid his body was found in our room in the hotel next door."

Avani gasped. I looked over to see her clutching her own bar towel. "That's terrible."

"It really was. Did you know him, too?"

She swallowed, and her eyes got shiny. "A little."

Hmm. Maybe Avani knew him better than she let on.

"If you're asking if anyone wanted to kill Edgar, I suppose the answer is yes because he's dead," Jai said. "Edgar had a lot of friends. He also had a gift for pissing people off, though he was harmless. He'd borrow money now and then and was slow to pay it back. He had kind of an easy come, easy go attitude, you know?"

I didn't really know, as I'd never been that laid-back, especially when it came to money. I was pretty careful except for the occasional splurge on a great dress. "Did he borrow money from you?"

Jai chuckled. "No, of course not. We were friends. We supported each other with business leads, but we didn't give each other money."

"Business leads? Like you sent customers to take his tour and he sent tourists to the bar?"

"Yeah, like that." He picked up the rocks glass again, then

set it down. "Edgar even created a haunted bar tour that stops here."

"Ever see the ghost yourself?"

Jai's dark eyes gleamed. "I saw a barstool float six inches off the ground once."

"No kidding?" I was pretty sure he was kidding, but my nerves prickled.

"Oh, yeah! Mostly I just smell him, though."

"Jai!" his sister exclaimed, and Jai laughed as she stalked off through the door that led behind the bar.

"Well, thanks for telling me about Edgar," I said. "I'm sorry about your loss."

"Yeah, me too." I felt him watching me as I headed into the lovely courtyard to see my friends.

I was surprised to see Kirby. He set his motorcycle helmet on the edge of the fountain at the center, pulled his porkpie hat out of his leather jacket and set it at a rakish angle on his head.

"How'd you get in?" I asked.

"There's an alley entrance they don't advertise. How's it going?"

"OK, I guess. Play any tuba lately?"

He grinned. "Maybe tonight. I thought I might try this street."

"You wouldn't dare."

He shook his head and laughed.

I looked around. "Now that we have a quorum, what have y'all found out about Edgar Poeville?"

Diana spoke first. "I think it's fair to say he was despised."

"Really?" I knew Mr. Joshi wasn't pleased with the tour, but I didn't think other people hated Edgar too.

"We heard the same thing," Barclay said. "Edgar was pushy, always trying to get his tours into places they shouldn't be."

"And he exaggerated a lot, one manager told me," Melody said. "But maybe she just didn't like her hotel associated with murder and prostitutes that turned into ghosts."

"She's the one who told us about the other tour, right?" Luke asked.

"Oh, yeah, the other tour." Melody pulled a phone out of her tiny purse, which could have been swallowed by my bag and never seen again. "Wilma Wells runs it. It's called True Bloody Ghost Adventures."

"What's the story?" I asked.

Barclay answered. "That hotel manager said Wilma Wells was planning to sue Edgar. She *hated* him."

"Sue him for what?" I asked.

"The manager didn't know," Luke said.

I took a sip of Sazerac. "Then it sounds like we need to talk to Wilma Wells."

Kirby spoke up. "Wilma's good people. She does Friday night tours. One starts in about thirty minutes outside Napoleon House. Maybe you can catch her."

Neil cast me a pleading look. "Not another ghost tour."

"We don't have to do the whole thing," I told him. "We'll try to catch her at the start and make it quick. Or I can go alone."

"No," several of my protective friends said at the same time, followed by chuckles.

"I'm coming along with you." Royce gave me a look. We still needed to talk about how his chat with his father went today.

"I'll come too," Aunt Celestine said. "Astra's snoozing after a fabulous chicken dinner."

I didn't want to ask. She loved spoiling Astra. But the gaseous emissions that followed my pup's occasional gourmet meals would asphyxiate a farting ghost any day.

"Maybe we can meet afterward and have a bite somewhere? I'm ravenous," I said.

After agreements and arrangements, Mark spoke. "Any more bad poetry from Beau?"

"No," I said, "but my parents did *not* send him the contents of their checking account, so that's something. And we saw him."

Surprise and chatter rippled through the group, and Neil answered their questions. "We saw him from a distance after getting a tip he might be in the Bywater. He stopped at a house in the Garden District and left. So *we* stopped to warn the woman who lived there who she was dealing with."

"She wasn't receptive," I added.

"One of my neighbors? Who was it?" Cray asked.

"Camelia Landry. Do you know her?"

Cray's eyebrows lifted. "I do indeed. She's quite the colorful character. I think Beau will have his hands full with her."

I smiled. "I got that impression, but she seems devoted to him."

"Speaking of colorful characters," Neil said, "has anyone heard from Mr. Mixy?"

"Why would we hear from Mr. Mixy?" my aunt asked.

"Because Neil had him follow one of the murder victim's friends, a sketchy guy named Alfie Boudreaux." I snickered.

Melody giggled. "If we're lucky, Mr. Mixy followed him on a long trip out of state."

"I wonder if we should worry." Neil sounded weary.

"I'll message him." I didn't want to, but we did ask Stephan to trail a drug dealer. Who knew what kind of trouble he was in?

As the others drank and chatted, I texted my ex-boyfriend and almost immediately got a message back.

"I'm fine. This Alfie guy is great. He spotted me following him, and it turns out he loves my TV show. I just left him after a couple of hours of drinking. You guys are all wrong about him."

I rolled my eyes.

"What?" Neil asked.

"He says Alfie is awesome and now they're drinking buddies and we're all wrong."

"Sounds like a good reason to look into Alfie further," Neil quipped.

I laughed. "First, the True Bloody ghost tour. Let me run to the bathroom before we go."

I headed inside and left my empty glass on the bar. Jai nodded at me but didn't speak.

The bathrooms were behind their own door, which stood open, revealing a hallway lined with raised rectangular panels in elegant dark wood. I stepped through.

It was dark in here. And it *did* smell weird. Maybe it was Jai's ghost talk, but this place gave me the creeps, so I walked carefully down the shadowy corridor, looking for the ladies'.

A loud creak behind me made me jump, and I whirled to see the door at the end of the hallway slam shut with a crash.

Chapter Fourteen

"Holy ..." My breath caught as the slamming door made the air tremble.

I jumped again as I heard another door open behind me. I spun to see Royce coming out of the men's bathroom.

"What was that?" he asked.

"You heard that?"

"They heard that in China," he said.

"The door at the end of the hall slammed."

"Did someone close it?"

I shook my head. "Not that I saw."

"Maybe it was the wind. You know, people are coming and going from the courtyard."

"Maybe." I looked around. "Does it smell weird in here to you?"

"Worried about a little farting ghost?" He looked amused.

"Seriously. Your sense of smell is probably as good as mine." I'd learned that about my brother in Kentucky.

"True." Royce paused, and we both stood there sniffing like idiots. "Besides a hint of bathroom cleaner, it kind of smells like a bar that hasn't been cleaned in a decade or two."

"Huh. Bar funk. OK, maybe. It was just powerful there for a minute."

"Relax, Pepper. I think the stress is getting to you. Do you want me to wait here while you do your thing?"

"Yes, please."

He smiled at my nervousness, and I found the women's bathroom and did my business. Royce was waiting when I came out. The slamming door at the end of the hall was stuck, and we had to yank on it to get it open, but finally it gave and we went out to the courtyard to rejoin our friends.

While most of them headed out to grab a drink at Jewel of the South while we went in search of the tour—I was *very* jealous—Kirby left for a gig with his band.

"I'd like to hear his band," Aunt Celestine said as she, Royce, Neil and I set out for Napoleon House.

I smiled. "Better than hearing him play tuba in the middle of the night."

"What, you didn't like the free concert?" Neil teased.

"When I was awake, yes. I didn't sleep much at Cocktailia. And not for good reasons."

Royce snickered, and my aunt smiled. I'd thrown myself at Neil during the cocktail convention, but it didn't work out. I had hopes that when I threw myself at him again, he'd catch me. If we ever got a break.

"So how did things go today with your dad?" I asked Royce.

He grimaced. "Not great at first. He was angry at my mom and me for doing the DNA test. Then she told him he shouldn't have kept such a big secret—adopting his own son, who was obviously conceived when he was still dating my mother, er, adoptive mom, just before they got married. Then he said she shouldn't have kept the DNA test a secret but soon realized his secret was kind of the secret to rule all secrets. Then he cried."

"Oh, my," my aunt said.

"I know. It was awful, but it was good, too. Then my mom cried and I cried and he hugged me. He doesn't do that much. He's only started to accept me for who I am."

"Wow," I said. "Did he ask about my—our mother?"

"Not really, actually. Though he said something about being relieved that I'd met her. He'd been too mortified over the years to reach out to her and was afraid she'd try to get me back."

"That's a lot of weight to carry around," Neil observed.

"So much," Royce said. "But I think it'll be OK."

I stopped mid-stride and gave him a hug. "We've got you, bro."

"Thanks." He smiled and accepted a hug from our aunt, too. I think we all had something in our eye for a second.

It didn't take much longer to get to our destination, where a small group of tourists was gathered at the corner of Chartres and St. Louis. A teenager with a clipboard walked around among them, checking off names. A forty-something woman stood nearby, watching him with approval. Her long, golden Victorian dress, trimmed with black lace, and a broad matching hat adorned with black roses complemented her umber skin.

She saw us approach, glanced at her crowd as if counting heads, then looked back at us.

"Ms. Wells?" I inquired.

"You don't have a reservation, do you? We can take you along if you want to pay Robert over there."

"Is he your money manager?" I asked with a smile.

She chuckled. "My son. He has a head for numbers and likes to help out."

"I'm Pepper. This is Neil, Royce, and my aunt, Celestine.

We're actually not here for the tour. If you have a minute, I'd like to ask you about Edgar Poeville."

Her humor evaporated, and a look of distaste crossed her face. "He's dead, of course. I saw it on the news."

"Unfortunately, yes. And since his body was found in our hotel room"—I gestured to Neil—"the police had a lot of questions for us."

Her eyes widened, but she didn't say anything.

I plunged on. "I understand you planned to sue him?"

She kept her voice low so her tourists wouldn't hear, but she wasn't happy with me. "Are you accusing me of something?"

"Not at all." *Not yet.* "I'm just trying to figure out why he annoyed so many people and if any of them might have killed him."

"You have that right. He had a way of crossing people. I think he enjoyed it. And he was a liar and a thief."

"What did he steal?" Neil asked.

"My work. All of it. He used it in his awful tours."

"You mean he stole your tour stops?" I asked.

"I mean he stole my historical research. I have a master's degree and work for a couple of museums in town. I started these tours for fun, but they've become an important part of my income, and they're based on my own work. I include information in my tour that's not easily found anywhere else. In fact, I've written a book that's under contract. But its publication is in jeopardy since Edgar sent his little spy to attend my tours and record me. The publisher is concerned about me being accused of plagiarism. Me! The man refused to stop when my lawyer sent him a letter. Suing the tour is my only option."

Or killing him, I thought. "You say he had a spy?"

"That little girl Sierra who did tours with him. I didn't realize till later that she'd been on my tour, without the costume. I had a customer tell me she heard some of my stories almost word for word on Ghostville Tours, including stories no one else in town has. I mean, history is history, but if you dig into original sources, you can find a lot more than what you get on the Internet. My research is deep and thorough."

"You're a historian? And you believe in ghosts?"

She quirked her mouth. "My history is accurate. And I share the ghost tales associated with these places. There's no harm in it."

"What about the farting ghost of the Fantome?" I asked.

Her laugh was bitter. "That's the one original story they have. I've never found anything about a farting ghost, but who knows? Maybe Edgar did some research after all."

"Who do you think might have killed him?" I asked.

"It wasn't me, if that's what you're asking. Maybe they just killed him because he's a horrible person." She nodded at her son, who now stood nearby, watching us curiously. "My tour's about to start. I would say I hope Edgar's spirit is chained to this earth in torment, but I have no desire to run into him again, ever. Have a good night." She walked away and greeted her tour.

Whew. Wilma Wells was angry, and I couldn't blame her. But it was interesting what she said about Sierra. If Sierra was as callous about stealing stories as she was about Edgar's death, I had little doubt she'd keep right on telling Wilma's tales. Then Wilma might still sue Ghostville Tours.

"Even if she did kill Edgar," Neil murmured in my ear, "it sounds like Ms. Wells still has a problem."

"So killing him wouldn't have solved anything. But she didn't know Sierra would keep doing the tours."

"True." His phone buzzed. He pulled it from his pocket and started tapping the screen.

I extracted my phone from my bag and texted Millie, our planner back home, to see if she could learn more about Carl the farting ghost. I had no doubt Wilma Wells was a clever historian, but maybe Millie could find the story Sierra mentioned about the writer's death in the *New Orleans Bee* and forward us the article. Millie had mad research skills.

"No problem," Millie texted back. "Be careful."

We joined Royce and Celestine, who'd drifted across the street. As Neil put his phone away, I took his hand.

He smiled at me. "Dinner?"

"Oh, God, yes," I answered.

"Everyone's headed for the Carousel Bar," he said. "The restaurant there has a great menu."

I shot him a mischievous look. "Not to mention a Vieux Carré. Let's go."

The Quarter came to life as darkness fell, all lights and music and interesting smells, from good food to bad booze. Some shops stayed open late to take advantage of the glut of tourists, and Royce stopped in front of one and stared at it.

"A voodoo shop?" I asked him.

"I think this is the one where that woman told me to find my missing piece. It's what convinced me to finally get the DNA test. And then I found you."

I exchanged a glance with Neil. Could it be the same woman who'd made sure I got the gator-tooth talisman?

Royce headed for the door. There was no discussion. One after another, we followed him inside.

The store was small but mazelike, and it smelled of

incense. Its moody purple and yellow lighting illuminated shelves overflowing with skull sculptures, books, crystal balls, voodoo dolls, African masks, candles, drums, jewelry—the jumble overwhelmed my senses.

A young woman sat behind the sales counter, not someone I recognized. So we wended through the shop until we came to a heavily decorated alcove in back where a woman in a turban and a flowing gown was saying goodbye to what had to be a tour group. As the dozen or so visitors left, some of them dropped a few bucks into a jar that sat on a table covered with flickering candles. For a minute, we dodged them like salmon swimming upstream, and then we were alone with her.

It was the woman who led the tour we encountered that night a year ago. The woman who made sure I had the token I now wore around my wrist. I couldn't quite believe it. Her layers of necklaces and bracelets glinted as she moved, and her ebony countenance brightened as she saw us.

She stared first at Royce, then at me. She stepped closer. "Ah, my brother and sister, you have found your missing piece." There was that island-touched accent I remembered. Her smile was like the sun breaking through the clouds, and her brown eyes sparkled.

She looked down and took my hand, lifting it, touching the bracelet. She closed her eyes, and something like electricity tingled in my wrist as she opened her eyes and released me. "You needed this more than I thought, eh?" She laughed, then looked at Aunt Celestine with a knowing nod.

Finally, she turned to Neil. "Stay close. A gray mist awaits. I cannot see inside, but in it lies danger."

Then she whirled and vanished behind a beaded curtain set in a doorway I hadn't even noticed.

"She knows how to make an exit," my aunt murmured.

"And an impression." Neil dug out his wallet. And even though the priestess had not asked for money this time, he left a fifty in her tip jar. Then he gave me a brief, fierce hug.

As we went on our way, I tried to tell myself the woman's touch was just static electricity. That her words were all for show. But her warning stayed with me, rattled me. If I got lost in the mist, would Neil find me?

Chapter Fifteen

I was in a much better state of mind on our walk back to
the hotel Saturday morning after a decadent breakfast at
a nearby outdoor cafe. I wore a pretty spring-green dress
with cute little bunnies on it, and I'd had an insanely delicious
pork-barbecue eggs Benedict served over garlic toast, with a
French 75 cocktail. Champagne in the morning made me
happy. It also made me want to nap, but then again, so did
staying out late the night before.

Rain was in the forecast, but for now, clouds scudded over-
head, chased by a fresh wind. I walked Astra as my aunt
chatted with Royce at the front of the group. The bartenders
and Kirby walked just behind her.

Mr. Mixy was here, too. He'd run into Mark—funny how
he kept doing that—who invited him along.

I figured I should take advantage of his unfortunate
proximity.

"So you got nothing out of talking with Alfie?" I asked Mr.
Mixy as we strolled. "Did he say anything about Edgar
Poeville?"

"Alfie said he was really broken up about the murder of his
friend and that he thought a couple who'd come into the gift
shop yesterday killed him."

I tilted my head at him. "He said that? Really?"

"Uh-huh."

"You know he was probably talking about Neil and me, right?" And maybe leading Stephan on.

Mr. Mixy seemed shocked. "Pepper, you didn't kill that man, did you?"

"Oh, for f— No, Stephan. That's why we wanted you to follow Alfie. To see if any of his sketchy activities might suggest a connection with Edgar's murder."

"What sketchy activities?"

"He tried to sell us drugs yesterday. Did he try to sell you any?"

"No, of course not," Mr. Mixy said. "But he gave me a pill he said would relax me if I got too stressed out."

"Did you take it?"

"Not yet, but I might if you keep haranguing me."

Ooo. *Haranguing.* Big word for Mr. Mixy. "You might not want to take that. First one's free, and then he gets you hooked."

"Don't be ridiculous. He's so cool. Look, there he is!"

We were getting close to the gift shop where Alfie worked, down the block and on the other side of the street. I hung back, and so did Neil and Mr. Mixy, along with Mark and Diana, who were right behind us. The rest of the bartenders, Kirby, my aunt and Royce kept going.

Alfie unlocked the door and stepped into the shop. A moment later, he plunked the scantily dressed mannequin outside the entrance and disappeared inside again.

But another person had caught my eye. It took me a second to be sure it was her. Camelia Landry walked toward us, and I didn't want her to see me, not after our uncomfortable conversation yesterday. If she was still hooked on Beau, she might report back to him about me.

I turned away toward a storefront and eyed her in the reflection. Following my lead, so did Neil, Mark and Diana, while Mr. Mixy continued to stare.

"Stephan!" I hissed. "Don't look at her. Look at this! This store sells vintage cocktail shakers. See them in the window? Maybe you need one."

He turned toward me, then looked in the window. "Maybe I do. It'll look good on TV." He strode into the antiques store.

"Sometimes he's weirdly vulnerable to suggestion," I muttered as Camelia entered the souvenir shop where Alfie worked.

"I think you've hypnotized him," Mark said.

"If I did, I'd convince him I turned into a cloud and blew away and he could never see me again."

"Worth a try," Neil said. "Was that Camelia Landry?"

"Yes. Good eye. Isn't it weird she's going into the souvenir shop?"

"That's the woman you saw yesterday who's being scammed by Beau?" Diana asked.

"That's her," I said. We all turned around now and waited, watching the souvenir shop.

In a few minutes, Camelia came out, looking preoccupied. Now she carried a brown paper shopping bag by its handles. Could she have bought drugs from Alfie?

She crossed the street and walked in our direction before we had a chance to move, then pulled up short when she saw me. A smile lit up her face, though I had no idea if it was genuine. She had the kind of Southern cordiality that came with a mask.

"It's Pepper, isn't it? Are these your friends? And is this your dog?" She bent down to pet Astra, who panted happily and tried to snuffle her way into Camelia's bag.

"Yes, ma'am."

"Oh, you don't need to ma'am me." She straightened, pulling the bag out of Astra's reach. "We're friends now, aren't we?"

"Sure," I said. Maybe she'd given my warning about Beau some thought. "You're out shopping early, aren't you?"

"Had to get going early so I could get around the race before it starts. I have a lot to do before my little Easter gathering tomorrow."

I was curious about the race, but I was more curious about what was in her bag.

I didn't even have to ask.

"If you want a very nice candy selection, that store over there is the best." Camelia pointed toward the mannequin, then opened the bag to show us her bounty. "It's the only place I could find Elmer's Pecan Eggs at this late date, and believe me, I called everywhere. I wanted some for these cute little goody baskets I'm making."

"Oh, yeah, I remember eating those as a kid." They were kind of a NOLA tradition.

She looked up and exclaimed, "Well, if it isn't Mr. Mixy!"

Stephan had emerged from the antiques store with his own shopping bag.

"Camelia!" he called out in a cloying tone, rushing over to give her a big hug. "What a coincidence! This is some of my bar team who will be working your party tomorrow."

His bar team? Wait—*what?* Our gig was Camelia's party? At her mansion in the Garden District?

"Is that right?" Camelia said to Mr. Mixy, then turned to me with a gleam in her eye before examining the rest of us. "Which of you is Neil Rockaway?"

Neil stepped forward and shook her hand. "That's me, ma'am. And this is Mark and Diana. *Not* on the bar team."

"Pleased to meet you," Mark said with one of his irresistible dimples.

"Oh, that accent! You must be Mark Fairman. Mr. Mixy told me about you and your distillery." She beamed at Mark, though she cast a judgmental eye on Diana's unfussy outfit.

Camelia turned back to Neil, eyeing him a little too long for my taste. "I just love your cocktail book. When Mr. Mixy said you were working for him, I couldn't have been more thrilled. I'll see you later today when you come by to look at the bar, yes?"

"Indeed you will." Neil managed a confident smile, but my mind was spinning like one of those frozen daiquiri machines on Bourbon Street. "You received the supplies we ordered?"

"I sure did. See you then. We'll make a cocktail hour of it. Have a nice morning." Camelia walked off with her bag of candy eggs in hand.

We resumed our walk to the hotel. This time I fell in beside Neil. "Did you know she was the one we were working for?"

"No idea. Millie handled the orders for supplies, so I didn't place the address. And Mr. Mixy was not forthcoming with details."

"What a surprise," I said dryly.

In a few minutes we were back in the lobby of Hydrangea House. There were two sets of doors to enter the hotel, which was on a corner. I walked across the lobby with Astra and looked through the doors we hadn't entered. A throng of people walked or jogged down the street, a few in costumes or pushing strollers or both, all of them labeled with paper numbers. This must be the race Camelia mentioned.

I went back to my friends, who lounged and chatted on the comfy furniture. Astra barked to see my aunt, who cooed and took the pup from me.

"Did you see all that?" I gestured toward the runners.

"Better them than me." Barclay rubbed his forehead as he lounged with one long leg over the arm of his chair. "Cray drank me under the table last night."

Luke, relaxing on a nearby couch, grinned. "That man is a machine."

"Maybe, but he's not here this morning, is he?" Barclay looked out toward the runners. "Is that a marathon?"

"It's a 10K. The Crescent City Classic. Has most of the Quarter shut down for another hour or so," Kirby said, walking back from the desk with his motorcycle helmet. They must've stowed it for him.

I glanced at the friendly clerk at the desk, a balding middle-aged man who might have once captained the Love Boat, and he recognized me.

"Ms. Revelle?" He held out a box with a smile. "You got a package."

I froze. In a moment, Neil appeared at my shoulder. "Not again."

"Maybe it's something nice," I said. "A corsage or a severed hand."

"Let me." He stepped up and took the small box of plain brown cardboard, with no return address, just a scrawl in black marker, *Pepper Revelle, Hydrangea House.* "How did this arrive?"

"Bicycle messenger, I think," the clerk said. "A little unusual, but I didn't think anything of it. Is there a problem?"

"What did the messenger look like?" I asked.

"Oh, just a kid. A teenager on a bike."

"Not Beau, then," I said to Neil. "But he might've hired the kid."

"He has before." Neil had the attention of all of our group now. Their chatter had fizzled to nothing as all eyes followed the box. He put it on the coffee table where I'd opened the last one and sat on the love seat. "Should I do it?"

"No. I really should." I sat next to him and pulled my cocktail knife out of my bag.

"I hate to keep asking this," Mark said, "but is it ticking?"

I huffed a much-needed laugh and held it up to my ear. "I don't think so." Feeling more at ease, I cut the tape and opened the box, only to find a shiny silver cardboard box inside that.

"Maybe it's a cupcake." That was Melody, always there to cheer me up.

"I do love cupcakes." The silver box had an elastic silver string around it, which I used to lift it. "It looks kind of like a bakery box." I sniffed it. "It smells like chocolate."

They all looked at me.

"Oh, all right. Here goes nothing."

Chapter Sixteen

I put my knife away and stretched the string over the corners of the silver box, pulling it off. I pushed the empty brown box aside and set the silver box on the table. Then, as all my friends watched in the quiet hotel lobby, I lifted the lid and looked inside.

"What a disappointment," I said. "I already had eggs this morning."

Luke stood and peered inside. "An Easter egg?"

"A big fancy chocolate one," Mr. Mixy said. "Can I try it?"

"No," everyone said at once.

I lifted it out and set it on the table. The dark brown egg, slightly bigger than a softball, was adorned with sugar decorations in pink and green—piped trim and flowers and music notes.

"Be careful opening it," Neil cautioned.

I wouldn't have to smash the egg like I smashed the bunny. It looked like its upper half was a lid made of chocolate. So it was hollow. It might hold Peeps or jelly beans or, you know, a hand grenade. The usual Easter treats.

"Detective Colby would tell me to use gloves, but I'd rather get this over with."

Neil frowned. "Beau didn't leave prints last time. I can ask the front desk—"

Before he could say more, anxiety took over. I lifted the chocolate lid and set it aside. Nestled inside the chocolate egg was another folded piece of paper. I pulled it out and unfolded it. "Another poem."

Royce looked worried. "What does this one say?"

I took a breath and read Beau's rhyme aloud:

> *I need to tell you what I want*
> *so that we're diamond-clear.*
> *Stay away from all my haunts*
> *to shield those you hold dear.*
>
> *I will let your parents be*
> *if you meet me, alone,*
> *in public, daytime, hassle-free,*
> *a totally safe zone.*
>
> *They call it the Music Box,*
> *a Village, not a maze.*
> *After this, the hare and fox*
> *will go our separate ways.*
>
> *Meet at ten or lose the chance*
> *to save your family.*
> *Don't tempt me to do the dance*
> *of death with them and ye.*

"This one's a bit better," Mark said, "but that last line is bollocks."

Chuckles relieved the tension.

"Agreed," I said, "but that 'dance of death' is kind of unnerving. He's warning me off."

"And asking to meet you," Neil said. "I don't like it."

"I don't either, but I don't see how I have a choice. What's this music box he's talking about?"

"Music Box Village," Kirby said. "That has to be it. It's a quirky art project in the Bywater where they have concerts sometimes."

"Like a stadium?" I asked. We didn't see a stadium when we were there yesterday.

He shook his head. "Much smaller. It's cool. All kinds of interactive musical installations."

"Great. Maybe he wants to play a duet. Too bad I'm not musical," I said. "Of greater concern is that if he means ten this morning, that's just twenty minutes from now."

"He did say daylight," Diana said. "That implies this morning."

I gazed through the doors to the river of runners. "How am I going to get there? It looks like the race has the hotel blocked off."

"Yeah, it goes right by the garage," Royce said.

"And you can't get a cab right now." Kirby looked thoughtful.

"Maybe that's a good thing. You shouldn't go anyway," Neil said.

"I agree," Aunt Celestine piped up. "No good can come of it."

"But if this is my chance to settle things with him, why wouldn't I?" I said.

"Let me text the detective." Neil tapped his phone. A minute later, he looked up. "He's also in the Quarter and says we're amateurs and should stay away from Beau."

"I don't think he's taking this seriously," I said.

"Maybe he doesn't need to," Neil replied. "Your parents

have protection. You foiled Beau's attempt to steal from them. You don't need to see him now."

"Not sure if you noticed, but he's unhinged." I waved the poem at him. "I believe he *will* try to kill them if I don't respond. I need to at least see what he wants. Maybe we can end this now."

"Yes, he's unhinged. Exactly. Don't go." As Neil dug in, I grew more desperate.

"I *have* to go."

"I could take you." Kirby patted his helmet. "I have my bike. I think I know a way to slip through the roadblocks."

Neil stood. "No."

"Yes!" I got to my feet so I wouldn't be arguing from a low altitude. I avoided my aunt's concerned gaze and focused on Neil. "I have to do this."

"Then I want to be with you." He turned to Kirby. "Let me take her. I can ride."

Neil rode motorcycles? And then that thought was eclipsed by the voodoo woman's warning yesterday: *Stay close. A gray mist awaits ... danger.*

"No offense, but no way," Kirby told Neil. "Besides, I know the quickest way to get her there. I'll keep an eye out for trouble. Usually there are people there playing in the exhibits. It should be fine."

"Right. What Kirby said. It'll be fine. I'll text you, OK?" I tried to will my urgency into Neil, but his jaw was set, and our friends stayed quiet.

"I can't prevent you from going," he finally said. "But please. Don't do it."

His deep concern moved me, but the pressure inside me was too great. If I could confront Beau, I could end the threat.

He'd offered to back off if I talked to him. I could let Beau win this battle, give in and go see him, and ultimately win the war. Or at least reach a truce.

"Why don't you tell Detective Colby where we'll be?" I suggested to Neil. "I can show up alone as directed, but if the cops come, maybe they can nail him."

"We'll let him know, and they can show up without you," Neil said. "There's no need for you to be there."

I shook my head. "Please try to understand. This is a real chance to end this nonsense with Beau. The only cost to me is feeding his ego. We're going."

I felt like crap for saying no to Neil. I supposed this was our second real argument as a couple. I could understand why he didn't like arguing with me. I didn't want to make him unhappy, either.

Neil's silence was a heavy weight on my shoulders as I followed Kirby outside. He'd parked his motorcycle in an alley next to a trash bin at the back of the hotel. Tomato red with black trim, the Honda looked old but in nice shape.

"Vintage?" I asked nervously as he detached a helmet from the back and handed it to me. I struggled to strap it on as Kirby stowed his cute hat in his jacket and donned his own helmet.

"Yeah. 1982. I fixed it up. It's pretty nimble. You ever ride a bike?"

"Once, on the back of a date's Harley. Mostly I remember how loud it was."

Kirby grinned as he boarded the bike and got it running. "This isn't a hog. It's more of a piglet. You all set?"

I'd finally secured the helmet, adjusted my bag across my body, and climbed on behind him, grateful for the pettipants under my dress and my practical sneakers. "Where's your tuba?"

He laughed. "At home. I have a car for that. Hold on. This could be bumpy."

Man, Kirby wasn't kidding. The bike rode smoothly enough when the road was level, but this was the Quarter, full of pavers and potholes and random hazards. I held tight to his waist, his leather jacket cool under my hands, as he buzzed away from Decatur and around Jackson Square, stair-stepping through the relatively quiet streets until he got to Esplanade and pulled up next to a cop standing at a blocked intersection. Runners trotted past us.

"Marcel!" Kirby called out to the officer, who turned around. Though the man was a bit heavier than Kirby, they looked a lot alike, right down to their smiles.

The cop walked over. "Hey, cuz. What's up?"

"I need a favor, man. I have to get through here. It's an emergency."

Marcel looked back at me and smirked, then at Marcel. "I see your emergency. But I have a job to do here."

"No, really," I shouted over the motor. "It's an emergency!"

Marcel looked back and forth between us, then stepped toward the road and peered both ways. He stepped back to us. "There's a gap coming up in a sec. Get across there quick and don't hit anybody."

"Thanks, man," Kirby said, rolling forward slightly to ease between the barricades. "I owe you."

A minute later, there was enough space between runners for Kirby to purr through the gap and zip across the divided street.

"My cousin," he shouted over his shoulder at me.

"A useful guy to know," I yelled back. The cousins had that in common.

A lot went through my mind in the next ten minutes as we wove through the streets on the way to the Bywater. Would we get there in time? Probably. Would Beau just want to talk? In spite of what I told Neil, I wasn't sure. But the burden of worrying about Beau had reached the exploding point. All the fear had snuck up on me, like lava rising under a placid mountain. Now I was ready to burst with all the bad feelings. I needed resolution, and Beau had offered me a chance to end this.

I also thought about Neil and how terrible it felt to argue with him. And I had a lot of second thoughts about myself. It wasn't too late to turn around. But wasn't a tranquil future worth the risk?

We rolled into the eclectic Bywater neighborhood. After a couple of minutes, Kirby turned down Rampart Street until it hit a dead end. He brought us into a parking lot by the train tracks that was more dirt than rocks. Well beyond the tracks were the spooky abandoned buildings of the naval base.

In front of us was Mad Max's dream house. The peculiar enclosed structure's tall walls were made of corrugated metal, a pastiche of rust and galvanized steel and green moss, occasionally adorned with painted flowers and upcycled glass pieces. A few crappy bicycles leaned against one wall. I wasn't sure if they were part of the exhibit.

One other vehicle was in the parking lot, a van. I didn't see the car Beau drove the other day. Was he even here?

Kirby killed the engine. As we dismounted and removed our helmets, the sounds of children laughing and strange clinking and mechanical moans and musical tidbits floated out to us, comforting but also unsettling.

"I told you," Kirby said in answer to my questioning look. "It's a musical place."

"Creepy, if you ask me."

"Wait till you play inside."

"I'm not here to play." Unfortunately. "Maybe you should stay here. He said to come alone."

"I'm going to at least escort you inside. I don't think either of us wants to tell Neil I just dropped you off in the parking lot."

I offered him a half smile. "You have a point. We might as well do this. What time is it?"

Kirby pulled a phone from the inside of his leather jacket. "Ten oh five."

"Damn."

"Close enough. That bastard can wait five minutes."

Kirby's bravado gave me courage, and we walked slowly around the outside of the structure along the dirt path, following the sign that promised an entrance. A few trees loomed over us. I couldn't tell if the chaotic green plants hugging the walls were neglected or just hadn't come into their own yet.

The eerie musical sounds bounced around inside the metal fence before coming out deformed. Or maybe that was my fear getting the better of me. I was about to find out. The tall, corrugated-metal gates were open, and we walked in.

I spotted two adults and five kids running around, beating on chimes, pulling on levers that made fartlike organ sounds, pressing buttons that honked horns, hammering on drums, squealing.

The father figure spoke. "Time to go. You heard the man!"

"Come on. Now," the impatient mom said. She gave us a funny look. And in less than a minute, kids wrangled, they were gone. Most of the sounds faded away, and the childish voices retreated down the path.

"Where is everybody?" I whispered to Kirby.

"This isn't good," he whispered back.

"Pepper, Pepper, Pepper," a voice boomed around the courtyard. "Didn't I tell you to come alone?"

Chapter Seventeen

I stepped in front of Kirby and tried to figure out where the voice was coming from. There were a lot of wild two-story structures in this place, mostly made of weathered old wood, with pieces shifting and groaning in the increasing wind. A treehouse-like walkway connected a second level of these weird little buildings, forming an outer ring. Peculiar staircases offered ways to climb up there.

I was just about to head for the nearest one to get a better view when I spotted the phone booth.

It wasn't a real phone booth, just a tall metal booth with open cutouts built on a tiny platform. Its door was open. It had a vintage phone in it, the old pay-phone type—and Beau.

"Pepper, Pepper, Pepper!" he said again into the receiver. Atop the booth, a pair of megaphones, facing outward and opposite each other, spun like helicopter blades as he spoke, throwing his voice loud and wide.

"I'm here!" I called.

"And who's with you?"

"My ride."

"Oh, you have a new ride these days?" His suggestive teasing ticked me off. Beau wasn't my friend. He didn't have the right to tease me.

"He gave me a ride here."

"Then he'd better leave." Beau stepped out of the booth, pulled a handgun from under his white T-shirt and shot it once in the air.

We both jumped. Kirby said a word I'd been trying to work out of my vocabulary.

Beau aimed the gun at him. "Tell him to leave, Pepper."

"Go," I told Kirby.

"But—"

"Go." I turned and faced him, whispering, "Get help if you can. I'll be all right." Louder, I said, "Go!"

"All right. I'm going."

"I'll be listening for your bike," Beau said. "Not a very quiet means of transportation. I heard you coming a mile away. If you don't go, I kill her. If the cops come, I kill her."

Kirby gave him a dirty look. "Don't hurt her." Then he walked out of the gate.

Beau and I stood and faced each other. A minute later came the sound of the motorcycle starting up and leaving.

"A wise choice." Beau stuck the gun back in his jeans waistband under his loose T-shirt. "I hate guns. No subtlety."

Beau's voice held a hint of Texas twang. He looked the same as I remembered, maybe a bit more weary—of medium build, handsome, with a square jaw and freckles. His shortish, dark-blond hair was tousled in an appealing way, and his pale blue eyes radiated innocence. His good looks and charm had helped him fool a lot of people.

He began walking toward me.

"Did you scare off that family, too?" I stepped to the side, avoiding his approach.

Not the smartest move. Instead of coming after me, he walked to the gate and closed it.

Crap, crap, crap.

"Now we're alone." He eyed me as I looked around for an escape. "Whatever you're thinking, relax. We'll be done long before the cavalry arrives. As for the breeders, I told them we were closing early to prepare for a concert."

"Why would they believe you?"

"I'm a volunteer here." He shrugged and smiled. "It's amazing what you can do when no one really wants to find you."

I stopped moving and hugged my bag. "What do you want with me? And what happened to the safe space you promised?"

He shook his head. "Even you, Pepper, believe what you want to believe. It's an epidemic. Fortunately, gullibility is an epidemic that benefits me."

"I'm willing to make a deal," I told him. "That's what you wanted, right? Why can't you just leave my parents alone?"

"Because they're like the parents I never had." His voice, so full of pathos, held a mocking undercurrent. It was like he was showing me his fake self and his real one at the same time. He grinned. "And your mom likes me more than she likes you."

"Can we end this now?" I asked. "I'll leave you alone, as long as you promise to leave my parents alone. And me."

"Oh, we'll end this now." He chuckled, approaching me again, and I scurried around the edge of the space, keeping structures between us—a tree, benches encircling leafy plants, a human-size birdcage on a pedestal. "Why run away, little Pepper?"

I *hated* when he called me that, but I chose to ignore his patronizing tone. "You said we could settle this. I won't interfere. Go on your merry way and leave me and everyone I know out of it."

I'd made it all the way to the phone booth. The air smelled different here, almost like fuel. I realized a metal building, like a barn or warehouse, bordered this space on one side, and its wide doors were open. Maybe they kept machinery in there. It might also offer another way for me to get out.

I hovered outside the phone booth, weighing my options, as Beau strolled over to a two-story shack near it that resembled a treehouse. It stood on four legs decorated with wood slats, forming four skinny pyramids. Ropes hung from the floor of the second story. The square metal roof had a peak in the center like a witch's hat.

"This is one of my favorites," he said, pulling on the dangling ropes. Fan blades and spinners with strange attachments—tubes?—whirled above the metal grate over his head, exuding alien whoops and whistles. The fans were mostly hidden behind multicolored, vertical wood slats, though parts of the spinners stuck out of holes cut in the walls of the second story. I glimpsed pulleys and other moving parts. Beau looked up at the machinery, smiling. "Do you like it?"

"It's cool. I'd enjoy it more if we settled our business."

He turned toward me, letting the strange sounds linger and echo. "You're right. That's why I wanted you to come. But I've realized it's far too late for me to let bygones be bygones. Especially since you've obviously coached my parents—I mean your parents. They're going to miss out on a *huge* investment opportunity." His eyes danced. "*And* you stirred up the cops against me. Was it your idea to kill Edgar Poeville?"

"What? What in the hell are you talking about?" It was as if, sociopath that he was, Beau thought everyone as capable of cold-blooded murder as he was. And I didn't like that he guessed my parents were finally on to him. "We thought you killed him."

He cocked his head and stared at me. "Interesting. Well, whether you did it or not, it hardly matters. In our little chess game, I'm ten moves ahead of you. I thought about using you for ransom, but that's so messy. It will be a lot easier to kill you."

Beau pulled out the gun again, and my heart skipped a beat, even as I wondered if he was screwing with me about Edgar Poeville. *He's always screwing with you and everyone else, Pepper.*

I jumped up into the phone booth, grabbed the handset and yelled into it, "Help! Help! He's trying to kill me!"

My amplified cries howled around the space and died away.

Beau laughed. "That's wonderful. Please, do it again. No one's here, little Pepper. Just you. Not even me, because I'm no one. No one knows who I am. And that's why I'm going to get exactly what I want. Now get out of the booth."

There was no point in staying in the booth. It had big cutouts in the side. It wouldn't stop any bullets. Still, I stepped down from the platform slowly, looking around for a way out.

I burst into a sprint toward the warehouse. Beau leaped forward and grabbed my arm, yanking me to a halt.

"Oh no you don't." He put the gun to my head, and I stilled. "Here's how this is going to work." He dragged me under the elevated shack with the spinning wheels and wailing tubes and to the other side, where a ladder leaned against the platform. The fuel smell was stronger here.

Oh, God.

I tried to wrench myself away from him, but he yanked me back and hit me on the head with the butt of the gun. It hurt like hell. I wavered, and he tightened his grip.

"Don't go passing out on me. That won't go well for you. I'm not going to shoot you unless you make me," he said. "Climb the ladder."

"I'm dizzy." *Gasoline.* That was what that smell was.

"Then I'll help you."

I struggled anyway, gun or no gun, until he wrestled me into a suffocating headlock and whispered in my ear. "Cooperate, or your boyfriend's next."

"I don't have a boyfriend," I gasped.

"Seems like you might have more than one," he said wryly, "but we both know who I'm talking about. Neil. This is one promise I'll keep, little Pepper."

I gulped for air. Then I nodded.

He pushed me up the ladder, then forced me through an opening cut in the wall of slats. I had to crouch among the rubbery black belts, ropes and pulleys that powered the instruments.

Beau didn't come in. "Stay or I'll shoot you." He climbed down, then tossed the ladder away.

Maybe I could jump. I was nine or ten feet up, and it would probably hurt. But if I tried to jump now, I was pretty sure he'd shoot me. And then he'd go after Neil.

Beau took a moment to pull on all the ropes, cranking up the eerie wails of the machinery. I ducked to avoid the fan blades and tried to figure out what to do. As they spun more slowly, their laments eased. And I heard something else. Sirens.

I looked down through the metal grate, hope warring with fear. Beau crouched, holding a lighter up to a pile of cardboard and newspapers packed around one foot of the structure. I hadn't even noticed it there. The gasoline smell was inescapable, and the newspapers caught fire right away. Then the wooden slats that decorated the metal legs started to burn.

The metal structure might stand up to Beau's fire. But that dry wood would burn all the way up to my perch.

"Goodbye, little Pepper." Beau walked away as flames raced

up the side of the structure where I'd climbed in. Jumping out was an even worse idea now.

Was this what an Easter ham felt like? The heat intensified as smoke rose around me. Flames licked up through the floor, and I jumped and skittered to the other side of the structure to get out of their way. I rubbed my head where he'd hit me and tried to think. When all the walls were engulfed, I'd be screwed.

Through the gaps between the slats, I watched Beau disappear into the warehouse as the sirens got louder. Were they coming for him? Would they catch him?

Would they be too late for me?

Chapter Eighteen

I couldn't wait around and find out if rescue was coming. More slats of the wall where Beau had forced me into this claustrophobic musical treehouse caught fire as the flames spread.

Staying low and maneuvering around the machinery above my head— the belts, ropes, pulleys and fans—I got as far from the flames as I could and rapidly assessed my options. The spinning gizmos partially stuck out of cutouts in the slatted walls. I'd have to get out of one of those windows.

The problem was, the fans and spinners were slotted in there, too, and while they weren't actively spinning now, they were definitely in my way. Could I take one down? I probably had a tool in my bag that could loosen a bolt or two, but how long would that take?

Maybe brute force was the answer. The machinery was clever and well installed, but those spinners weren't made to stand up to the weight of this cheese-of-the-month-club-enhanced body.

I chose the lowest spinner near me, a hoop with fat flexible black tubes lashed to it in arcs to catch the wind. It stuck out of a gap cut where two walls of slats met—a corner. I looked closely. The framework for this spinner was light wood, not metal as I'd feared.

With a silent apology to the artists, I used a cross-support beam on the wall to hoist myself up so I could lean against the hoop that held the tubes. After a moment of creaking in protest, the whole spinner collapsed, dumping me on the metal grate floor.

I cursed and coughed, trying to breathe through the smoke and rising heat. The sirens sounded close now, but the flames crawled closer, creeping around both walls that met at this corner. I clambered to my feet. I had to hurry.

While part of the spinner's axle and hoop remained, I now had room to squeeze out of the gap in the wall. Probably.

I yanked off my bag and tossed it to the ground first. I looked down. Maybe I could use the leg of the structure as a kind of slide. It was slightly angled, shaped like a tall, two-sided pyramid made of wood. But it would be rough. The leg's decorative slats pointed to and almost met at the corners, but there were no smooth edges.

Then again, it wasn't on fire. Yet. My ass was getting hot, and not in a good way.

I used the crossbar on the wall to hoist myself up again and squeezed into the "window," getting stuck halfway through.

Rip. "Damn it!" Now there was a nice tear along the waistline of my cute bunny dress. But the flames were close enough at my right that I knew I didn't have a choice. I sucked in my stomach, pushed farther through and hoisted my left leg over. I grabbed onto slats sticking up at the bottom edge of the opening and pulled my other leg through so I was facing the shack.

A scene of horror lay before me, a chaotic inferno of disintegrating wood. The wind blew hot air and ashes around my face, and I freaked out.

I wanted to lower myself down the leg gently, but there was no time. I chose falling.

Before I could plunge all the way to the ground, I caught the top of the leg's skinny pyramid with my hands. *Good.* From here I could drop, and I did, hearing the skirt of my dress rip on the way down as it caught on the boards.

I fell hard on my side with an "Oof!" Heat baked my back, and I scrambled to grab my bag and scurry away from the shack. I stumbled to the steps at the base of the giant birdcage several feet away, out of breath, my head hurting. I dropped onto a step and sat and watched my prison burn.

Flames had reached the window I'd tumbled out of and now spilled down the leg that had been my runway to the ground. The blaze engulfed the entire two-story structure, and in the strange currents created by the wind and fire, the tubes inside whispered death moans as they made their final gasps.

"Pepper!" came a familiar voice from behind me.

I turned my head. "Neil?" I croaked.

He ran toward me from the now-open gate, trailed by Kirby and two uniformed police who got on their radio and called for help.

And then it started to rain.

Neil helped me to my feet and hugged me, smoke and stupidity and all.

I held him close as tears leaked from my stinging eyes. "I'm sorry," I snuffled into his shoulder.

"It'll be a lot easier to forgive you since you're alive." He held me at arm's length and surveyed my torn, smudged dress and no doubt dirty face. He used his thumb to wipe a tear away. "It's not your fault."

"You know it is. At least a little."

A corner of his mouth turned up. "But understandable. I guess you didn't make a deal with Beau."

"The deal was that he wanted to kill me. I guess you can say 'I told you so' now."

"I would never," Neil said.

His words made me smile. "Any sign of him?"

"Police are looking, but no, I think he's long gone. Kirby called 9-1-1, then me, as soon as he got out of the neighborhood. I might have yelled at Detective Colby, who picked me up and brought me over."

"I guess he had no trouble getting through. Where is he?"

We broke apart and looked around. The detective had just entered the gate, wearing a black rain jacket and an air of defeat. He stopped to have a word with the other cops.

I waved to Kirby and mouthed "thank you," and he gave me a thumbs-up. I glanced back at the shack. The top had partly collapsed. The dry wood had gone up fast, and now it burned itself out with the help of the rain.

Firefighters had arrived, and they stood and talked and kept an eye on the dying fire. The cables draped above the hut didn't look so healthy, though. It might be a while before another concert happened here.

We all pretended we weren't getting soaked as Detective Colby walked over to us. I looped my bag over my head, cross-body, and faced him.

"Did you get him?" I asked.

"Of course not," he said. "It figures, when he finally shows up and performs a criminal act, I'm not here. You'd better tell me what happened."

So I did.

AFTER MANY THANKS to Kirby and a flurry of texts to our friends and my aunt, Neil and I summoned an Uber back to our hotel, which was no longer besieged by runners. I took a quick shower, declared my dress dead and changed into jeans and a T-shirt advertising my bar, Nola. Then I met Neil, Royce, Aunt Celestine and Astra in the lobby.

As we waited out front for the valet to bring Neil's car around, a familiar sight caught my eye—Sierra Felt in her cape, leading a group of tourists to her spot in front of the Fantome. Only another group was already there. I looked closely and saw it was led by Wilma Wells in her Victorian gown and wide hat. She turned toward Sierra and scowled.

"And this is the young lady who uses all of my research to lead her ghost tours," Wilma said loudly enough for all of the tourists to hear.

"Hey!" Sierra shouted back. "That's not true. Nobody owns history."

"But you don't own my copyrighted words and unique discoveries!" Wilma snapped.

"But you don't even have the story about the farting ghost!" Sierra returned as some of the tourists smiled. Maybe they thought this banter was all part of the tour.

Wilma Wells just rolled her eyes. "You'll be hearing from my lawyer—again. This way, folks. I have some wonderful, *original* ghost stories to tell you."

Sierra shook her head in a dramatic fashion as Wilma led her people away. As Sierra started her spiel, the valet arrived with Neil's car, and we piled in, heading toward my parents' house.

"That was ugly," I noted from the co-pilot's seat while I petted Astra. I needed some cuddly dog time. Even if my aunt had dressed our dog in the equivalent of an Easter clown outfit: a purple onesie dotted with yellow and pink eggs and a fluffy collar of multicolored ribbon, accented with tiny pompoms and bells.

"Both of them are angry," Neil said of the tour operators.

"Wilma justifiably so, if Sierra really did come on her tour expressly to steal her material," I said.

"You know, I think I've seen Wilma Wells before," said Royce from the second row, where he sat with Aunt Celestine.

"Of course you did," my aunt replied. "When Pepper and Neil talked to her last night."

"No. Not then," Royce replied. "I arrived at Hydrangea House before you did on Thursday. My flight got in late morning, and I came over to see if my room was available yet. While the clerk was checking the computer, Wilma Wells came in from the garage entrance and walked through the lobby. She was dressed in modern clothes, moving quickly. I didn't realize it was her when we saw her again last night in her fancy duds."

"Holy crapnoodles," I said. "What was she doing?"

"I have no idea," my brother said.

"We should tell Colby. He can ask her," Neil suggested.

"Could she have arranged to meet Edgar there?" I wondered. "Maybe talk about her dispute with him? And then the discussion got out of hand?"

"If so," my aunt asked, "how did they end up in the hotel room? It was obviously not Edgar's room, since they let it out to you."

"Unless they mixed up our reservation," I said. "But we should let Detective Colby know anyway. That's too much of a coincidence. You don't think she's connected to Beau somehow, do you?"

"I don't want you anywhere near that man," my aunt exclaimed, bringing me back to this morning's encounter. "You'd better not scare us like that again."

"We're all going with you next time you decide to do something that ... risky," Royce added.

"Stupid," I said. "You can say stupid."

"You're not stupid. You just wanted to fix things," Neil amended. "I understand that. But don't do that to us again," he echoed my aunt.

Celestine and Royce chuckled.

"I'm sorry. And embarrassed." Astra licked my hand, making me feel a teeny bit better. "I really thought he would make a deal with me. I thought we could put all this behind us. Or maybe it was wishful thinking."

"You're a good person who wants to solve problems," my aunt said. "It's who you are. But you're dealing with a dangerous criminal who doesn't have your standards of behavior."

"He has *no* standards of behavior," I huffed.

"Where do you think he went after he left you?" Neil asked.

"Somewhere in the Bywater, probably. His car wasn't in the parking lot. Then again, it might've been parked on one of the side streets."

"So he walked?" Royce asked.

"Now that I think about it, there were a few old bicycles outside the Music Box. Maybe he took one of those. I really think he's in the Bywater somewhere, given his choice of meeting places and what Jezebel told us. And Camelia said she helped him with rent sometimes. Maybe he has an apartment there."

We were in Lakeview now, its neat, comfortable houses

lovely in the spring sunshine that had broken through the scudding clouds. All seemed calm.

Until we turned onto my parents' street.

Chapter Nineteen

"What's happening here?" Neil asked as we rolled up on multiple police cars blocking access to the street, their blue lights strobing. A white, technical-looking truck sat next to them.

I looked down the street. More than two blocks away, more police cars and a fire truck had formed a barrier. "My parents' house is in the middle there. Whoa no. I hope nothing happened to them."

"Try calling." Neil pulled over to the curb just shy of the roadblock.

I called my dad's phone. He answered after a couple of rings. "Pepper? Oh, my. We've had some doings here."

"We're parked on your street. What's going on?"

"The police say there's a bomb threat. Your mother and I are waiting at the end of the block."

I looked around and spotted them huddled with other neighbors and one of the cops. "I see you. We'll be right there."

We piled out of the car with Astra, who took a moment to pee on a fire hydrant.

My parents stood in front of a charming cottage that sat well above the ground, its stilts hidden by latticework—insurance against the next flood. As we approached my parents, the neighbors who'd been talking to them wandered off. The female police officer remained.

"I'm Pepper Revelle. These are my parents," I told her. "What's going on?"

Petite, wearing her brunette hair pinned up and a skeptical expression, she looked us over. "I'm Officer Newbold. There's been a bomb threat."

"Are you guys OK?" Royce asked my folks.

My mother took an extra moment to consider Royce, her newfound son, emotion softening her face for a second before she turned stoic again. "I'm sure it's nothing. We didn't see anything odd in the house."

"The bomb threat is for *their* house?" I asked the officer.

The cop regarded me for a moment. "Pepper Revelle, did you say? Didn't you just escape being turned into a charcoal briquette?"

"Uh ... yes?"

"I heard from Detective Colby, and he filled me in. Since we had a security detail on your parents' house, he wanted us to know what we're dealing with."

"You mean Beau," I said.

"Maybe," Officer Newbold replied. "The threat was called in to the police station about an hour and a half ago. The caller said there was a pipe bomb in your parents' house that was timed to go off at 1 p.m. So we evacuated within a two-block radius."

I pulled my phone out and checked the time. "It's one twelve."

"Could the threat be fake?" Neil asked.

"If it's Beau, who knows?" Royce said.

"That man is a snake." Aunt Celestine wore a livid expression that would have turned Beau to stone.

"We have to play it safe," Officer Newbold said. "The bomb squad didn't have enough time to go in before one. Now they're considering sending in a robot—"

KA-BOOOOOM!

I screamed and ducked along with half the residents of Lakeview as an explosion rattled the neighborhood and threw out a shockwave that blew our hair back.

Astra barked furiously, and I picked her up. She trembled in my arms even as she barked, the bells on her collar jingling. Poor puppy. I looked in the direction of my parents' house as small bits of debris and insulation fell around us. A column of dusty smoke rose from the blast site.

Officer Newbold paled. "That was no pipe bomb," she muttered, then turned to the people on the street. "Everybody OK?" She stepped away and got on her radio as first responders scrambled. A frantic woman ran past me clutching two kids in her arms. A couple ran to their car, jumped in and drove away. A short man with a hobbit physique stared and laughed out loud—maybe from shock? There was a lot of shock to go around.

"Is everyone all right?" Neil echoed the police officer, checking on our little band.

My parents, stunned, didn't say anything. They stared open-mouthed down the block but seemed physically fine.

"I'm OK," Aunt Celestine said, taking the panting Astra from me and hugging her.

"I'm fine, too," Royce said. "Not so sure about your parents' house."

My heart raced. I tried to see through the smoke. "You know, I'm not sure that *was* my parents' house."

As the stiff breeze cleared the smoke somewhat, we could make out a severely damaged structure. The roof was on fire. The house wasn't obliterated like in the gas explosions I've seen on the news, but the whole thing seemed to be sagging, its windows blown out, its porch hanging off.

My parents' house never had a porch.

"Do you see what I see?" I asked Neil.

"I think so. Your parents' house looks OK. Some dings in the brick and window damage, maybe."

"The house next door took the brunt of it," I said. "That wasn't the house with the kids, was it?"

Neil knew immediately which house I meant, the one where we'd seen children playing in the yard yesterday. "No, it's the other one. The one that blew up was that cottage that was for sale."

"What is he up to?" I mused.

"Beau?" Neil's eyebrows lifted. "Assuming it's him—"

"It's him."

"I don't know. Intimidation?" he guessed.

"Seems like there'd be an easier way."

"I want to go check on our house," my mother suddenly said. "All this fuss and it didn't even explode."

"Evangeline," my father said, "the house next door to ours just blew up!"

"I don't care," she said. "Officer! I need to get into my house."

Officer Newbold came back over. "Ma'am, it's going to be a while. The bomb squad is reconfiguring. They'll want to survey your house and then check out the neighboring houses just to be safe."

"A little late for that," Royce said, earning a severe look from the cop.

The officer turned back to my parents. "They're going to

send a drone into your house first. We'd like you to watch the video, tell us if you see anything unusual."

"Don't be ridiculous," she said.

"I can watch, if you like," my father said.

"I want to see it too," I added.

It was half an hour before the bomb techs set up the drone. A fire truck moved a little closer to get the house fire tamed first so it wouldn't spread. Then a fully suited bomb tech approached my folks' house and opened the front door before retreating to a safe distance.

Neil and I joined my father and stood behind the man operating the drone. He sat at a table next to the white bomb squad truck. The pilot's control device included a monitor and was plugged into a larger screen so the officers and we could see what the drone's camera saw.

The drone lifted off the ground and flew down the street, buzzing through tendrils of smoke, then approached my parents' open door.

Slowly, it floated into the house, its light illuminating the interior.

"Limited battery life," the drone pilot said, "but we should have enough time to survey the structure. If you see something out of place, anything, speak up."

"All right." My father seemed fascinated. "It's so strange to see our house on TV."

The pilot chuckled, maneuvering the drone into the kitchen, a bathroom, a utility room, the living area, then up the stairs, peering into all the rooms before it descended again.

"Anything?" he asked.

"Wait," I said as the drone hovered in the living room again. "Can you turn it around?"

"Sure." The pilot had the drone do a three-sixty turn.

"Stop! Dad, have you been redecorating?" I pointed to the wall with the big rustic cross on it.

"No." His forehead creased.

"That little sparkly cross you had. Did you take it down? I don't see it."

His eyes widened. "Oh, no. No. It can't be."

"What?" the pilot asked with irritation.

"The cross is gone," my father said.

"Maybe the explosion shook it off the wall," Neil said. "Can you look down?"

"We're supposed to be looking for explosive devices," the pilot grumbled, but he had the drone do a slow sweep of the wall and the floor all around it.

"It's not there," my father and I said at the same time.

"I'll double-check with Evangeline," Kevin Revelle said, "but I don't think she'd move it without talking to me."

I looked at him in puzzlement. "Why not?"

"Oh, it's extraordinarily valuable. This is bad. Very bad."

"How valuable?" Neil asked as my neck prickled.

My father looked at us as the pilot finished his sweep and flew the drone out of the house.

"It's worth more than a million dollars. It's very special. And now it's gone."

Chapter Twenty

My parents had a million-dollar blinged-out cross in their living room?

"Let's ask Mom," I told my father as we walked away from the bomb techs. "Maybe she moved it."

But Evangeline was as horrified as my father had been when we explained to her, my aunt and Royce what we saw.

"It's missing?" my mother asked. "Are you sure?"

"It wasn't on the wall or the floor," my father said.

I had a really bad feeling about this. "Why do you have a million-dollar cross?"

"Beau said it was a good investment," my mother said. "He connected us with an antiques broker in town."

"We bought it directly through a reputable dealer," my father added. "Beau did not participate in the sale, if that's what you're wondering. It's authentic."

"But he coached you to buy this thing," I said.

"He suggested that besides real estate, a valuable item like this would be a good way to build on the money we'd received," he said. "It used to be owned by the pope. Multiple popes. The resale value will be tremendous."

How odd. They owned a papal cross. And they weren't even Catholic.

"And you hung it on your wall why?" Aunt Celestine asked.

"Hiding it in plain sight," my mother said. "That was Beau's suggestion. He's such a clever boy."

Well, I did think it was a piece of junk when I saw it, so maybe it was a good hiding place—if a con man hadn't told them to put it there.

"Beau's the one who suggested we put in the alarm system," my father said.

Color me shocked. "You have an alarm system?"

"Yes. And he didn't have the code for it. In fact, I changed it just last week."

I turned to my mother. "You didn't give him the code, did you?"

"Please," she said. "I don't even know how that ridiculous thing works. Kevin handles all of that."

"He suggested the doorbell camera, too," my father said.

I shook my head. "And yet somehow he's stolen the cross."

"Of course he hasn't," my mother said.

Neil grimaced, and Royce and Aunt Celestine exchanged glances.

"He almost killed me *again* today," I told my mother. "I might have neglected to mention that. He's figured out you're not giving him the money. This has to be his doing, his way of getting his hands on your fortune."

"How did he get in?" my father asked. His face changed. "Oh."

"What?" I asked.

A little wrinkle formed in his brow. "The bomb squad had us turn off the alarm system and unlock the doors, front and back, so they could check out the house."

"That's why he called in the bomb threat," I guessed.

"I'm confused," Kevin Revelle said.

"He planted a bomb next door to you," I told him. "He

issued a threat to make sure you were out of the house, but the cops evacuated multiple blocks, providing a distraction while he slipped into your house to grab the cross. Exploding the bomb was just the cherry for him."

Neil added, "Maybe it created enough confusion for him to get away unnoticed."

"But where was he hiding?" my father asked.

"I don't know. A neighbor's yard? He's crafty. It was him! He's the only one who knew how valuable it was, right?" I looked back and forth between them. "And he knew about the alarm system. Even if you hadn't disarmed it, he must've known he could break in without repercussions during a bomb evacuation."

"Tell us a little more about this cross," Neil said in a much calmer tone than mine.

"Oh, it's very pretty. Not that we believe in using the church's money for material things," my father said. "It was just an investment."

"What's it made of?" I asked. "What's its history?"

"Oh, now let's see," Kevin Revelle said. "It's carved of eighteen-karat gold and is inlaid with sixty carats in gems. I think that's right—emeralds and very large diamonds. It's about eight inches tall. Vatican artists designed it around 1920. The pope gave it to the U.N. in the sixties to raise money to end human suffering. It's been owned by all sorts of famous people since then. It's quite exciting."

"And you sank half of your spanking new fortune into it." I was starting to feel helpless. Beau must have planned to steal my parents' trinket if they didn't wire him the money for his fake real-estate scheme. Maybe he planned to steal it regardless.

"Not quite half our fortune," my mother said. "We'll just have to carry on."

"Evangeline, do not be a martyr," Aunt Celestine snapped. "We have to do something."

"Was it insured?" Neil asked.

"Oh, well, we didn't want to pay all that money for insurance," my father said. "The plan was to let it accrue in value for a couple of years and then sell it. Diversifying, Beau called it."

Royce looked as pained as I felt, and Neil's lack of expression told me he was concealing a great deal of frustration, too.

"I'm not going to let him get away with this," I said.

They all looked at me with concern.

"*You* aren't going to let him get away with this?" Neil said in disbelief.

"This time, it's personal," Royce intoned in a movie-trailer voice. Aunt Celestine chortled.

"We have to get it back," I said. "It's that simple."

Neil crossed his arms. "It's not that simple. One, he's an armed lunatic. Two, we don't know where he's holed up. Three, we are not the Guardians of the Galaxy."

"Wouldn't that be cool if we were, though?" Royce said.

I raised an eyebrow at my brother. "Let's just get the gang together and talk about our options, OK? We'll see if Detective Colby wants to get involved. After all, Beau just tried to blow up a whole neighborhood. They'll try a lot harder to find him now."

"First, I think Evangeline and Kevin should make a report to the officer here," Aunt Celestine said. "When the police are done with their robots and their searches, they can double-check and make sure the cross isn't in the house. I can make sure they're taken care of."

"I do not need your help," her sister said.

"Too bad," my aunt replied. "You're going to get it. Don't worry," she said to me. "Astra and I will get a cab."

"I'll stay, too," Royce added. "Maybe I can help."

I gave them a thumbs-up. "Be careful. I'll text our friends and call a meeting at Hydrangea House, OK? Maybe we can't do anything, but if we can, we should do it quickly. He may already have a buyer lined up for the cross."

Neil appeared resigned to his fate. "Don't forget we have an appointment later with Mr. Mixy to see Camelia Landry's party setup for tomorrow."

"I wish I could forget it, but we'll make it work," I said. "Want me to drive?"

"I've got you." Neil's glance said a lot. He was there for me. But he wished I wasn't always going somewhere he didn't want to go.

IT TURNED out our friends wanted to meet at the Fantome, since it had a decent bar. Of course.

Neil and I rolled in to find Barclay, Luke, Melody, Mark, Diana and Kirby hanging out, drinking their potions of choice and scarfing appetizers. I grabbed a burger slider topped with Swiss cheese and caramelized onions at Mark's invitation and ate it in about four bites. Apparently dealing with a psychotic con man makes a girl hungry.

To my displeasure, Mr. Mixy was there, too. I was pretty sure he was stalking Mark now that he'd learned the Englishman was a soft touch and invited him to everything.

Jai Joshi was behind the bar. Just before I ordered, a chill ran through me, my hairs lifted, and I caught a whiff of something strange.

I looked at Jai.

He raised his thick eyebrows. "The ghost, right?"

A door slammed, and I jumped. I looked around. It was the door to the bathroom hallway again.

"You have some angry doors in this place," I told Jai.

He chuckled. "It's Carl. Maybe he doesn't like you."

I ignored his remark and ordered a soda water with lime.

I turned away, enjoying the cold fizzy water, to see Detective Colby hustling in behind us. He'd traded his black rain jacket for a wrinkled sport coat and gave off a harried vibe.

"What you done to my town?" he asked me.

I raised my hands. "What? Me? Talk to Beau Reed—I mean Beau Moritz."

"Now the FBI is interested, and so are my bosses. They're giving the pharmacy robbery to someone else so I can find this screwball."

A bell rang inside my brain, and I led the detective away from the bar to make sure Jai couldn't hear us. I didn't want the bartender to discuss our chat with his good pal Alfie.

"The robbery you were investigating earlier was at a pharmacy?" I asked Colby. "Did they take money?"

Detective Colby cocked his head at me. "Pills and money. Professional job. Why?"

"Alfie Boudreaux tried to sell us drugs when we talked to him about Edgar Poeville's murder. And Sierra Felt said she thought Edgar was selling pills. Just wondering if it's connected."

He stared at me for a minute. "She told you that? And Boudreaux tried to sell you pills? Did you see them?"

"No, but he wasn't trying to sell us candy, that's for sure.

Maybe he meant something else. Just seemed like a coincidence since they're friends."

"Thanks for the tip." The detective pulled out a notebook and scribbled in it. "Now stop interviewing my suspects."

Neil, who'd grabbed a plain water from Jai, interrupted. "We're here to talk about Beau, right?"

"All right." The detective pocketed his notebook. "I need to find him."

"So do we," I replied. "He stole an extremely valuable jeweled cross from my parents. It's worth over a million dollars, and we want to get it back."

"I saw the preliminary report. I have questions." Colby was in full skeptical mode.

"So did we," I said. "The important thing is finding Beau, right? We think he's in the Bywater."

"Because he tried to burn you to death there earlier?"

I tried to quell my shudder as our friends gathered to listen. "Not just that. We talked to Jezebel Harlow, who owns a shop in the area. She knows Beau, and she thinks he's still in the neighborhood. And we saw him get into a car after getting out of a bar there. That's when he drove to see Camelia Landry, who he's also lured into his real estate scam."

"Speaking of whom, we saw her in the hotel this morning," Barclay said.

"You mean after we saw her on the street? What was she doing here?" I asked her.

"Maybe she needed a drink," Mark joked.

"I saw her, too," Melody said. "She was quiet-yelling at poor Avani at the front desk. The girl was in tears."

Colby held up a hand in the "stop" position. "Back up. How do you know about Jezebel Harlow? Oh ... the fingerprints on the bunny ribbon." He rolled his eyes. "Somebody's got some explaining to do."

"Never mind that," I said, hoping I hadn't compromised Jane the fingerprint tech. "He's got to be in the Bywater."

"Maybe," the detective acknowledged. "But where?"

"If I may," Kirby interrupted, "I'm Kirby Banks. My cousin's with NOLA PD. He used to be assigned to that area, so I called and asked him a few questions. He remembers one of his informants, a homeless guy, telling him about a slick dude holding court in the abandoned naval base. He'd hole up in some theater. Here's the kicker: People called him the Baron or Baron Beau. All the homeless people talked about a treasure box he had there, and either the Baron or one of his devotees guarded it at all times."

"That's it!" I exclaimed. "The base! Of course. He could've taken a bicycle from Music Box Village and headed right over the tracks and into the heart of the base and disappeared. We have to go in there and look!"

Detective Colby's eyes widened. "Are you out of your little mind? That place is a nightmare. Sure, some homeless folks are there because they have nowhere else to go, but it's also been a crime scene over and over. We've found bodies in there. Mysterious fires happen there. You can't just walk in there like you're going to the mall."

"Some of those bloggers who go into abandoned places have gone in there," Kirby said. "I saw the videos."

"Then they're not too bright either," the detective complained.

"You want him," I said, "you have to go get him. Don't you have SWAT teams and helicopters and stuff?"

The detective shook his head. "You're talking about a major security operation. That place is a rabbit warren, and he's armed, possibly with explosives. As much as we want Beau Moritz for questioning after the bombing, I can't just throw together a small army with so little to go on. I need buy-in from my bosses, which means I need real evidence that he's there, not outdated fanciful hearsay from some vagrant C.I. who just wanted Kirby's cousin to buy him a sandwich."

Just when my hope sagged like a wet potato chip, I got a boost from an unexpected quarter.

Luke spoke up. "I love those abandoned-places videos. I'm up for it."

"Sounds interesting. I'll go," Barclay said.

Melody put her hands on her hips. "I'd love a chance to punch Beau in the mouth. I'm in."

"I want to go!" Mr. Mixy added. "Besides, I need to make sure we're on time for our appointment with Camelia. She's sweet on me, you know."

Kirby endured his ego with a smile. "I went into the base once during my more mischievous days. Why not?"

"And of course Mark and I are at your disposal," Diana added.

Mark blinked at Diana's declaration, then addressed the detective. "We can flush him out for you. We'll go in, roust him from his lair, and you can nab him."

"I can *nab* him," Detective Colby repeated in a dry tone.

"Maybe show up with lights and sirens and everything," I said. "He'll think you're coming in to get him even if you aren't. He'll have to make a move. You can get him when he comes out."

The detective scratched his chin and looked into space as he considered the idea. "Even if we don't *nab* him, he might think his hideout is compromised and go on the run. That could be good for us. Assuming he's there, of course."

"What do you have to lose?" I prodded.

He focused again on me. "Dead tourists are bad for business. And bad for my career. And you are a tourist hell-bent on getting dead. What do I have to lose? All of you. What do you have to lose? It could be your life."

Chapter Twenty-One

Neil stayed silent, but he put a hand on my shoulder. I wasn't sure if it was in support of my quest or if he was subconsciously trying to hold me back. Maybe both.

The detective looked around at us. "If you go into that base, it won't be as an emissary of the police force. I can check it out, say I got a tip, which indeed I have. But I can't go leading a tour group through that hive of villainy."

I noted the *Star Wars* reference with amusement. "We'll be careful. We'll do our best to find him. We'll be safe enough."

"Why does this sound painfully familiar?" Neil interjected.

I tried to reassure him with a smile, though nerves threatened to undo me, too. "It'll be fine. Safety in numbers."

Neil crossed his arms. "I'm not that worried about the rest of us, especially if we don't corner him. If Beau wanted to kill a bunch of random people, he could've bombed an occupied house. But he has a particular desire to torment and kill you, Pepper. I don't want you coming into direct contact with him."

"But—"

"Why don't we distract him, draw him out?" Mark suggested. "Then one small team can go into this alleged lair and look for the cross."

"If we can find the lair," Kirby said. "I have some ideas, but it's going to take some doing."

"Not to mention all the interesting people we'll meet along the way," Barclay added.

"But how do we draw him out?" Melody asked.

"Blow something up?" Luke's suggestion prompted a few snickers.

I looked at Melody. "This might sound crazy, but hear me out. He likes music. He might be curious enough to look if someone starts singing in there." We all knew "someone" meant Melody. She had a beautiful voice.

"I can sing!" Mr. Mixy said. "I'm really good."

I shot him a dark look and turned back to Melody. "Melody can sing like an angel. And Beau even sang with her back in Kentucky. He won't be able to resist."

"Don't remind me of that night." Melody's angry tone held a hint of vulnerability. She often had whirlwind relationships, but she'd fallen hard for him before he showed his true colors.

"We just need him out of his lair long enough for us to get a look," I said. "Then the police can come and hopefully get him as he comes out, or they'll catch him inside. Either way, we can get my parents' million-dollar investment back."

"That *is* crazy," Detective Colby agreed.

"But it just might work?" Luke joked.

"I don't know." Melody seemed nervous. "I can sing, but do I want to do it by myself?"

"I told you, I can sing," Mr. Mixy said.

"No," I told him. I turned to Melody. "You can do it."

"I can accompany you," Kirby interjected.

I balked. "On the tuba?"

He chuckled. "I play other instruments. How about guitar?

That's what your wonder boy plays, right? He won't be able to resist the Bard of the Hotel Lebeau."

I laughed, surprised Kirby remembered what I called him last year. Then I looked at Neil. "Can you live with this plan? We'll basically get Beau out where the cops can find him and then get a look at his hideout. I don't ever have to meet him again."

Neil's jaw clenched. Then he lowered his shoulders slightly. "I will be with you at all times."

I smiled up at him and slipped an arm around his waist.

"Great. It's a date." Detective Colby was a font of sarcasm. "I won't stop you from going in. And I'll see if I can get a few officers off the Lakeview scene to help me. If you narrow down Moritz's location, we can get into position. But our little chat here is unofficial. Do you hear me? We'll just 'happen upon' your little group. I know *nothing* about your scheme. I can't be seen as ordering a bunch of drunk out-of-towners into the heart of a zombie movie."

"We're not drunk." Mark smiled and set his empty gin and tonic glass on a table, then flexed one muscular arm. "One drink is just enough to prepare me for anything."

"And to prevent you from thinking too hard about it," Diana teased him.

The others chuckled as I tried to push down my apprehension and focus on the goal. I didn't want to expose my friends to a dangerous situation. But together, we might be able to get the cross from Beau and help the detective arrest him, too.

What could go wrong?

WE DROVE by the base once to get a look—Neil, me, Mark, Diana, Mr. Mixy and Barclay in Neil's big black SUV, and Melody and Luke with Kirby in his little purple one.

I'd tried to convince Mr. Mixy to stay at the hotel, but he kept reminding me that he'd had a vision that he was supposed to stay with me and help me, whatever that meant. Dealing with him was like trying to get gum off my shoe.

I didn't talk to Aunt Celestine at all. I didn't want her to worry, and I knew she'd be apoplectic if she knew what we were doing.

And now we were in the Bywater, looping around the block, driving past the gloomy complex one more time. A misty drizzle had returned, keeping pedestrian traffic down, though a man walking a couple of black labs walked right by the base as if it weren't there. For the folks here, that hulking eyesore was a constant, uneasy presence.

Kirby parked a few spaces closer than we did. At least his Louisiana plates didn't stand out, and his purple car matched the purple trim on the bar with all the cats stenciled on its walls.

Neil found a space on the street away from the main entrance, then had me grab a couple of flashlights from his glove compartment and hand them to Barclay and Mark.

"All seems quiet," Mark observed.

"I don't like it," Neil replied.

"You keep saying that," I noted as we climbed out. "You know, he might not even be in there. I didn't see his car anywhere."

"Neither did I," Neil said, "but he could have it stashed somewhere, especially now that we've linked him with the car and talked to the police."

"True."

"No police yet," Diana noted calmly, intrepid adventurer that she was.

"This place is cool," Mr. Mixy said as we approached the main gate and the others joined us. "Maybe I should film me in front of it. Gotta feed the social media beast, you know."

"Not now!" I snapped. "We don't want to give ourselves away."

"Geez, chill! I won't post it till later."

"It's not a bad idea, actually," Barclay said. "Maybe it will make us look like just another bunch of video bloggers."

"If Beau doesn't recognize us," I replied.

Neil wore a grim expression. "Let's hope he's not watching."

Mr. Mixy winked at himself and shot a selfie.

"If he has minions, they might keep an eye out and share what they see." Kirby adjusted the strap of the acoustic guitar he carried. "Probably everyone who stays in there knows each other. You gotta work things out in a situation like that. Territory. That kind of thing."

Everyone had taken time for a quick change into jeans and T-shirts before we'd driven over here, except for Diana in her adventure khakis and Melody. My blond friend's rockabilly-style halter dress, white splashed with red flowers, stood out like a flare against the gray afternoon.

"If he sees me, I want to burn his retinas out with my glamour," she'd explained back at the hotel. "Maybe he'll die of regret."

The stocky buildings of the naval base, six or seven stories tall, might have been white once, but now they were a dingy gray marred by black mold and broken windows. The extensive graffiti at every level spoke of many visitors before us. If that many people had passed through here, maybe it wouldn't be so bad.

"You want to lead the way since you've been here before?" I asked Kirby.

"I can at least get us in."

The chain-link fence had started to rust, and the chain closing the gate together had just enough give to let us squeak through. We walked forward, past a decrepit, graffiti-covered guard hut and over the wet pavement, until we could see the first canyon between the big buildings. Pedestrian bridges connected them a few floors up.

"Parking garage." Kirby gestured. "Office building."

A distant cough froze us all in place. We weren't alone. Intellectually, I knew that, but to hear someone else in this desolate complex—that put me on a whole new level of alert.

I swallowed and mentally pulled up my big girl panties. "You said you heard Beau was in some kind of theater?"

Kirby nodded. "If it was Beau and *if* it's true, yeah. Prepare for disappointment."

I ignored his comment. "So where is this theater?"

He shrugged. "I didn't see it the last time I was here. I guess we'll just have to go in and look."

Chapter Twenty-Two

It wasn't hard to get into one of the abandoned office buildings. There were busted doors and windows at regular intervals. We chose a door with the least amount of debris around it, but it still smelled like pee. And mold. And rot. And something burning. My supernose would suffer for this little jaunt.

A short corridor led to another hallway, and then it got really creepy. Neil pulled a headlamp out of his pocket, turned it on and adjusted the strap on his head. Oh my God, nerd alert. He was such a Boy Scout. It was kind of sexy anyway.

Luke used his phone light and helped Melody navigate a pile of broken glass in her chunky sandals—not ideal footwear for this kind of thing. And then we began the search.

It was hard to make time when we startled at every noise, and there were plenty—skittering, banging, rustling. In every office, we found new sources of these sounds—Venetian blinds swaying as wind blew in through a broken window. Scurrying cockroaches. Dangling wires and frames from stripped lights rattling against each other.

Once, a rat ran out in front of us and Mr. Mixy screamed. Then we all turned to stone for three minutes while we waited for zombies to come.

They didn't.

But there were people here. We saw a few. In one office, a woman lay on a piece of cardboard, snoring, bundled up in spite of the balmy temperature, surrounded by what was left of her life—candles, a pile of rags, half-empty soda bottles, a puzzle book, snack wrappers, a couple of shirts hanging on a line. Like everywhere else here, there were piles of trash. We backed out quietly.

Office furniture remained in many of the rooms—desks with the drawers pulled out, cushioned chairs, computer monitors, even white boards with writing that probably dated from the last time the Navy used this place. A meeting room still had its long table surrounded by executive chairs—and mist blowing in through the broken windows. I imagined every derelict chair held a ghost.

In one office sat a desk with an old-school phone with lots of buttons, like something a secretary might use. When Luke lifted the handset, it still had a dial tone.

"Bloody eerie," Mark whispered.

"This is taking too long," I whispered back.

"Maybe we can approach a different way," Diana suggested.

So we took one of the pedestrian bridges and found ourselves in a parking garage marked by garbage, hanging wires, and stunning murals of mystical women, punk monsters, aliens, praying hands, kitschy toons, and a big sun and earth with the words "the Earth has not swallowed me yet."

"Pssst," Neil said, and we gathered close. "I got a text from Colby. He's outside. He'll stay there. He's sending a handful of officers in to look around."

"We have to hurry!" I said. "Let's get back into the offices. We have to find the theater."

"And a place for us to set up nearby," Melody said. "I'm losing my diva energy."

I knew what she meant. All the tromping up and down stairs and through the dystopian cityscape had just about depleted my adrenaline. But a different route led us into a new area we hadn't seen yet. And in a stairwell, we ran into two pallid, skinny teens who looked like they weren't here on a dare. I had a terrible feeling the boy and girl lived here.

"Hey," Kirby said when they tried to look cool even as they were clearly terrified. "We're just looking around. We hear there's a theater in here somewhere. Know anything about that?"

They looked at each other, and the boy scanned our group. "Whatcha got in exchange?"

Mark pulled a twenty-dollar bill from his pocket—just to be safe, we'd all left wallets and bags behind, even me—and handed it over. "What do you know?"

The boy shrugged and took the money. "You're talking about the Baron, right? He's two up, straight ahead, at the end of the hall."

"But he'll be salty. He doesn't like visitors," the girl said. "We stay out of his way."

"Two floors up?" I asked. "What else is up there?"

She smirked. "An ice cream parlor. Whaddaya think?"

I felt bad for her anyway. "Thanks. Sorry to disturb you."

"No problem," the boy said.

"Is there any other access to that floor?" Neil asked.

"There's a bridge with access to the garage up there. End of the hall, turn left, and it's down there. And another staircase at the opposite corner of the building, but it's hard to get to."

"Appreciate it," Neil said.

"If you're going to see the Baron, we're outta here," he answered, and the teens headed down.

We climbed silently to the next floor—one shy of the

Baron's hive—and left the stairwell, pausing inside the corridor to confer.

"Where should Melody and Kirby set up?" Luke asked.

"The tunnel to the garage?" Barclay wondered.

"Those bridges aren't that big, and I don't want them trapped in a small space with him," Neil said.

"Or anyone else," Melody agreed.

"So maybe they start in the bridge and draw him toward the garage?" I suggested. "This is more complex than I thought it would be."

"Let's see what's up there. Then we can figure it out," Diana said. "Adapt and overcome."

"You're so smart," Mark said, and she smacked his arm. "I mean it!" he protested.

"OK, everybody be quiet," Neil said. "We'll go up and go slowly."

We crept up the next flight like Royce's distillery cat stalking a rat. And we *were* stalking a rat—a rat who called himself the Baron. Or maybe other people made up the name. Was Beau the Baron? He'd better be, after all this. My sense of smell had all but shut down in protest.

Somehow Neil, the least enthusiastic of all of us, reached the door first.

"Your light," I hissed.

He nodded, reached up and turned off his headlamp. Then he opened the door slowly.

It emitted a long, low squeak. This place really was like a massive haunted house.

I held my breath, listening, but heard no one, and no one came. If Beau was at the other end of this shadowy corridor, he either didn't hear us or didn't care.

We moved into the hallway and looked around. We were at

a junction of two hallways, actually; one, filled with debris, headed off into darkness at our left. Presumably, the theater was straight ahead somewhere, if our informant was correct.

As we stepped forward, we found the entrance to a fitness room to our left. At least, that was what it said on the glass windows surrounding the doorway. If there'd been doors, they were long gone.

Kirby held up one finger in the "wait" position, handed Melody his guitar, then gave me a shock when he sprinted down the hall on silent sneakered feet. He vanished into the shadows. It was a long, suspenseful minute before he reappeared, jogging back to us. As he caught his breath, Melody pointed to the gym, and we all eased inside.

The room was big and bright and still full of exercise machines that could have been abandoned yesterday. But all over the floor were slats from the blinds that had once covered the wall of windows.

We huddled and whispered.

"There's a door that says *Theater* down there on the right," Kirby said. "It's closed, and I didn't hear anything. This hall runs into another one. If you go left, the doors to the garage bridge are down there on the right."

Melody looked around. "Well, if he's in the theater, he should be able to hear us if we set up in here. This looks like a good, resonant space, and the stairs offer an escape route if we want it."

"That and the door at the other end." Neil gestured toward a closed single door at the far end of the gym that led out to the hallway.

"Were there any offices across from the theater?" I asked Kirby. "Someplace we can hide and watch the theater door?"

"A small laundry room," Kirby said. "It has a closed door

with a frosted glass window—cracked, I think. You might be able to see through it."

"We'll check it out," Neil said.

"I'll stay with Melody and Kirby." Luke pointed to a wooden booth of sorts in the corner. "I can hide in that old sauna and jump out if you need a distraction."

Our strategy sounded pretty lame when he put it like that.

Neil tapped his phone. "I'm texting all of you Detective Colby's number. Message him if you see Beau or see where he's going. Do not engage if you can help it. Just get him moving so the cops can find him."

"That's a good idea," Barclay said. "Mixy and I can go into the garage. That way if Beau heads in that direction, we can pass on the info."

"But I want to stay with Pepper," Mr. Mixy whispered.

"*I'm* staying with Pepper," Neil declared, to Stephan's disappointment. I was glad Barclay, who was calm under pressure, was babysitting my idiot ex.

"And no screaming," I told Mr. Mixy.

His beard bobbed as he gave me a resolute nod. "You can count on me."

"I saw an office across the hall here," Diana said. "Mark and I can huddle inside to see if Beau heads down these stairs or takes the other corridor."

"All right." I turned to Melody. "Don't start singing until we get into position. Count to a hundred or something, then start. When Beau leaves the theater to check out your music, we'll dash in there and do a quick search for the cross."

"*If* he leaves it and no one's guarding the place," Neil noted. "*If* he's there at all. And we'll inform Detective Colby so the cops can sweep in and get him."

"Think positive," I said. "Worst case, we go in there even if he doesn't come out. He might not even be there."

"We do *not* enter his lair if we think there's any possibility he's there," he argued. "That's for the cops."

I knew he was right. I shouldn't give Beau another chance to kill me. But he'd stolen an artifact worth more than a million bucks from my parents. I wanted it back. My stomach hurt just thinking about letting Beau win.

"Very well," Mark said. "It's a plan. It's not a good plan, but it's a plan."

I suppressed my chuckle. And then we headed for our posts.

Neil and I trailed Barclay and Mr. Mixy down the hallway as I asked the gods of abandoned places not to send another rat into Stephan's path. To my relief, they successfully made it to the other end and turned left. A moment later, I heard a metallic *ker-thunk*, presumably the doors that led to the enclosed bridge and the parking garage.

Neil and I looked both ways. It was darker here, though a little light still filtered in from the gym at the other end. The theater was behind a set of wooden doors to our right.

We pushed open the door marked *Laundry* across the hall, and I closed it carefully. Kirby was correct: The windowless room was small, with a couple of commercial washers and dryers still in place, and it had a skinny window of cracked frosted glass.

"Is it enough to see through?" Neil murmured in the near-darkness as we both looked it over.

I pulled my phone from my pocket and turned on the light to take a quick look. "See this? It looks like a bullet hole." Ugh. A bullet hole. "I think this will work as a peephole. We just have to make sure he doesn't see us."

"The hallway is so dark, I think we'll be all right. Hey, do you hear something?"

We stopped whispering, and I turned off the light. The clear sound of a beautiful voice accompanied by guitar drifted down the hall.

I smiled. "It's Melody!"

"What's she singing?"

"'Cry Me a River.' A perfect go-to-hell song. Now let's see if we get any action."

We stilled and hovered by the peephole, taking turns looking into the dim hall as our eyes adjusted. I hoped so hard that Beau would take the bait. Hell, that he was actually here.

I grabbed Neil's arm as the door to the theater opened.

Chapter Twenty-Three

A man emerged from the door marked *Theater,* but it wasn't Beau. This guy was short and round, hobbit-like, with a ruddy, jowly face. He walked with a limp.

Wait. I remembered that hobbit guy. Didn't I see him at the bombing scene? Maybe he'd been keeping tabs on my parents—and us—for Beau.

The hobbit stepped into the center of the hall and looked toward the other end, where Melody sang along to Kirby's guitar in the erstwhile fitness center.

The hobbit shook his head, then went back into the theater. He did not close the door; in fact, it appeared the room had two sets of doors, illuminated by the weak light inside, and he left both of them open.

I couldn't see what was inside, but I could hear him.

"Boss, sounds like you got fans. You're getting a serenade."

"Don't be stupid," came a responding voice, and my spine prickled. *Beau!*

"Seriously. You have to hear this. They sound really good. Maybe she's hot," the hobbit joked.

This time, the hobbit wasn't the only man who entered the hallway. Beau followed him. He didn't look like a vagrant. He looked like he'd looked this morning, a regular guy, handsome in his jeans and white T-shirt.

Beau looked around in suspicion, and we shrank back from the window. We leaned in again when he spoke to his minion. "I swear I've heard that voice before."

And he started down the hallway, followed by the hobbit.

Yes. Beau *and* his henchman, distracted. My hand grasped the doorknob.

Neil grabbed my arm. "Wait," he breathed.

"No time. Once he sees her, the jig is up," I whispered back, and opened the door.

Beau and the hobbit were halfway down the hall. I ran across the corridor and through the still-open doors of the theater, then pulled up short inside.

"Whoa." I'd expected some kind of movie theater with plush red seats, but that wasn't what this was. Or had been.

A couple of small windows in the back of the fifty-seat theater offered enough light to reveal gray theater chairs laid out in rows. They faced a big, shattered video screen. Graffiti covered the walls. But this place had been cleaned up more than most of the ramshackle spaces we'd seen so far. The floor was free of debris.

A big speaker's stand was set up in front of the broken screen. Beyond the screen in the corner, a mishmash of blankets hung from the ceiling, forming a partition that hid whatever was behind it.

Neil entered the room behind me. He immediately pulled out his phone and tapped, presumably texting Detective Colby. Then he flipped on his headlamp and scoped the room, focusing on the shattered screen and the jumble of projectors and equipment behind it. As he moved forward to see if anything was stashed there, I ran to the blanket fort in the corner and looked inside.

The makeshift room held a cot covered in nice-looking

bedding, a desk with a tablet computer and a glowing battery-powered lamp, shelves stocked with food, a full clothes rack, and a guitar. Pretty nice for apocalypse head-quarters.

I wasted no time in tossing the bedding, feeling inside the pillow and running my hands under the mattress. I moved everything I could around on the shelves and looked all around the tiny space. I checked jacket pockets on the clothes rack and even picked up the guitar and shook it. Nothing. No trea-sure chest. No cross.

I popped out of the blanket fort. Neil stood there, frozen, listening.

"What?" I stage-whispered.

"Screaming," he said back. "I think it's Melody. We have to go!"

I heard it then, an incoherent high-pitched jumble. Melody was in trouble.

"Come on. Now!" Neil called, sprinting out the door.

I hated to go. But I'd found nothing. "Coming!"

I followed him into the hall, thinking about the other door to the gym that was closer to us. He was way ahead of me, his hand on the knob, and he went in just as I had an inspiration.

The speaker stand. I hadn't looked inside the theater's lectern.

It would take only a minute. Melody had plenty of backup. I turned and ran back into the theater.

I crouched behind the lectern, shifting around piles of newspaper clippings, mostly pieces about the wealthy set of New Orleans. Was this how Beau found his victims? What-ever. The cross wasn't there.

The distant sound of a different scream struck me—Mr. Mixy?

I stood up straight, ready to leave, and gasped as Beau ran into the room.

He pulled up short, and a wicked smile crept over his face. "I knew you had to be behind this, little Pepper."

I backed away. What had he done to Melody? Where were my friends?

I frantically looked around for another exit. On the same wall where the main entrance was located, there was another door in the back of the theater. But I'd have to go through Beau to get to it.

"Looking for something?" he asked as I slid sideways. He matched my movement, in perfect position to stop me from going to either door.

Maybe I could get him talking. "I am looking for something. Something you stole from my parents."

"Now how could I steal anything from your parents?" he asked. "I haven't seen them in weeks."

"You set off the bomb, didn't you?"

He laughed. "Oh, Pepper. Let it go. This isn't your world. Your world is the pretty bars and the fruity drinks and the drunks staggering up and down Bourbon Street."

"You made your world mine when you tried to scam my parents and kill me in the process."

"I have what I want, for now," he said. "You could have just walked away." As he rambled about how I'd stumbled into the dark side, time seemed to ice over, freeze. I almost didn't think the shadow I saw emerge from the far doorway was real—a dark figure in a hoodie, crouching, creeping forward. Was it a friend? A cop?

The figure lifted a handgun. On pure instinct, I ducked. The shot seemed to shatter the air as the blast reverberated in the big room. Beau fell silent.

When I peeked over the podium a moment later, the figure had vanished. And Beau had collapsed into a theater chair, holding his side. Blood bloomed scarlet on his white T-shirt. He looked up at me, his pale blue eyes wide. Surprised.

I didn't hesitate. I ran like hell.

As I burst out of the theater, Neil ran toward me. "What happened?"

"Somebody shot Beau! Is Melody OK?"

"She's fine. Apparently, when Beau showed up, she started screaming at him about what a jerk he was. But by the time I got to their end of the room, he wasn't there. I didn't realize he'd doubled back—or that you didn't follow me. Not at first. Are you trying to scare me to death?"

"I'm sorry, but I had an inspiration."

"Did you find it, then?"

"No," I said glumly as Mr. Mixy and Barclay appeared from the direction of the garage tunnel.

"You OK?" Barclay asked. "We heard a shot."

"I'm fine." I looked at Mr. Mixy. "Did I hear you scream? I told you no screaming."

"That was my war cry," he said. "This round little man wobbled into the garage. He looked like he was running away, so I tackled him. One of the police showed up right away and grabbed him."

I blinked, then looked at Barclay, who shrugged. "I didn't have a chance to tell him not to. It might've been some poor homeless guy."

I shook my head. "If he had a limp, it was probably Beau's buddy."

"Yeah," Mr. Mixy said, "he did have a limp."

"Did he have a gun?" The shadow who shot Beau seemed

thinner than the hobbit, but they'd been crouching, so it was hard to tell much more than that.

Mr. Mixy blanched at my question. "Uh, I don't think so?"

"The cops didn't find a gun when they patted him down," Barclay said.

A noise at the other end of the hall caught our attention. Two more cops had appeared. "Hey! This way!" I called, and they trotted our way, a man and a woman. "Beau Reed—I mean, Beau Moritz is in there, and someone shot him." I pointed at the theater.

They drew their guns. "Is the shooter still in there?" the woman asked.

I shook my head. "I don't think so, unless they hid. I got out of there."

"All right. Stay back. We're going in."

The officers proceeded with caution. Where *did* the shooter go? This place was such a maze.

Still shaken, I retreated to the gym with Neil and our other friends.

Melody sat on a weight bench, as pretty as a daisy blooming in the middle of a parking lot.

"Are you all right?" I asked her.

"I feel great. I finally told that scumbag what I really think of him. Of course, he ran off a minute after I started yelling, but I got some good ones in."

Kirby grinned. "She sure did. She scorched my sensitive ears. She can really sing, though."

"Yes, she can." I grinned back.

The male cop appeared in the doorway of the gym and looked at me. "Are you sure Moritz was in there?"

"Yes." The bottom dropped out of my stomach. "Why?"

"He's not there now. All that's left is a fresh bloodstain."

"How is that possible? There are only two doors to that place, right?"

He shook his head. "Three. There's one in the corner behind that blanket room. Goes to the other hallway. Maybe he got away." He grabbed the radio affixed near his collar and spoke into it. "Moritz was shot, witness says, but we can't find him."

Detective Colby's voice came back. "Who shot him?"

"Unclear."

"Keep looking. I'll call it in. Now we'll have to search the place in earnest. Did you run into the tourists?"

"The witness is a tourist." The cop lifted his eyebrow at me. "What's your name?"

"Pepper Revelle," I said, and the cop passed it on to the detective.

"Great," Colby said in exasperation. "Send her out. Send them all out right now, and tell them to see me before they go home. Then keep hunting for Moritz and the shooter."

We obeyed orders and kept an eye out for trouble, exiting the complex a lot faster than we got in, now that we had a sense of the place. When we reached Detective Colby outside the gate, he was pacing and smoking.

"Look at what you did to me," he complained. "I haven't had a cigarette in three months. My wife is going to kill me."

"Sorry?" I didn't want to mention that the cigarette might kill him, too.

He looked at the smoke in disgust, dropped it and ground it out with his heel. "All right. What happened?"

We told him about finding Beau and his henchman, who sat in the back seat of one of the patrol cars parked outside. I described the shooting. Then Colby told us to get lost before reinforcements arrived.

"You still might get him," I told him before we left.

"And muffulettas might fly out of my butt," he rasped. "I'll be in touch."

"Well, at least that's over," Mr. Mixy said from the rear seat after climbing into Neil's car with Mark, Diana and me.

"Over? He's still out there!" I said. "And he still has my parents' bling."

Neil, his headlamp stowed, started up the car. "But at least we're not still in there." His spirits seemed restored now that we weren't tramping around the derelict base. "We'd better change before we head to Camelia's."

"I could use a shower," Diana said, "even if we're not joining you."

"A shower and a drink," Mark agreed.

"I think your drink got us into this muddle," she said, and Mark laughed.

"So what do we think happened to Beau?" I asked as Neil drove down the street, following Kirby's purple SUV with the rest of our crew. "There was a lot of blood. I can't imagine him just running away."

"He went somewhere," Neil said. "Maybe he's incapacitated enough that he won't bother you now."

"But he still has the cross. I don't know how we're going to get it back."

Neil looked over at me. "You might have to accept that you're not going to get it back."

I didn't want to admit that he was right. I looked out the window, frustrated. Not only didn't I have the million-dollar cross; my nemesis still wasn't in custody. "And who the hell shot him?"

"The Easter bunny?" Diana suggested, and even I laughed.

"It's all quite peculiar," Mark said. "At this point, I wouldn't be surprised."

All I knew was that I'd broken a lot of eggs trying to track down Beau, but that was how you made an omelet, right? And this cracked Easter egg hunt was far from over.

Chapter Twenty-Four

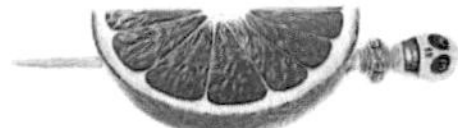

It was good to feel like a bartender again and not an urban explorer. I loved seeing new places, but abandoned ones harboring the man who wanted to kill me were not what I had in mind.

As Neil drove Mr. Mixy, me and the rest of Bohemia Bartenders to Camelia's house in the Garden District, I texted Aunt Celestine the bare minimum details of our adventure. I wanted her to know that our attempt to find the cross in Beau's hideout was unsuccessful and that Beau was wounded and on the run again.

"WHAT DID YOU DO?" was her response. I could never get anything past Aunt Celestine.

"How are my parents? Any news?" I texted back.

"They are back in their house and under guard," she wrote. "Royce and Astra and I are back at the hotel. And we WILL talk later."

So much for avoiding the subject. "Love you," was all I typed back, and she responded with "xo."

As the bad weather moved off and the sun dropped toward the horizon, we caught a glow of gold, pink and orange in the last threads of storm clouds scattered across the sky. The light cast Camelia's white mansion, with its oaks and porches and wrought-iron railings, in almost sepia tones, like a photograph from another era.

She welcomed us into the roomy entrance hall in a creamy wrap dress that matched the walls. A steep staircase, gold-framed paintings and mirrors, chandeliers and dainty antique furniture set the tone. She hugged Mr. Mixy and gave him a big kiss on the cheek, unbothered by his fountain of beard.

"I'm surprised that you answer your own door," I told her. "I figured a house this large must have a staff."

"Oh, I do have people who come in to help me. Sometimes Zeke answers the door. But I have the cameras so I can pick and choose. I only answer the door for people I want to see." She radiated a gleaming smile and smoothed her white-blond hair as I wondered who Zeke was. "I'm so glad y'all could come by. May I take you on a tour before I show you to the parlor where you'll be working? I'm a bit house-proud. This place has been in the family for more than a hundred years, though I've added one or two amenities."

"We'd love that," Mr. Mixy said. "My crew deserves a little treat after the day we've had."

His crew? I bit my tongue and shot Neil an *Are you kidding me?* look.

"I also had a trying day after I met y'all. I expect you saw me at the Fantome." Camelia glanced at Melody as she led us into a dining room. "They royally screwed up one of my guests' hotel reservations. What happened to you?"

I didn't want Mr. Mixy spilling all the ghastly details of our doomed escapade to a woman who'd already been targeted by Beau and thought he was little more than a sweet music teacher with great business tips. I cut him off before he could talk.

"Unfortunately, we ran into your friend Beau," I told Camelia. "The police are after him now."

Camelia's friendly smile flattened. She ran a finger along the back of one of the fine antique chairs surrounding the polished wood dining table. Then she looked up at me. "I've seen the police. They had some questions for me. I'm afraid I've been a foolish old thing. Rest assured, I'm well aware of Beau's intentions now, and he no longer has my confidence."

I ignored Melody's soft "hmph" and replied. "I'm sorry I had to be the one to tell you about him, but I'm relieved to hear you say that. We didn't want him to hurt anyone else."

A half smile touched her lips. "Thank you, Pepper. And now, let's move on to more pleasant topics, shall we? These are family portraits and a few art pieces I've collected ..."

By the time the tour was done, I was blown away by Camelia's glamorous three-story home. No wonder she was house-proud. While it didn't seem huge from the front, it seemed to go on and on with a massive modern kitchen, garden room, game room, lots of bedrooms. The master bath was bigger than my living room. The grounds included a poolside guesthouse, though we didn't get to see inside. She called it a "dependency," once a servant quarters.

The pool courtyard was where Camelia introduced us to the aforementioned Zeke, a broad-shouldered man of well over six feet with heavy eyebrows and unruly black hair. As he raked leaves, he gave us all a dark look that made me think he wasn't thrilled to have anyone else in his boss's house.

Camelia led us back around the ground floor and into a long, large room decorated with more chandeliers, art, fancy old chairs and tufted couches upholstered in pale green, cream and pink. "This is it—the parlor. It began as a ballroom and becomes one again any time I have a party. I'm having some of the furniture removed tomorrow morning to facilitate easy movement. This is where you'll work."

At one end of the parlor was the bay window visible from the street, framing a baby grand piano.

"Do you play?" Melody asked her, gesturing toward the instrument.

"Not a bit," Camelia answered. "Go ahead if you like."

Then what had Beau been teaching her? Guitar, maybe. Melody sat at the piano and began playing a breezy jazz tune while we took in the rest of the parlor.

At the opposite end of the room, filling the wall, was a fabulous bar of dark carved wood. Gleaming wood columns with ornate capitals framed the back, complete with fully stocked shelves and an arched mirror at the center.

"It's beautiful," Neil said in awe. "Antique?"

"It is indeed. Mahogany. A family heirloom." Camelia waggled her eyebrows. "I have a colorful family. Now can I make you something?"

"Allow me." Neil moved smoothly behind the bar, and I followed. It was nicely equipped with a small fridge, had a tap for beer, and had even been plumbed for a wet bar, so we had everything we needed. He smiled at me, then turned back to Camelia and the bartenders. "We'll make you all something if you like."

"Excellent," she said. "I have some very good rye back there. Why don't you make me a Sazerac?"

Camelia eyed Neil with interest as he made her the classic New Orleans cocktail, and I worked on a Vieux Carré for him. Luke popped behind the bar, too, and made drinks for Melody and Barclay. Mr. Mixy asked me for a vodka tonic, which I presented to him with a disdainful glance.

When I was finished making the drinks and Camelia had

hers, I saw Neil had made me a Sazerac, too. We exchanged cocktails and lifted our glasses in a silent toast and sipped as the others chatted.

"Very nice," we said at the same time, then laughed.

"This is more like it," Neil said softly as we came out from behind the bar and began a stroll around the room.

"I can't disagree with you." The rye didn't taste as fancy as Camelia claimed it was, but the cocktail was lovely.

"Hey, look at this." Neil stopped in front of a framed poster in tones of sepia and brown. The border was full of sketches of people drinking, with round seals and ornaments drawn on the corners and in the center of each side. A circle in the middle of the poster showed various drink recipes in a wheel, compass points at its heart, faint numbers over it like a clock face. The wedges of the wheel were inscribed with lots of tiny lettering and drawings of glasses. Filling out the design were drawings of famous New Orleans watering holes, including the Sazerac Bar.

"Oh, wow," Neil said. "See where it says, 'we're for toleration and down with Prohibition'? It's an anti-Prohibition poster. Look at all the clever sayings and rhymes in the border. This is so cool."

"You and your obsession with Prohibition."

"You should be obsessed with it, too. It just about ruined the culture that makes New Orleans so wonderful." Neil scanned the poster more closely and laughed. "Oh, this is one of my favorite toasts by Wallace Irwin, though they've tweaked it a bit. 'I used to know a clever toast but now I cannot think it. So fill your glass to any thing and damn your souls I'll drink it.'"

"That's perfect. But you always have a clever toast to share."

"Do you, Neil?" came Camelia's voice from behind us. "I'd like to hear a toast."

Neil startled and turned around, as did I. How long had she been listening to us?

"A toast usually bubbles up from my memory, depending on the occasion," he told her.

"Well, this is an occasion, having you here in my home," she said. "Indulge me."

The request felt strange. Neil glanced at me, then back at Camelia. He thought for a moment. "Will a quote do?"

A corner of her mouth turned up. "I'll allow it."

"Thank you." Neil made a little bow. "'There is no bad whiskey. There are only some whiskeys that aren't as good as others.' Raymond Chandler."

She giggled in delight. "So very true. Thank you for coming today. I look forward to having you tomorrow."

I hoped she didn't want to *have* Neil in any way but as a bartender.

"We'll serve New Orleans classics, as you requested, as well as a special cocktail or two of our own," Neil said.

"Remember that quote about the whiskey," she said. "I do love a good rye."

"Your wish is my command," he said.

Mr. Mixy, hovering nearby, seemed anxious that Neil was getting all the attention. "My crew and I will make you happy, I promise."

I glared at him again as Camelia turned to him and ran a hand down his arm. "I do hope so."

Boy, Camelia was on the prowl. First Beau. Then Mr. Mixy? As long as Neil wasn't the intermission, I really didn't care.

We cleaned up the bar and headed out into the purple

twilight. I touched Neil's elbow on the way to his car, and he fell back a step to listen to my whisper.

"She was interesting, wasn't she?"

He smiled. "Not as interesting as you. But yes, very interesting."

"Should we visit Cray, since we're in the neighborhood?"

His eyes lit up. "Great idea. Maybe we can talk him into going to dinner. He's only a couple of streets away."

The other bartenders were more than happy to go, especially Barclay, who shared Cray's affinity for rum.

"I'd rather get a cab," Mr. Mixy said. "I want to go back to the hotel and relax before we go out tonight."

He assumed a lot—one, that we were going out tonight, and two, that we wanted him to go with us.

Neil gave Cray a quick call first. As he started up his car and we all buckled in, I looked in the side mirror and watched Mr. Mixy loitering on the sidewalk, tapping on his phone. When we were almost at the end of the block, he looked both ways and strolled back up Camelia's walkway to her front door. We turned before I could see whether he got back in.

Or was he invited?

Chapter Twenty-Five

Conan Cray's mansion looked like the evil twin of Camelia's. Well, fraternal twin. It was impressive but probably half the size of hers. And as darkness fell, it really did look haunted.

Far more gothic than most of the grand houses in this neighborhood, the house loomed gray-green like the moss hanging from the oak trees. Their branches swayed in the wind and cast eerie shadows under the streetlights. Lots of peaks, spires and wrought iron completed the *Munsters* look.

We passed through the gate in the cast-iron fence and approached a gray porch some clever designer might call "distressed," especially under the glow of the lantern-style light hanging from the porch ceiling. The jumble of big and small planters I remembered still covered most of its surface, filled with vivid green life, complemented by the dark green front door. My aunt would've loved to explore this potted herb garden.

Cray didn't have cameras or a modern surveillance doorbell. Instead, there was a substantial iron door knocker, a sinister gargoyle face that held a hoop in its teeth. A delighted Barclay stepped up to wield it, announcing our presence. I figured he wanted to get to Cray's famed rum collection as soon as possible.

It took a minute, but Cray, in a light blue sweater and tan trousers, opened the door with a drink already in his hand. "Come in, my dears, come in! I've already pulled a few bottles I think you'll love." He looked at Barclay. "Especially you, young man."

"Thank you so much!" Barclay led the charge, and we entered the impressive two-story front hall, with its curving staircase and behemoth chandelier, before heading into the Victorian parlor. Smaller than Camelia's, it looked like a set from a Sherlock Holmes movie with its bookcases, fireplace and old furniture, but it had been spiffed up since we were here last.

Cray caught my smile. "I have a housekeeper now, Kayanne Pepper. She comes in every two weeks and de-dusts. Old houses like this just seem to create their own environment, and it is *not* clean."

I laughed. "I love this house, though."

"As do I, my dear. Enough room for my rum collection and a chemistry lab. It's everything I need. Now who would like a drink before we go to dinner?"

A few minutes later, he'd fixed us all up with a glass of choice rum—he had several fine bottles set out on a table with a bucket full of fat ice cubes. Barclay grilled him about each label until Cray reached into his pocket and held up a key. "Would you like to see the vault?"

"The rum collection?" Barclay beamed. "Yes, please!"

Cray gave him the key and directions and told him to have a look. I was kind of eager to see the rum room myself, but it was nice to sit down with Neil on the creaky settee, with Cray in a chair next to us. I smiled to see Luke and Melody talking and laughing in a pair of soft chairs in the corner.

"So you went to see Ms. Landry's house? Quite the pile, isn't it?" Cray drawled.

"It's massive," I said. "And surprisingly up to date. Not that yours isn't."

"Oh, mine isn't, except for the lab and the kitchen. Well, if twenty years old can be considered up to date." Cray chuckled. "She inherited that house and put a lot of money into it."

Neil sipped his rum—he'd taken a very small pour, since he'd be driving—and set the glass on a side table. "She said she'd inherited the bar. It was part of the house?"

"Oh, no, not at all," Cray said. "I suppose she didn't divulge her family's rather interesting history."

"She said she had a colorful family," I replied.

Cray nodded. "Oh yes indeed. They were known for their saloons and houses of ill repute back in the golden days. Even had a couple of establishments in Storyville back when the city tried to corral vice into one location lest the delicate sensibilities of our citizens be jarred by such doings. Finally the city legislated Storyville out of existence.

"Ms. Landry's people ran a few speakeasies during Prohibition. They were doing a public service, in my opinion. Many restaurants set up private dining rooms and other ways to hide their booze, but the alcohol ban nearly destroyed our finest drinking establishments."

"We were just talking about that," Neil said.

"Jazz was particularly hard-hit. It barely survived Prohibition. It was already hurting with the crackdown on vice, especially as ill-informed prudes tried to tie jazz and sin together. Prohibition made a bad situation worse." Cray sighed. "Where were the musicians to play with all the bars shut down? Louis Armstrong left the city for Chicago during that time, in 1922. Did you know?"

"I didn't realize that," I said. "He's so associated with New Orleans."

"Indeed. He only came back when he was famous." Cray sipped his rum and sighed with pleasure.

"Is Camelia Landry musical?" I asked him. "She has a nice piano but said she didn't play it."

Cray's eyebrows lifted. "Not that I know of. Why do you ask?"

"Because Beau—who is still eluding the police, by the way —was her music teacher. Maybe he was giving her guitar or singing lessons."

"Perhaps," Cray said. "Would it be less than gallant for me to say that she could use a few singing lessons? I attended one of her parties where she sang drunken karaoke. It was bad enough to make my few remaining hairs stand on end."

We laughed as he smoothed his flyaway white hair.

"Are you invited to her party tomorrow?" I asked.

"I am. I'll expect good whiskey, since I doubt rum is her drink."

"She had some nice bottles of rye," Neil said, "but the one I tasted this afternoon was a little disappointing."

I turned to him in surprise. "I thought the same thing. But the cocktails made the most of it."

Neil smiled. "True. It was fine. I just wouldn't call it a sipping whiskey."

"She certainly has a nice selection of liquors and a beautiful house," I said. "I can see why she'd be a juicy target for a con man like Beau. He didn't give up on ripping off my parents, and he might not give up on her, either. We should keep an eye out. Though I really hope I never see that man again."

Neil squeezed my shoulder. "I'm glad to hear it. I don't want to have to worry about you like that again."

"And I don't want you to." I gave his knee a squeeze in return. "Meanwhile, I'm wondering who left the body of Edgar Poeville in our room at Hydrangea House."

Cray's shoulders shook in a dramatic shiver. "I don't know how you can even stay in the same hotel."

"Expedience," Neil said.

"I'm still trying to figure out who could've killed him." I sipped my rum and considered the possibilities. "Sierra Felt seemed glad to get rid of Edgar because she got to take over the ghost tour. And Wilma Wells was going to sue him for stealing her material, but now Sierra's using the same script, so offing Edgar would not have helped Wilma. But she had no way to know that for sure. What's weird is Royce spotted Wilma at Hydrangea House the day of the murder. You told Colby about that, right?" I asked Neil.

"I told him, but maybe the detectives have been too busy to follow up."

"Ms. Wells is a historian, isn't she?" Cray asked. "I've read an article or two by her. She seems like someone who's more likely to sue than kill."

"She was hopping mad at Edgar, though," I said. "Then there are his drinking buddies Alfie Boudreaux and Jai Joshi. Both of them mentioned Edgar owed people money, which would expand the list of suspects beyond those we've heard about. Plus we think Edgar might've been selling drugs, pills maybe, based on what Sierra said. Alfie seems to be in the same business. It's all so sketchy."

"Don't forget Beau," Neil said.

"How can I? I don't believe anything he says, but weirdly, I almost believed him when he implied he hadn't killed Edgar."

"There's something we're missing," Neil said.

"Dinner, I think," Cray suggested, and I grinned. He was right. I was hungry after our trying day.

Barclay came back in the room with stars in his eyes. He handed the rum room key to Cray. "You have so many fascinating bottles! And I have so many questions."

"You can quiz me over Oysters Rockefeller," Cray said, setting down his empty glass. "Shall we go?"

"Let me text the rest of the gang." Neil pulled out his phone. "Where did you have in mind?"

As Neil and Cray discussed the options, my phone buzzed in my big bag. It took some digging, but I pulled it out, stepped into the entrance hall and answered it. "Hey, Millie. How's it going?"

"I'm fine," said our planner and finder of facts and things. "How about you? Any more dead bodies?"

"No, but not for Beau's lack of trying."

She must've heard something in my voice. "Uh-oh. Are you OK?"

"More or less." I gave her the abridged version of my run-ins with Beau. "What have you got for us?"

"I searched the newspaper archives for all of New Orleans and couldn't find any stories about a writer who died eating oysters and drinking too much. Of course, those are difficult keywords to search for because there are so many stories about drinking and food, but I included the Fantome's previous name—the Fantome name change was a pretty recent marketing tactic—and I searched for Carl, too. Basically, no searches came up with the drunken farting ghost story."

"So it's not true," I said.

"I'm not a big believer in any ghost story, but the story behind the story is elusive. Doesn't mean it didn't happen. It could be I just haven't found the right source. And the *New*

Orleans Bee also published in French, and given my French skills still aren't great, I might have missed something."

"Rats. Anything interesting about the Fantome and ghosts in general?"

"Oh, it's had hauntings or tales of hauntings. An opera singer who fell to her death, a wounded Confederate soldier."

"I heard about those on the ghost tour."

"It once was known for its wine cellar," Millie said, "but I understand their wine selection is more modest now."

"There are no cellars to speak of in the Quarter."

"Ah, but this was more of a half basement. Not totally underground. I've also read the city is sinking, so when it was built, maybe a partial basement wasn't that hard to keep dry. There was also a story, more of a legend, really, about a tunnel built to smuggle items from the hotel to the river and back."

"They say the same thing about Lafitte's," I said. "Probably a myth given the water table."

"Probably. Sorry I couldn't find more."

"Your *not* finding anything about the farting ghost may be telling," I told her. "Though I have to say, I've had one or two creepy moments in the Fantome bar."

Millie chuckled. "Seems to me you've had enough scary encounters in real life that a little ghost fart shouldn't bother you too much."

"Maybe, but I have such a keen sense of smell," I complained, and she laughed. "Thanks again for looking."

"Let me know if you need anything else. Later!"

We ended the call, and I joined our crew and Cray in Neil's SUV, my brain working overtime and coming up empty. Maybe food and sleep would help. We had a big day tomorrow— Easter fun, then Camelia's party. But I didn't like having so many potentially dangerous mysteries gnawing at me—Beau's vanishing, the million-dollar cross, and Edgar's murder. Murder was always disturbing, but this one felt especially so, probably because the victim was left in what was supposed to be my bed.

Our bed.

Leaving a corpse for us just seemed so ... *personal*.

Chapter Twenty-Six

I slept like a boulder after an exhausting day and a pleasant evening with our friends, but one of my strange dreams dragged me into wakefulness.

I was back in the bowels of the abandoned naval base, only I walked through the halls by myself, and I could hear music. I followed the sound and found a sparkling ballroom bursting with light and color and clashing melodies. A big band played jazz, with Kirby on the tuba, Royce dinging a triangle and Aunt Celestine shaking a tambourine. Beau stood at the microphone, singing, looking at me with one of his handsome smirks. The song was like one of his strange poetic threats, only to a bouncy beat. Melody stood at a microphone across the room with Luke and Barclay, singing "Blues in the Night," while Jai and Avani made drinks at a bar that looked like Camelia's.

Camelia and Alfie sat at the bar with a vaporous entity dressed in nineteenth-century clothes who must have been Carl the farting ghost. Then Edgar Poeville joined him, looking just as translucent, and they laughed and clapped each other's backs and made a toast. Their drinks poured through them and onto the floor, and Astra ran over and lapped up the glowing puddle. I tried to stop her, but I was interrupted by Sierra, who stalked in and demanded Edgar and Carl behave and appear on her tour. Then Wilma walked in with a small army of tourists chanting, "I don't believe in ghosts!" while Edgar and Carl laughed at everyone. And where was Neil? I couldn't find him, and Beau and Melody kept singing louder and louder, and just when my head was about to explode like the bomb in Lakeview, I sat up with a whimper, sweating under the thick comforter of the hotel bed.

"Bad dream?" came a voice to my right, and I looked over to see my roomie Diana sitting at the desk, already dressed, writing in a journal. She set down her pen and looked at me with concern. "Are you all right?"

I blinked and blew out a big breath. "Yeah. I have weird dreams sometimes."

"I understand. I had one about Mark."

"Do tell." I smiled. "That had to be good."

Her amber skin went a shade pinker. "Oh, it wasn't like that. He was driving me through the jungle in an enormous Range Rover."

"A big, virile, hunky Range Rover that wants to carry you away?"

She laughed. "Ah, I see. My subconscious is telling me something, then?"

"Was it a stick shift?" She laughed louder as I added, "All I can say is that Range Rover would probably be a hell of a ride."

"Its motor is always running. I'm still deciding whether to jump in," she said coyly, then turned back to her journal as I headed to the bathroom to get ready for the day.

It was Easter morning, I realized. This was supposed to be a day for joy and renewal, no matter what you believed. It was spring. A time of hope. But dread crept into my thoughts. Easter wasn't over. Beau had vanished. Where was he?

Our group met in the lobby in late morning. Aunt Celestine emerged from the elevator with Astra on a leash. Our dog wore a silly hat with flowers and a fluffy dress. She seemed excited about the outfit because it meant we were going somewhere, and she licked my hand when I petted her.

My aunt wore a perky little hat topped by lavender ostrich feathers that matched her flowing dress. She carried two more hats, the "Easter bonnets" Melody had designed when she found out they were a thing in New Orleans, the crazier the better. We'd brought them in the car. My friend had made me promise not to peek in the boxes, only told me the color scheme so I could dress accordingly.

I could see why. They were wild.

Melody donned hers first. Her broad-brimmed hat was a study in pink and white froth, with folds of tulle, little white birds and a birdhouse, and a veritable garden of flowers. Mine was more of a blue top hat wrapped in a sparkly turquoise-and-blue ribbon printed with peacock feathers and an additional band of pale blue gems. Glitter-coated fake peacock feathers sprouted in a fan out the back, like a peacock's tail—only not as big, fortunately. An adorable small peacock sat in the center of the hat, looking out with a cocky expression, as if it had nested there.

"That's—" I struggled for words.

"Fabulous, right?" Melody enthused, fluffing her tulle. Her hat went perfectly with her sleeveless pink dress with its white lapels, big white buttons and rather daring V-neck.

I gingerly took mine from my aunt, whose eyes twinkled, and set it on my head. It was a little heavy, but it did match my ruffled turquoise-and-blue floral dress.

Diana had dressed in khaki and white again, no hat, but she'd added a scarf in pretty pastels. Mark wore a cream-colored jacket and brown trousers with a light blue shirt.

Royce looked good in a light green jacket and khakis. Luke and Barclay had gone tropical. And Neil arrived in dark blue pants and a gorgeous subtly shiny vest in the same colors as my dress, over a blue shirt.

He smiled at my shocked expression, or maybe at my hat, and came over and kissed me.

"You've been talking to Melody, haven't you?" I asked him.

"Maybe. What do you think?"

"I think you're the only Easter candy I need."

Barclay and Luke snickered, and I raised an eyebrow at them. And smiled. Because it was a beautiful day, and we were going to put aside our troubles for a few hours and have fun. And I was with Neil.

"Where's Kirby this morning?" I asked him.

"Playing tuba on one of the floats."

I was about to ask where Mr. Mixy was, as he never showed up for dinner last night and I hadn't seen him, when a blinding apparition in bubble-gum pink stepped out of the elevator.

His beard preceded him and his outrageous suit. He lifted his head to Melody. "Hey, we match."

She just shook her head at him in a way that said *In your dreams, furry face.* Besides, her pink wasn't quite as neon as his.

"So," Royce said to me with a mischievous smile, "Aunt Celestine and I went to your parents' church early this morning and did our best to pray for all our souls. Now the drinking can commence."

My aunt looked amused. Her spirituality was more fluid than formal, but it was nice of her to support her sister.

"How are they?" I asked.

"They're fine," she said. "Though I think they are more bothered by the theft of their million-dollar 'investment' than they let on. And a cop is still trailing them, though I don't know for how long, given everything that's happened. No word on Beau?"

I shook my head. "I've got nothing. Neil?"

"Nothing from Colby. No news."

"No news is good news?" Royce said hopefully. "Shall we grab brunch? We've already missed the first dainty little parade. A big one starts at one, and if we have time, the gay parade later today is supposed to be awesome."

"Let's do it," I said.

My aunt had made reservations at another restaurant that allowed dogs outside, so we went and stuffed ourselves. Then we found a nice shady spot under some scaffolding outside a building under renovation that was along the parade route. There was scaffolding across the street, too. An old city that was often in the path of hurricanes was under constant construction.

Lots of people crowded the sidewalks: adults, many in festive wear and carrying drinks, and shrieking sugar-fueled kids in wee suits and flouncy dresses that were already on their way to ruin.

Then came the parade—bands and krewes marching in costume, but mostly floats, big boxy rolling wagons pulled by tractors filled with gaily dressed people tossing out strings of beads, candy and other gewgaws. It was like Mardi Gras without the debauchery. I snagged reflective turquoise beads that matched my dress and considered it a win.

There were a few too many furry Easter bunnies, though—people in bunny costumes, that is. Why were they so creepy? The big dead pupils and the buck teeth were more hideous than huggable. And there was a rabbit loitering across the street who kept giving me the eye as he handed kids plastic eggs from his basket. Not that I could tell where the giant costume eye was really looking, but that was what it felt like.

So it seemed like a strange dream when the bunny abruptly stepped into the street in front of a gorgeous old pink Cadillac convertible filled with mature ladies in outrageous hats. And the dream became a nightmare when he walked in my direction.

"Get out of the way! This is a parade!" hollered the driver, waving a gloved fist at the rabbit.

That's when the bunny shook off a mitten, reached deep into his basket, and pulled out a handgun.

Chapter Twenty-Seven

The Easter bunny aimed his handgun at the Cadillac's angry driver.

She screamed, this time in terror. So did the other three women in the rolling aircraft carrier as the driver wrenched the wheel to the right to avoid the rabbit and the gun—and plowed right into the three-story scaffold across the street.

The structure collapsed in slow motion. Metal bars and boards spilled into the street and hit the hood of the car with a mighty crash, sending up a cloud of dust as everyone in sight ran, shrieking. Even the rabbit leaped out of the way. My instinctive duck probably saved me as the bunny turned toward us, aimed his gun and fired. I heard breaking glass and looked up to see a hole in the window behind me.

"Pepper!" Neil shouted, grabbing me by the arm and hauling me down the street as our group scattered. Astra barked as she and my aunt went one way and Neil and I went another.

"Bunny man! Halt! Police! Drop the gun!" came a deep voice behind us.

I looked back over my shoulder as we ran, dodging panicked pedestrians and askew parade vehicles. As the women climbed out of their trashed Cadillac, a big, ebony male cop sprinted after the demented Easter bunny. The buck-toothed baddie looked toward me, then the officer, before hopping away into the crowd.

Neil guided me right at the corner, and I looked back again. The cop ran in the opposite direction, chasing the rabbit, so I tugged on Neil's arm and brought him to a stop.

"We're fine now." I gasped for breath. "The cop's on him. He's heading the other way. Check and see if everyone is OK."

Neil looked around, reassuring himself that no evil rabbits were in sight, then pulled out his phone and tapped.

"They're checking in …" He rattled off the names as his phone pinged. Everyone was fine. "Maybe we should take a break somewhere quiet till we're sure the crisis is past."

The parade was definitely taking a break. A woman with a clipboard shouted at the floats that hadn't yet turned down the street we'd been on, which was now blocked by the collapsed scaffolding and an evolving crime scene.

"New route!" She shouted directions. "Leave room for these guys to back out. Careful!" More police showed up to handle traffic and look out for armed Easter bunnies.

After more group texts and a circuitous stroll, we found ourselves in the Backspace Bar, sharing hugs with all of our friends before decompressing with a drink. This place gave off a dive vibe with its dark atmosphere, writer theme and cheap deals, but its cocktails were solid, as I learned when I ordered a Manhattan, another rye favorite and always a comfort when I needed a soothing sipper.

Barclay leaned against the fireplace, holding a mojito. "Now I've seen everything."

"Don't tell me you've never seen an armed Easter bunny before," Luke replied.

"Well, there was that time in Miami," Barclay answered, and we laughed, losing some of our tension.

"Imagine how many innocent people in Easter bunny outfits are being shaken down by the police right now," Melody said.

"There are no innocent people in Easter bunny outfits," Barclay deadpanned.

"Pepper! Your hat!" Melody peered at my top hat as I sat at a small table opposite Neil. "Your little peacock lost his head."

Yikes. Had the bullet come that close? "Better him than me."

"Still, it's a shame. He was so cute."

"Why did the Easter bunny shoot at us?" Royce asked.

"You mean, why did he shoot at Pepper," Neil said.

"Royce has a point." I tipped my glass in his direction. "We don't know for sure he was aiming at me. Who can tell with those freaky costume eyes?"

"He was aiming at you, darling," Mark said with concern. "You're a magnet for trouble."

"Could it have been Beau?" my aunt asked. Astra, too cute to be denied entry to the bar, sat on her lap.

"I don't see how," I answered. "He was shot yesterday. No matter how minor his injury was—and there was a lot of blood —there's no way he could run down the street like that with a gunshot wound."

"Since he got away yesterday, maybe he's more mobile than you think. Who else could it be?" Mark asked.

"Someone who thinks Pepper is dangerous to them." Neil reached across the table to hold my hand.

"He almost hit *me!*" exclaimed Mr. Mixy as he worked on a two-dollar beer special.

I glowered at him. "What's worse is that he could've hit anybody. There were little kids there."

"It's no wonder that creature missed you," Diana said. "Rabbits' eyes are on the side of their head. You can wave a piece of lettuce right in front of their nose and they can't see it."

It took a second for us to realize she was kidding. My friends' humor restored my spirits. As they chatted, I asked Neil if he'd heard from Detective Colby.

"I messaged him about what happened, and he said he'd talk to us later. They're still trying to unravel the bombing and pick up Beau's trail. 'Keep your heads down' was his advice."

"Great," I said dryly. "Anything else?"

"They talked to Jezebel Harlow. She admitted to helping connect Beau and your parents to a high-end antiques dealer. But she denied helping him fence the cross."

"So maybe Beau still has it."

"Maybe," Neil said. "Oh, and Colby had info on Beau's license plate. The car was borrowed from an eightysomething woman in the Bywater who almost never used it."

"Borrowed as in stolen?" I asked.

"No. She actually lent it to him."

"Smooth talker," I muttered. "I want to take him down."

Neil shook his head. "Our priority at this point is to keep you safe."

"Agreed," Aunt Celestine said. "I don't think Pepper should go to the next parade. She might get hurt."

I smiled at her. "I'm not going to hide. Beau's incapacitated and probably fleeing. By now the police surely have the rabbit on the run, whoever he is. Even if they don't have him, there's no way he'd be stupid enough to try again."

"I don't know ..." Neil's eyes were full of worry.

"We can't stay long anyway," Mr. Mixy said. "We have to work Camelia's party."

Ha. As if Mr. Mixy would actually work.

"We'll look out for Pepper," Royce said. "Everyone keep your eyes peeled for rogue rabbits."

There *were* a lot of bunny ears hopping around the French Quarter, but eventually I stopped flinching when I saw them and began to enjoy myself, especially as we got near Dauphine and St. Ann. A kaleidoscopic street party was in progress, with bubbles drifting over a pastiche of wild costumes and elaborate hats and glitter and rainbows as the crowd danced to thumping music and awaited the gay parade.

As the floats and their attendants flowed through the neighborhood, the riders tossed adorable prizes to eager spectators—I added a few more strings of beads to my outfit—and happiness filled me. This scene was pure joy.

"My people," Royce said, wearing a big grin.

"You need to juice up your wardrobe if you want to fit in here," I told my brother.

He laughed. "True."

Aunt Celestine caught a fuzzy stuffed bunny and showed it to Astra, who grabbed it by the ear and started to teach it a lesson. Astra didn't like bunnies much right now either.

Mr. Mixy was the one to tell us what we weren't ready to hear. "Time to work, bartenders!" he called out.

"Now that's scarier than a deadly Easter bunny," I said to Neil as we Bohemia Bartenders began to make our way back to the hotel so we could change, pick up our gear and get Neil's car.

"What?"

"Mr. Mixy being our boss."

"Never," Neil said. "We're merely hired consultants."

I laughed. "He'd better watch it, or there'll be a mutiny."

Neil smiled. "I'm sure you'll keep him in line."

CAMELIA'S HOUSE looked like a tornado in progress when we arrived, with caterers and decorators running around, prepping the place for the party. Vases full of showy flowers in dreamy pastels had sprouted everywhere, including a huge arrangement on the baby grand piano. And dozens of adorable miniature Easter baskets were lined up as favors, complete with Elmer's Pecan Eggs and mini whiskeys, on a table in the front hall.

As Mr. Mixy wandered off to be Mr. Mixy and we headed to the kitchen, I stopped at the sight of Kirby. He and three other guys on clarinet, banjo, and trumpet were setting up in the sun room next to the parlor/ballroom that held the bar.

"How'd you end up here?" I asked him. "Is this your band?"

"Sometimes." He looked around before continuing, making sure no one else was in earshot. "Once I knew you all would be here, I thought it might make sense for me to be here, too. Just in case."

"Cool. And I can't wait to hear you play."

"For real?" He seemed pleased. "I thought you disliked my tuba."

"Only when it's playing at 3 a.m. outside my hotel."

I joined the other bartenders in the kitchen to do some quick prep—squeezing lemons and limes, making fresh simple syrups and creating lemon-peel garnishes. We staged the first batch of specially ordered ice balls and smaller cubes in the bar fridge. And we gobbled up the sandwiches the caterers left for us.

We would focus on classic New Orleans cocktails at Camelia's request, but there were a lot of classics to consider. We'd narrowed them down to the Sazerac, a Brandy Crusta, and a Ramos Gin Fizz (so lots of cream and eggs were stocked in the bar fridge). Each Fizz would require up to five minutes of shaking—first a dry shake without ice, then a longer one with it—to get that trademark foamy top, so having five bartenders today wasn't a bad idea.

To capture the Easter vibe, Neil had created two variations on Crescent City cocktails. The Parisian Pink was a spin on the champagne-and-gin French 75. It came out a lovely color worthy of an Easter egg thanks to the addition of an Italian strawberry liqueur. It wasn't French, but it was good.

His invention A Mint of Spring, inspired by a classic Milk Punch, used rye instead of brandy or bourbon. A dollop of homemade crème de menthe gave it a delicate pale green color. We prepared fresh mint for the garnish and had nutmeg ready to grate over the top.

Camelia's hired man Zeke loomed over us with a scowl as we transported our ingredients and gear to the ballroom bar. Didn't volunteer to help, though.

Soon after, our grand hostess arrived in the ballroom, now dotted with high-top gnoshing tables and devoid of most of its fancy furniture. Elegant and slightly daring in a low-cut floral dress that seemed to float around her, Camelia approached the bar as we set up our *mise en place*. She looked us over. We all sported pastels to fit the theme, with Melody and I in simpler floral dresses than earlier, with flower clips in our hair instead of hats. Luke and Barclay wore button-up shirts in lavender and pale green, respectively. Neil looked adorable in white suspenders and a bow tie striped in yellow, pink and blue. A blue button-up shirt and dark blue pants emphasized his lean figure.

"You look marvelous." Camelia's eyes lingered on Neil. Then she gave me a smug look that lit up my jealousy circuits before her eyes slid back to him. "Everything ready?"

"All set." Neil pointed to a couple of small stand-up menus he'd placed on the bar. "Classics and their variations, as you requested. Can we make you something?"

"After I do one more round of wrangling. I'll let you know." A tinkling bell sound floated through the room. "Ah, there are the first guests now."

As she scurried out, Mr. Mixy drifted in, still wearing his pink suit. The look on his face was even more smug than the look on Camelia's. He approached me as my colleagues made the first cocktails for guests and the first server passed by with a tray of crudités.

"Go, team!" he said to my friends, then leaned against the bar and told me in a low voice, "Camelia is very happy with us. *Very* happy."

"Not because of anything you did, I presume."

"You presume wrong. The premium experience is all about *me*, Pepper." Mr. Mixy pressed a hand to his chest in a dramatic gesture. "It's my job to keep the client happy. And I have." He smirked. "Last night. And today—"

I held up a hand to stop him. "I don't want to know the details." But I could guess. Was Camelia's taste really that bad? "Anyway, kissing and telling is extremely ungentlemanly."

"Oh, there was a lot more than kissing."

I worked on making garnishes out of an orange peel and tried not to listen.

"I told her that you were sweet on me," he said, "but that didn't stop her from jumping my bones."

"What the— You are *delusional!* And seriously, Stephan, I have to work."

But he was caught up in romantic reminiscence. "It was a beautiful night. We were having a midnight swim. The pool is heated, you know? And I didn't have my bathing suit with me, if you know what I mean." Ugh. I was going to barf in the garnishes if he didn't shut up. "Though she got kinda weird when I wanted to use the bathroom in the guest cottage. I thought she was joking, but she grabbed me when I went to leave the pool and attacked me—in a good way. Heh heh. And then she kicked me out." He stroked his beard in an unseemly fashion. "I think she was just overwhelmed with emotion because she wanted me so much. Women get like that around me sometimes. I mean, look at your reaction just now."

I resisted the urge to fling a scoop of ice cubes into his face as he continued. "She asked me yesterday if I could handle the bar myself if anything happened to you guys. Of course, I told her I could. I'm a professional, not just a TV star. I told her you serve at my pleasure. She seemed to like that."

Neil interrupted before I could stick a spoon up Mr. Mixy's nose. "Pepper, can I get you to make a Brandy Crusta?"

"Sure, no problem." *Thank you, Neil.* "Goodbye, Stephan."

"Bye, Pepper," he said in a smarmy tone.

I tried not to imagine him with Camelia. Seriously, why did he have to plant those images in my head? Did he think I cared about his conquests? Camelia got plenty of action without Mr. Mixy. I mean, look at her fling with Beau, even if Beau *was* trying to scam her.

I finished the cocktail, garnishing the sugar rim with a spiral of orange peel, and smiled as I handed it to a guest. The room was filling up. Cray came by, dapper in a cream-colored suit. He made off with a Ramos Gin Fizz, its towering foam head jiggling, after watching Luke and Barclay engage in an enthusiastic cocktail-shaking duel.

Then a well-dressed couple approached me. The man looked oddly familiar, but not. I knew I hadn't met him before.

They ordered drinks, and the man smiled as I handed them over. "Pepper?"

"That's me. Do I know you?"

"Not yet. But you know my son. I'm Royce Doucet—Royce J. Doucet. RJ to my friends. And this is Teresa. Royce told me you might be here." Implied was: *He also told me you are his sister*.

I was speechless for a moment before my wits returned. Of course! RJ looked a lot like Royce. "Mr. and Mrs. Doucet—it is so nice to meet you. And I'm so glad you and Royce were able to talk."

"It's been an interesting weekend." Royce's mom's smile held a touch of irony. "I'm very glad to meet you. I hope we see one another again."

We agreed that would be a good idea, and they left me to deal with the queue of partygoers. I got into the rhythm of making drinks as my mind wandered, my thoughts bouncing along to the tunes of Kirby's jazz band in the next room.

First, I thought about Royce. Then about Mr. Mixy's annoying chatter. Something had bugged me about what he said—not just his icky bragging. Something about the guest cottage.

Camelia, who kept turning up in unexpected places. Camelia, who was sweet on Beau. Why was Camelia so secretive about the guest cottage?

I needed to find out.

Chapter Twenty-Eight

The party was a success, judging by the happy drunken people coming back again and again for our cocktails. We ran out of a couple of them, but as Camelia had lots of booze, there was still plenty to drink. Mr. Mixy was one of our best customers, in between mingling with guests and signing autographs on a sheaf of eight-by-ten head shots he carried around with him.

The crowd was pretty much gone by eleven, and Kirby checked in with us before he left with his crew.

"All is well," Neil told him with a smile. He seemed relieved we'd avoided any major disasters on this disaster-prone weekend.

Camelia returned from her hostess wanderings and thanked us. "Your cocktails were wonderful. Mr. Mixy is lucky to have you."

That was the truth. Mr. Mixy, sprawling on a soft chair, half looped, waved and grinned through his beard as we cleaned up the bar.

"Glad to help," Neil said with a barely perceptible side-eye toward the indolent Mr. Mixy.

"Zeke will make sure you get your stuff out to the car. I have to run an errand," Camelia told us. And then she was gone.

An errand? This late on Easter Sunday? Whatever. Halfway through our cleanup, I told Neil I had to go to the restroom. That part was true.

What I didn't tell him was that I had another purpose. With the bartenders stowing supplies and packing up and Zeke keeping an eye on them—what, did he think they were going to steal the silver?—I stopped in a bathroom, then slipped out to the poolside patio.

It was quiet out here now, though I knew from a previous foray to the kitchen that during the party, several revelers had enjoyed the evening out here. It was a beautiful night, and the air smelled like flowers. Camelia even had pretty pink, purple and yellow spotlights aimed at the house and plants in the garden to reinforce the Easter theme.

On the other side of the pool, lying in darkness with no spotlights on it and no lights inside, was the guesthouse.

"This is ridiculous," I told myself. But there was something about Mr. Mixy's story that piqued my curiosity and rearranged the puzzle pieces in my head. Could the guesthouse hold a secret?

Or a person?

I hoped I was wrong. Camelia wouldn't harbor a violent fugitive, would she, in spite of all his devious charms?

I trotted around the pool, trying to stay to the shadows. I looked around and saw no one. Then I approached the cottage and tried the door.

"Damn." Locked. Not surprising, really. If she didn't want people in there, of course she locked the door. I snuck around the side of the house. The windows were conveniently low to the ground, given the small stature of the building. I peered through the first one I found.

It was dark in there and hard to make out the contents, but

my eyes adjusted enough that I could see a couch, a chair and a small credenza with a dark television, a fireplace, and beyond the living area, a tiny open kitchen. Nothing odd at all.

Go back, the guilty part of me said. *Neil will worry about you.*

I was about to listen to the little voice when I heard a noise from inside. I wasn't sure what it was, but I was pretty sure it was human. Now was I just a voyeur? Not if I didn't actually want to see what I was looking for, I reasoned.

I slid along the wall to the next window, which presumably led into the bedroom. The cottage wasn't that big, and there had to be somewhere to sleep besides the couch. But inside this window, a shade covered the surface edge to edge.

Almost.

There was a tiny nick in the shade, and a dim light flickered beyond it, colors changing as I watched. A television?

Somebody was in there. I was sure of it. It could be a drunk guest from the party. But I thought it more likely that Beau was in there, hiding under Camelia's protection. What if Camelia herself was in there and the errand was just a ruse?

It might make sense to call Detective Colby, but I didn't want to drag him out here on a hunch. He already thought I was flighty. Better to make sure Beau was there. Maybe I could slip through a window, take a peek and then dash out the front door.

I eased back to the living room window and tried to open it. It resisted. I was about to give up when it suddenly gave way and shot up with a low *thunk*.

I cringed. This wasn't good. But I had to hurry. I hoisted myself up, getting halfway over the windowsill. I flashed back to awkward gym class moments in high school. Most of my gym class moments were awkward, especially during the gymnastics unit, an extended torture session that went on for weeks. I was never good at mounting the balance beam. That moment when I had to swing my substantial legs up and over the beam was always touch and go. And when I swung my leg over the windowsill of Camelia's cottage, I kept going and fell with a *thwump* to the floor.

I bit back a curse and sat up and listened.

"Camelia? Is that you? I'm glad you came back. I want to talk to you."

Beau. His voice made my hairs stand on end. But he sounded a little funny through the closed door, like he was wheedling. Maybe he didn't feel well. He'd been shot, after all. I needed to get out of here and tell the cops where he was.

I flinched as the bedroom door latch clicked. The door opened inward with a creak, casting a shaft of light into the living room.

The flickering glow of the television backlit the figure beyond the doorway. Oddly, he sat on the floor just inside the bedroom.

"Well, well, look who it is," Beau said after a moment. "Little Pepper. Maybe you can help me."

"Would you stop calling me that!" I scrambled to my feet, switched on a lamp on a nearby table, and grabbed a poker from the collection of tools by the fireplace. I couldn't help noticing its brass handle was shaped like the head of a court jester, which seemed appropriate somehow. I wasn't sure who the jester was here—me or Beau.

I stayed where I was, wielding my ridiculous weapon, watching Beau in the other room. He seemed to struggle to rise. Unkempt and pale, he pushed himself up with a grunt and sat on the bed in the other room. Why didn't he come after me? His wound?

"Come on, Pepper. I was just teasing you with that fire thing. I knew you'd be OK."

He delivered this absurd line with such conviction, I almost wanted to believe him. He was a mesmerist, this guy. Everyone fell under his spell.

"Stay away from me." I brandished the poker. "I'm getting out of here and calling the cops. Camelia should've known better than to hide you here. How'd you talk her into it?"

Beau looked at me for a second, and then he laughed, a bitter, strange laugh that turned into a croak of pain. He pressed a hand to his stomach and winced. His shirt—a fresh black T-shirt—rode up, revealing the bandage on his side. Something flashed at his wrist.

He let out a breath and looked up. He lifted his hand, revealing a stout manacle attached to a chain secured to a beefy eyebolt in the wall. The chain was just long enough to let him open the door and, presumably, reach the bathroom.

"I didn't talk her into hiding me," he said. "She had one of her cronies take me here after she shot me."

I blinked. "She shot you? That wasn't her at the old naval base, was it?"

"Technically, no, it wasn't. Her crony shot me on her behalf. You've probably met him. Zeke? Tall guy? Looks like Lurch?"

I tried to process what he was saying. "Well, you did try to con her after you seduced her. Can you blame her for wanting to shoot you?"

Beau started to laugh again, then put a hand to his mouth and coughed. "Oh, little Pepper, you really don't get it, do you? I never tried to con Camelia. I might've tried to do an end run around her, but it's not like I wanted her job. I just wanted my fair share for doing all the work."

I took a step forward. "What are you talking about?"

He shook his head. "I thought you had more brains than this. She's the boss, or at least she thinks she is. Her empire is fraying at the edges, and she's cleaning house."

"You're saying you work for her?"

"I have, when convenient. She has connections. She hooked me up with investors, but I'm the one who made it work. I felt I deserved the largest cut. Camelia didn't."

"So it wasn't just my parents?"

"I had half a dozen greedy bastards on the hook for my real estate project, worth several hundred thousand before I got your parents on board. I was counting on your parents to make it worth my while; Camelia had no idea how much they were going to give me. Fortunately, I found a way to get back what I was owed."

I'd almost forgotten the cross. "Where is it?"

"Ah ah ah." Beau held up the manacled hand again. "Get me out of here first."

"Not happening."

"Do you want it or not?"

I took a guess. "So you have it with you."

He didn't say anything for a moment, and then his eyes slid away and back. I was *sure* he had it with him. And he knew I knew.

"Let's negotiate," he said. "You release me, and I give you the cross."

I was keenly aware I'd been here for too long. Even if Camelia didn't return from her errand, Zeke would come looking. I needed answers fast. "Where's Camelia?"

"I told you, cleaning house. She's tired of punks who can't do anything right and keep skimming off the top. Too bad poor little Avani will be collateral damage. But that's what happens when your brother is a screwup. He'll be lucky if he doesn't end up like Edgar."

Jai? What did Jai do? "Wait—are you saying Camelia killed Edgar?"

"Not exactly." Beau smiled. "But she knows who did. She told me she arranged it to teach me a lesson, to show me she could do anything to anyone at any time. She doesn't like my— what did she call it?—*obsession* with you. She really didn't like me sending you the eggs."

"If what you're saying is true, why did you tell her about them? About me?"

Beau shrugged. "She found my rhyming dictionary." *Ha!* "It spurred a conversation about writing songs and poetry, and I thought she'd be amused by the Easter eggs. But she took offense that my attention should be drawn away from her for one lousy second." He rolled his eyes. "I think she thought you might be arrested or at least distracted by Edgar Poeville's murder and that I, out of a sense of self-preservation, would leave you alone. She didn't understand my compelling need to bring an end to our quarrel."

"Our *quarrel?* You've tried to kill me at least twice for no reason."

He smiled, but his eyes were frosty. "I always have a reason."

Yeah, being a psychotic whack job. Though to be fair, he thought if he got rid of me the first time, no one would get in the way of his swindle of my parents.

Now Beau, still bent on vengeance, had just painted Camelia as a criminal mastermind responsible for Edgar's death. Could it be possible? If so, she must have an intense need for control to kill Edgar just because she didn't like Beau's sick game to get me to New Orleans.

I had one more chance to end this. "Throw the cross to me and you'll never have to see me again."

"And you'll set me free? She keeps the key in that stand by the front door."

"Throw it to me," I said again. "You know I'll do the right thing."

Beau's pale blue eyes held mine for a minute. Then he used his free hand to reach down the front of his jeans and pull out the cross. Its gems caught the light as he turned it in both hands, considering. Then he looked up at me and tossed it over.

I caught it with my free hand, gripped the poker with the other, and tried not to think about where the cross had been hiding. Maybe diamonds were antibacterial.

He held up his hand with the manacle clamped on his wrist. "Key?"

"Where's Camelia going?"

"The Fantome, of course. Get the key and toss it to me. If you don't trust me, you can run. It's all good. You'll be fine."

The Fantome? I stuck the cross into my bra, where it fought with the girls for space. The pope would have to have this thing steam-cleaned if he ever wanted it back.

"Not happening," I said to Beau's pleading look.

"Pepper." He didn't say "little" this time, but his voice had become low and dangerous.

I stood my ground. "No fun being on the other side, is it?"

The charming mask bled away, and fury took over his features. "She's going to kill me. You can't leave me here."

"Like you left me in that bourbon barrel?"

"Bourbon under the bridge. You're here now, aren't you?"

"Only because I have good friends. Maybe, if you're lucky, the cops will find you first."

I stuck the poker back where I'd found it and left Beau there. I exited the front door of the cottage and ran across the courtyard, hiding behind a column as Zeke emerged from the house and looked around. I held my breath. He walked around the pool and tried the door of the cottage—I'd locked it behind me. Satisfied, he never walked around the corner to find the open window, but he did head off into the bushes. I didn't know if he was searching for me, checking the perimeter or what. All I knew was that I had to get out of here.

And we had to get to the Fantome.

Chapter Twenty-Nine

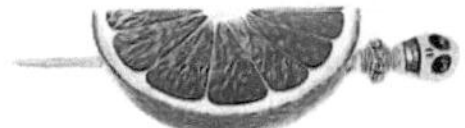

"What's going on?" Neil asked after I grabbed my bag and rushed the Bohemia Bartenders to the car. I told Mr. Mixy he had to come, too, or risk getting killed. I didn't know if he thought I'd be the one to kill him, but fortunately, he responded well to commands.

"Beau's back there, and we have to get to the Fantome," I told Neil as he pulled away from the curb. I grabbed my phone out of my bag and dialed Detective Colby. The phone rang and rang.

"What? You *saw* him?" Neil sounded half shocked, half angry, half concerned. OK, that's thirds, but whatever. He had at least half of each.

"I saw him. And look." I reached into the top of my dress and pulled out the cross.

"I thought your boobs looked weird," Mr. Mixy said from the back. "I know her boobs pretty well," he said to everyone else.

I shot him a dirty look as Barclay spoke. "That's awesome, but what's at the Fantome? What did Beau tell you?"

I held up a finger as Colby's voicemail came on. "Detective, it's Pepper Revelle. Beau Reed, I mean Moritz, is being held in Camelia Landry's guesthouse. She's got him chained up. But this is more urgent—she's on her way to the Fantome, and Beau said she's cleaning house. He said she's his boss, though I'm not sure what to believe. He suggested she's killing her partners in crime. I don't know what's going on, but we're going there to stop a bloodbath."

"We are?" Neil seemed overtaxed.

I put my phone in my bag, along with the cross. "Beau said Avani would be collateral damage and that her brother is a screwup. I don't know exactly what's going down, but we can't let her get hurt. We have to at least warn her."

"Try calling the hotel," Melody said from the second row. "See if you can get her."

"Good idea." I pulled the phone out again and dialed the Fantome. A voicemail came on that said all staff were busy and to leave a callback number, so I ended the call. "No answer, and I don't want to leave a message in case the wrong person gets it."

"How did Beau end up at Camelia Landry's?" Luke asked.

"He claimed Zeke shot him and then whisked him away from the naval base," I told him. "I don't know what her plans are. If he's right, is she just playing with her food before she takes a final bite out of him?"

"Ew," Melody said.

"Sorry," I replied.

We'd reached the edge of the Quarter. "So what's the plan?" Neil asked. "Seems to me we should, for once, let the cops handle this."

"We don't even know if they'll be there," I said.

"What happened to dialing 9-1-1?"

I raised my eyebrows at his question. "Valid. OK. They're going to think I'm a ditz."

"But they don't know you like we do," Luke teased.

I dialed the emergency number and tried to tell the dispatcher that we expected a crime to happen at the Fantome but couldn't tell her what. Exasperated in her pursuit of details, she finally said she'd send a squad car but they might not get there right away because of the huge crowds in the Quarter.

I saw what she meant as I stowed my phone again. Neil navigated through flocks of revelers at a crawling pace as we got closer to our hotel and the Fantome. The beautiful weather had drawn everyone out into the street.

"Here's what I think," he said. "We should not all go in there like the SWAT team. Most of you should wait in the lobby for the cops to arrive. Pepper and I will go in like we just want to have a drink and see if we can find any of the players."

"Really?" I was stunned he actually wanted me to go in.

"You're going to go in anyway. I want to be there to back you up. And I figure discretion is the better part of valor in this case."

Aw. Neil was going to back me up. "Thank you," I said. "I think that's a good plan."

He left his car with the valet at Hydrangea House, and we all walked next door and stopped just outside the Fantome.

"If anyone asks," I told the other bartenders and Mr. Mixy, "say you're waiting for our other friends before you go to the bar. Or waiting for a taxi. Just in case the person asking is one of the bad guys."

"But if it's the cops, send them in," Neil added.

I looked up at the sound of a familiar voice asking, "Are you finally off the clock?" It was Aunt Celestine and Astra, striding toward us with Royce, Mark and Diana.

"What ho," Mark said with a smile. "After-dinner drink? Or after-job drink?"

"Not exactly," I said as they joined our group. I explained the situation as quickly as I could.

"And you weren't going to tell me?" Aunt Celestine frowned.

"I'm telling you now."

"There's no chance we're waiting in the lobby," Mark said. "We're going in for a drink as well."

I rubbed one temple and sighed. "All right. But someone needs to stay in the lobby to talk to the cops."

"I will," Melody said.

"So will I," Luke was quick to add.

"I will too," Barclay said.

"And someone should stay outside to direct them. Mr. Mixy?" Neil suggested, to my relief.

Mr. Mixy, still tipsy, looked glad to have a way out of confronting potential killers. "Sure. I'll stand guard out here."

I handed my bag to my aunt. Her eyes widened as I told her, "The cross is in there."

She looped the bag over her head, cross-body, and patted it. "I'll take care of this."

"Good. Do you think they'll let you take Astra in there?"

A corner of her mouth lifted. "If you're correct, they have bigger problems than an adorable dog in their bar."

I smiled at Astra, whose eyes sparkled with excitement. Then I looked up at Neil. "Ready?"

Our group walked into the Fantome lobby as if nothing was wrong, though surely anyone with a decent sense of smell could sniff out my fear. That is, if they could smell it over the weird Fantome funk, which seemed particularly strong tonight. The farting ghost must've had a big dinner.

No one was at the reception desk. While Luke, Melody

and Barclay sat on a tufted bench, the rest of us entered the bar.

It was empty except for a guy slumped on a barstool, his elbows on the bar, his hands clutching a half-empty glass of beer. With his curly red hair, rosy nose and flowery purple jacket, he looked like a clown on his night off. He barely glanced at us as we all pulled up next to him and waited a moment.

"No bartender?" I asked.

"Haven't seen 'em for twenty minutes at least. Two of 'em went to the bathroom at the same time." He pointed toward the restroom hallway with a wavering arm. "Never seen 'em since. Shelf-shervice works for me," he slurred. He slid off his stool and stood, leaned over the bar to one of the taps, and refilled his glass. Then he settled back in place and took a long sip, leaving a cloud of foam on his upper lip.

"Have you seen a woman come through here?" Neil asked.

The man scrunched up his brow. "Maybe? Might've been a ghost. This place is haunted."

Neil and I exchanged a glance and moved away from the bar with the rest of the group so he wouldn't hear us.

"So where do we go from here?" I asked. "I still feel like I'm missing something. Like there's a reason Camelia was coming to the Fantome, and not just to mess with Jai."

"Does Jai live here? Maybe she went to the family living quarters," Neil suggested.

"Maybe, but if the bartenders were Jai and Avani, apparently they 'went to the bathroom' and never came back."

"That could mean anything," Aunt Celestine said. "Maybe they slipped out the back."

"Or they actually went to the bathroom. Or toward the bathroom." I pondered for a moment. "What if they went somewhere else, someplace *near* the bathroom? Millie told me there was a legend about tunnels under this place used for smuggling in the old days, but with the city sinking and the water table so high, it's unlikely tunnels survived if they ever existed. And I don't know about the half basement either."

"Half basement?" Neil asked.

I nodded. "Supposedly this place once had an excellent wine cellar they kept in a half basement."

Neil looked thoughtful. "Could there be remnants of that still around? The French Quarter has a pretty decent elevation compared with the rest of the city. Maybe that's where they went. Maybe they still use it for something. Maybe even wine."

"By 'they' you mean Jai and Avani?" Diana asked.

"Possibly," Neil replied.

"Beau implied Jai and Camelia were linked somehow," I said. "That Camelia was running some kind of criminal operation, including the real estate con. But Beau lies all the time."

"It's hard to imagine Camelia running a crime syndicate. It might be as real as the farting ghost," Neil pointed out.

A little spark popped in my brain. "You know, maybe it is real. The farts, anyway."

"Explain," Aunt Celestine said.

"Millie couldn't find any evidence of that ghost story being real—I mean, even of the supposedly real events involving the drunk, depressed writer. But the smell is real. I've smelled it multiple times. Maybe the ghost story is just a cover so people won't question the smell."

"But a cover for what?" Mark asked.

"I don't know." I pointed a thumb toward the restrooms. "But I smelled the funk pretty strongly in the hallway to the bathroom, the same hallway where the door keeps slamming."

"So did I," Royce said. "And that hallway is where Jai and Avani went, right?"

"If we can rely on that guy." Neil nodded toward the barfly.

A thrill of excitement ran down my spine. "Let's check the hallway. Maybe there's more to it than a slamming door. Maybe there's a draft from somewhere that makes that happen—a draft with the funk. We can follow our nose."

"I'll follow your nose," Neil said. "It's better than mine."

"Just a moment," Mark said. "Diana and I will look around for the family quarters, if there are family quarters. Maybe check in the office. See if your missing brother and sister bartenders are hiding somewhere else."

"Good idea," Diana said.

"Excellent." Mark smiled. "Diana says I had a good idea."

We laughed.

"Text me if you find anything," Neil told him. He pulled out his phone and tapped on the screen. "I'm texting Colby right now and telling him something's going down. Hopefully he'll send reinforcements."

Mark and Diana headed back out to the lobby. Royce and my aunt agreed to stay in the bar with Astra, though my pup whined as Neil and I walked toward the bathroom hallway.

I hoped my dog didn't know something we didn't. And that whatever we found didn't slam us the way the farting ghost always slammed the door.

Chapter Thirty

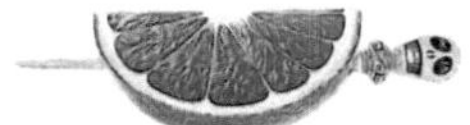

The door to the bathroom hallway stood open.

"Do you smell it?" I whispered as I led the way inside.

"I smell something," Neil whispered back.

The Fantome funk was more intense here than I'd ever smelled it. And it didn't smell like farts—more like that mold that formed on buildings downwind from the Kentucky distilleries. Maybe this hotel had a secret black mold problem.

We eased past the closed restroom doors toward the shadowy end of the hall, looking around.

"I don't see another door." Neil turned on his phone light and looked up and down. "Nothing above, nothing below."

"What about straight ahead? Does that paneling seem off to you?"

The rectangular wall panels in glossy dark wood, trimmed with molding, spoke of the historic nature of this building. They were perfectly aligned except for one at the end. I'd thought it strange that this hallway continued to nothing. But maybe this wasn't nothing.

Neil and I stepped forward. The panel seemed slightly bumped out on one edge. Could it be?

I reached out, slipped my fingers under the edge and pulled.

The panel opened by a few inches. A door!

And at the other end of the hall, the door slammed shut with a *BANG!*

"Drat," Neil said.

I couldn't help chuckling. "I love that word." It reminded me of the historical romances I liked to read. "I guess we've announced ourselves. But hopefully they'll blame the ghost. If 'they' are here."

"You ready?"

I nodded and pulled the door wider. A swirl of smells and dust tickled my nose, and I clamped a hand over my face to muffle a sneeze.

"Bless you," Neil whispered.

I kissed him on the cheek, and a spark lit in his eyes.

Then I surveyed our route.

A stairway descended in front of us, a short flight to a landing, where the stairs turned and disappeared out of sight. Dim light coming from the bottom made it possible to see, so Neil turned off his phone and pocketed it.

Before I could stop him, he'd gone ahead of me. Sigh. Always so gallant.

We reached the first landing and looked down and to our left. The stairs continued to another landing lit by a wall sconce. How many floors down did this go?

We descended to discover the stairs ended there. Was this one floor down or two? Or just a half—a half basement? A closed door awaited us at the bottom. It looked old. It even had an old-fashioned keyhole.

I crouched and looked through it. "It's kind of dim," I murmured. "I see shapes. Machines, maybe. And I hear voices."

"Boiler room?" He crouched and looked, too. "I don't see

anyone, and I can't make out what's being said. Let's go quietly. Hide behind the machines."

I nodded, turned the knob and pushed the door open. We paused there in the doorway, where we still had a chance of escape, assuming there was anything to escape from. A woman's voice echoed in the long, tall-ceilinged space, which was about the size of a small ballroom and enclosed by brick walls painted white.

Neil closed the door silently, and we moved forward, getting behind one of the big, dark shapes in front of us. It was a cylinder, made of shiny metal. I looked to the left. There, growing out of another cylinder, was a copper thing that looked like a giant finial. A pipe ran to another piece of machinery with vertical pipes. Small portholes and dials punctuated the tallest column.

Farther to our left was a stainless-steel vat, and the telltale yeasty odor of fermentation filled the air. Metal racks filled with small barrels lined the wall across the room.

I exchanged a quick glance with Neil, who grinned at me. A still! And it was steaming and gurgling. This was a modest distillery operation, and probably not a legal one. Beyond the gear, in the middle of the room, were irregular pyramids of boxes. They had all kinds of whiskey labels on them, real brands, most of them hard to get—some bourbon and a lot of rye.

The hum of the equipment prevented me from hearing the voices clearly. I gestured to Neil and scampered through the shadows down the row of machines to get closer. Then I hid behind a tall, deep metal shelving unit filled with glass bottles of varying shapes. He followed, and we stayed low. At the far end of the room, a ramp led up to a garage door that faced the street. Was that how they got the goods out?

At least now we could see who was talking.

Avani sat at an old wooden desk in the central open space next to the piles of boxes and a couple of filing cabinets. The desk held a laptop computer and a laser printer. Sheets of printed labels of varied design littered the surface.

Avani's posture was stiff in the desk chair, her hands clasped tightly together. She wore simple black pants and a white blouse and a shiny name tag, hotelier garb. Anxiety creased her brow. Her brother, Jai, stood nearby next to a tower of boxes in a patterned hipster button-up shirt, his arms crossed.

The siblings faced Camelia, still in her floral dress, now topped with a long, pink jacket. But despite her froufrou clothes, her face was hard.

"You couldn't get one thing right." She directed her venom at Jai. "Now the entire city is looking for a gun-toting Easter rabbit."

"How else was I supposed to get close to her?" he retorted.

I gripped Neil's arm. *Holy crap! Jai is the killer bunny!*

"Do you have the gun?" she asked Jai.

He nodded at Avani, who pulled open the top drawer of the desk, withdrew a handgun and nervously handed it to Camelia. When the older woman stuck it in her jacket pocket, brother and sister both seemed to sigh in relief.

"I don't understand why you wanted to off her anyway," Jai said. "She doesn't know anything."

"Maybe. Maybe not," Camelia replied. "But Beau's preoccupation with her was interfering with his work for me. Just as your little operation with Edgar Poeville was."

Jai's face shifted, and he held up his hands. "Now, I don't know anything about that. Whatever you're talking about."

"You thought I wouldn't notice? A few pills here and

there, no biggie, right?" Camelia stepped closer, and Jai tried to step back but bumped into the stack of liquor boxes, prompting the telltale clinking of bottles jostling one another. "Your buddie Alfie told me everything, because Alfie has a healthy sense of fear. This operation wasn't enough for you? It's more of a hobby for me, I'll admit, but I like the idea of making whiskey. My ancestors would have approved. We're selling plenty to the eager taters on the collectible market. As you know well, because you were skimming here, too."

"I was not! And I deserved it! This was my operation to begin with, and you know it. I was going to go legit." Jai didn't seem to realize he'd contradicted himself.

"We had a nice thing going," Camelia said. "And you had to ruin it."

"I didn't ruin anything!" Jai protested.

"Where is Beau?" Avani cut in, her voice trembling. Maybe she was trying to distract Camelia, but bringing attention to herself probably wasn't a great strategic move.

And what were we going to do? Just hope for the cops to arrive? Would they even know where to go?

Neil must've had the same thought, because he was trying to send a text. He shook his head at me and mouthed, "Bad signal."

Camelia was answering Avani's question. "Ah, Beau. He's in a safe place. Very snug. He's all tied up at the moment." Camelia cocked her head and smiled. "He's pretty, isn't he? You like that?"

Avani visibly swallowed. "I—I don't know what you mean."

"Don't you? I would have asked Beau to convince you to kill Edgar, but I was trying to send Beau a message—that Pepper Revelle was a distraction that he'd best leave alone.

This was one job I didn't want him to get involved in. And making you kill him was so satisfying."

"Avani?" Jai asked in shock. "You killed Edgar?"

"Because of you!" Avani snapped. "Ms. Landry said she'd let you live if I did it. Ugh—I had to steal the maid's key card and lure him up to that hotel room. I had to let him touch me, like he'd tried to do so many times before." She shuddered. "He was an ugly person. It could have ended there. But then you conspired with the crew to dip into the stash from the latest robbery, didn't you?"

"How do you—I mean, no," Jai said. "Of course not."

Avani looked at Camelia, then back at her brother. "She told me you did when she stopped by the hotel yesterday! She knows! And you had one chance to clear the debt, and you screwed that up too!"

"Do you know how hard it is to see out of a bunny head?" he asked helplessly as I tried to breathe. Neither of these two seemed like killers. Yet Jai had tried to kill me, and Avani not only seemed OK with his plan; she had killed Edgar.

"Why did you get involved with Ms. Landry in the first place?" she cried to her brother. Tears rolled down her cheeks as she looked from Jai to Camelia.

The older woman stepped even closer to Jai, whose dark eyes tracked her as if she were a tiger stalking her prey. She lay a hand on his cheek, then slid it down and rested it on his bare chest, in the open V-neck of his many-hued shirt. "Jai and I had an understanding." She grabbed a fistful of his shirt, pulled him to her and kissed him hard before releasing him. "And now I'm going to have to let you go."

She pulled the gun from her pocket.

Avani gripped the arms of the chair. Jai tried to back up.

"Stay put," Camelia said in a low, cool voice. "Or I'll kill your sister, too."

I didn't have time to think through my response. Why would I want to save the guy who tried to kill me? Maybe because I preferred he get justice the legal way. Maybe I felt pity for Avani. Or maybe I didn't feel like seeing any more corpses on this trip.

I put my hands against the shelves that held the bottles, glanced at Neil, and raised my eyebrows at him.

A bunch of emotions crossed his face in a microsecond, then finally, acquiescence. He nodded.

Three, two, one, I mouthed, and we stood up and pushed.

Chapter Thirty-One

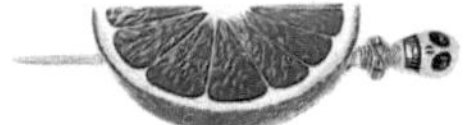

After our push, a long second passed in which I held my breath. The towering metal shelving unit twisted like a skyscraper in an earthquake, and then the whole thing fell forward in a mighty crash of bottles and metal.

Avani screamed and stood. Jai jumped back. In Camelia's haste to get out of the way, she tumbled to the floor amid the cacophony of breaking glass and avoided a direct hit.

Jai leapt forward and tried to grab the gun, but Camelia wrestled him for it. As they grappled, Avani realized they were distracted, saw Neil and I standing there, and bolted for the exit.

She'd gotten away, though now I had mixed feelings about her escape.

A moment later, I was sure I heard barking.

Jai came up with the gun, and Camelia climbed to her feet like a boxer who wouldn't let one punch keep her down. Slightly rumpled, she looked at me with venom in her eyes, and my blood froze.

"Shoot her," she said to Jai.

Jai turned and aimed the gun at me. But he hesitated. "Why bother? We can both get out of here." He didn't sound very convincing.

"Shoot her, or I'll track down your sister and kill her anyway," Camelia said.

Jai pivoted and brought the gun to bear on Camelia. "What if I shot you?"

"Do you think I'm the only person you have to worry about? Ha." Camelia ran her hands through her hair, straightening it after her fall. A sprinkle of sparkling shards fell to the floor. Her hands were speckled with red—blood from the broken glass. "You kill me, my soldiers will have you in the ground before dawn."

Man, she was scary.

Jai gulped and aimed the gun back at me.

"You don't have to do this," I said. "If she had an army of enforcers, don't you think one of them would've shot you already?"

"Of course not, Pepper," Camelia said with a malevolent smile. "I like to do the things I enjoy myself."

Neil made an incoherent sound of distress but didn't say anything. Maybe he was trying to tell me to be quiet, too.

"You have a chance," I told Jai. "You haven't killed anyone yet. You can inform on her. Make a deal." At least, that was what they did on *Law and Order.* Where the hell was Detective Colby?

"Pepper, what is it about you that men find so fascinating?" Camelia said as Jai's hand trembled. "Not that Beau was interested in you in that way. He just wanted to kill you." But strangely, Camelia's words held a note of doubt—doubt that must have fueled her jealousy, her desire to muck with my life. The very idea of Beau being interested in me in *that* way was almost more creepy than him wanting to kill me. I decided it was her imagination and nothing more.

"I have no idea why this handsome, talented guy here

would give you the time of day." She lifted her chin at Neil as I gritted my teeth. "I'll have you know I slept with your other boyfriend." She caught my look of puzzlement. "Mr. Mixy."

"Oh, dear God. You can have him!"

I could've sworn Neil snorted a laugh as Camelia's eyes narrowed to slits.

"Are you going to shoot her or what?" she asked Jai, sounding as if she'd lost her temper for the first time.

Jai held my gaze for another second, and I grabbed onto Neil—and pushed him away and out of the line of fire.

And Jai turned to Camelia and pulled the trigger.

CLICK.

Time stood still. Jai looked incredulously at the gun, then up at Camelia. Her mouth had formed a perfect *O* that slowly flattened and curved up at the corners.

Click. Click. He tried again, but nothing happened.

"Well, isn't this interesting?" Camelia said.

And then the stairway door burst open, and six police officers poured in, brandishing guns, followed by Detective Colby.

"Drop the gun! Down on the floor! Now!"

At their shouts, I dropped to the floor, and so did Neil, a few feet away from me. He gave me a stunned look, like he couldn't believe I'd pushed him away. Or that the gun hadn't worked. Or that I was still alive.

It took Jai a second, but he not only dropped the gun; he slid it toward the police and hit the floor amid the broken glass. Camelia just stood there with her arms crossed.

"I am not lying down in all this broken glass," she said. "These people tried to kill me."

"I think you mean you tried to kill everyone else!" I shouted from my spot on the floor.

"Pepper?" Detective Colby said.

"Ma'am, get down on the floor!" another officer said to Camelia.

The detective looked at me for a second, and at my fervent nod, he made a decision and addressed the closest officer. "Cuff Ms. Landry and read her her rights. We're going to take this downtown."

"Gun's empty," said another officer who'd picked up the weapon.

"What?" Jai and I exclaimed at the same time.

"Avani. She must have emptied it," her brother said as he was cuffed, too.

"Clever woman," I said.

Jai aimed his big brown eyes at me as he was yanked to his feet. "I'm sorry."

"Are you, though?" I figured he was more sorry that he'd been caught. And I had no patience left for another liar.

"You two can get up," Colby told Neil and me. "Give me the short version. Your phone message was garbled."

"I have an excellent lawyer who will make mincemeat of you," Camelia called to the detective on her way out.

"Yes, ma'am," he called back wearily as Jai was hauled off as well. Then he looked at me. "This had better be good."

I explained about Beau being locked up at Camelia's, about the pill operation and that they were making whiskey here, too.

"So it's bootleg booze?" the detective asked.

"Actually," said Neil, who'd been eyeing the desk while one of the officers opened the filing cabinets to find bag after bag of pills, "I think it's not just a bootleg booze and pill operation.

There are a bunch of labels here for different collectible whiskeys, rye and bourbon. I think they were flippers, but instead of selling real collectible bottles, they sold counterfeit liquors to collectors. Maybe they sold the whiskey outright, too. I don't know."

"Jai Joshi would know," I said. "He started the whiskey operation. His sister, Avani, escaped. She killed Edgar Poeville. Camelia blackmailed her into it."

The detective seemed bemused for a second. "Huh. Maybe Avani is the one who ran out through the courtyard. Your aunt said your dog almost took a bite out of whoever it was." Colby called over his shoulder to a blond female cop. "Moore! Take Mathias and search the hotel for Avani Joshi. Arrest her for the murder of Edgar Poeville. Call in and request an APB for her in case she flew the coop. And get them to send a car over to the Landry place to look for Beau Moritz. He's supposed to be chained up in the guesthouse."

"Kinky," Officer Moore said.

"And be careful with the butler or whatever he is," I said so Officer Moore could hear. "Zeke."

"Zeke," Colby echoed. "Uh-huh. What did Zeke do?"

"Beau said that's who shot him at Camelia's request," I said. "Over at the naval base."

The detective sighed. "I think you two should come downtown and make a statement. Your file's getting a little too thick for my liking, Ms. Revelle. Bombings, shootings, thievery—"

"I didn't do any of those things! And oh, yeah. I got the cross back. Beau had it."

"Nice," he said, a small smile touching his lips. "And now I'm finally going to get the man himself."

Chapter Thirty-Two

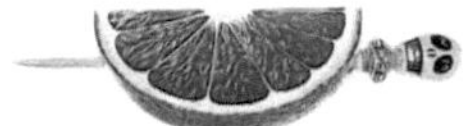

Detective Colby did not get Beau. No one did. The officers who raided Camelia's guesthouse found only an empty metal cuff—and Avani's hotel name tag. Which we learned during our seemingly endless brain dump at the police department so the detective could get our statements.

At last, we summoned a cab and headed back to the hotel.

"So Beau got to Avani, too." I rested my head on Neil's shoulder in the back of the cab. Even the party crowd had thinned out in the Quarter, it was so late. Or should I say early?

"She was a killer. Maybe she was more devious than she let on."

"Smart, yes. Devious when she had to be. But I think she was forced into it because she cared about her screwed-up brother."

"Maybe," he said, "but will she go on the run with Beau?"

"Don't remind me. He's still out there."

"But now he's probably on multiple most-wanted lists," Neil said. "Everybody's going to be looking for him. I don't think he has any reason to go after you now."

I lifted my head and looked at him. "Are you crazy? I left him there in chains. He's going to be pissed."

A corner of Neil's mouth lifted. "Well, yeah. But the feds are involved. Even Bohemia police will look for him now. With everybody on alert, the last thing he's going to do is come after you."

"I hope you're right."

Neil slipped an arm around my shoulders and kissed me lightly. "I'm right. I'm always right."

"I know," I said, and he laughed.

I AWOKE WITH AN UNSETTLED FEELING, not sure if I should be worried or happy. At least I got some sleep. The bedside clock said ten fifty-nine, and Diana's bed was empty. By this time of the morning, she'd probably written a research article on some plant she'd discovered growing between bricks in the French Quarter. Or maybe she was hanging out with Mark. The thought made me smile.

Ah, romance.

Oh, yeah. Romance! Neil and I were supposed to get a room together tonight. Could it actually happen? Would I finally see if he really had a tattoo? What weirdness would get in our way?

I was relieved that Easter was over. It wasn't like we were truly free of Beau, but those creepy poems of his had built up Easter Sunday as the scary culmination of all his threats. And in a way, it had been, only it didn't turn out the way anyone expected.

Now it was over, and we had a chance to have one normal day in New Orleans. If there was such a thing.

I took a shower and put on a clingy black knit dress with a flattering V-neck. Big coconut-shell buttons ran all the way down the front to where the hem fluttered above the knee. I added a little eye makeup, lipstick, my hot nerd glasses and bling, including my good-luck bracelet. It had not failed me—maybe because it had received a recharge from the voodoo priestess? Or maybe I was just insanely lucky.

I hauled my suitcase toward the elevator to meet Neil downstairs. I had my messenger bag, too. I wasn't sure how it got to the room I'd shared with Diana. Maybe my aunt had handed it off to my roomie.

On the elevator, I remembered the bejeweled cross. I felt around inside the bag, but it wasn't there. I tried not to worry. I'd text Aunt Celestine about it as soon as I got out of the cellular dead zone of the elevator.

But I didn't have to text. "Pepper!" my friends and my aunt called as I stepped out. Our whole group was there: Melody, Luke, Barclay, Diana, Mark, Royce, and Aunt Celestine. Mr. Mixy was gloriously absent, thanks to his celebrity appearance on a local radio station.

"Hey, guys!" I left my suitcase with the front desk so the staff could move it to the new suite and turned to greet them.

Astra, wearing a mercifully demure scarf, jumped up on her hind legs until I picked her up and gave her a cuddle. When I set her down, lots of human hugs followed, maybe because yesterday could have turned out so badly. I was really lucky to have these wonderful people around to support me.

"Hey, Aunt Celestine—do you have the cross?"

"No. Don't fret," she said to my aghast expression. "I visited your parents this morning, and we took it to a safety deposit box. We've also set in motion paperwork to have it insured. And your mother actually said a bad word or two about Beau."

I blew out a breath of relief. "All of that is good to hear, especially because, as of last night, Beau was still on the run."

"It's too bad I never got a chance to kick him," Aunt Celestine said. "Astra, stop eating that pillow!"

As my aunt dashed off to rescue the lobby upholstery, Melody sidled up to me. "Girl, that dress looks fabulous on you. What's the occasion?" Then her blue eyes widened. "Wait … is this the day—night—finally?"

"Shhh," I said, looking around. "I hope so. I really hope so. Where's Neil?"

"Not sure. He was here, then he disappeared."

A few minutes later, Neil showed up with a big bouquet of red, pink and yellow roses and handed them to me.

"Neil—these are beautiful. But why?"

He looked a little sheepish. And damn handsome in black jeans, blue shirt and dark patterned vest. "I thought we could start over. Pretend this weekend never happened."

"At least parts of this weekend." I inhaled the heady scent of the roses, then brushed his lips with mine. "These smell a lot better than the Fantome's ghost."

"Speaking of which," Mark said, "have you heard what's happening to the bootleg operation?"

Neil nodded. "Detective Colby told me this morning they'd shut it down. They're questioning Mr. Joshi, the hotel's owner, and he claimed he knew nothing about it. Who knows?"

"Poor guy," I said. "His kids got tangled in Camelia's web. You talked to Detective Colby this morning? Have they caught—"

Neil shook his head. "No Beau. But they found Avani. He abandoned her at the bus station and took her car. She was a wreck, apparently. She's in love with Beau, Colby thinks. But she told them everything. So did Jai. His testimony alone is going to make exoneration very difficult for Camelia Landry. And he's to blame for the farting ghost tale. He told it to Edgar Poeville as a cover story for the distillery smells."

"Seems a shame to liken distillery smells to farts," Royce mused. "I wish farts smelled that good."

"So why was Wilma Wells at Hydrangea House the day of the murder?" I asked.

"She told the detectives she was replenishing her tour brochures in the hotel's display of attractions," Neil said. "Total coincidence."

I left the splendid roses at the front desk with a request they be taken to our new room, then joined the crowd. "Where's lunch?"

"I don't care, as long as I get to Latitude 29 before the end of the day," said Neil. "I need a Mai Tai."

"We *all* need a Mai Tai. I'll make reservations for late this afternoon," Barclay said, "and I'll ask Cray to meet us there, too."

"And lunch is where Kirby's band is playing. They're going to let me sing a few songs." Melody beamed.

"And there's an outdoor courtyard for Astra," Aunt Celestine added.

Astra barked in joy. And I knew exactly how she felt.

"So. This is it." Neil gestured around him to the splendors of the eighth-floor suite. We were here. Finally. Alone. No body in the bed (I checked that first). We'd had a wonderful day of eating and drinking and walking around the French Quarter. I'd had a civil phone call with my parents, who were out of crisis mode, and a great time with my friends. No Beau. No psycho bunnies. Just fun.

We'd even run into Wilma Wells, just finishing up a tour, and spoke with her briefly. She'd resolved her dispute with Sierra Felt by offering to buy out Ghostville Tours. Sierra, who was overwhelmed by the debt Edgar had left behind, as well as the threat of a lawsuit that would break her, had agreed to become a guide for Wilma's expanded company.

And now—now, after visiting the bathroom, checking out the view from the balcony, sniffing the roses and watching Neil pop the cork on a chilly bottle of champagne, compliments of the hotel, I was nervous.

Why was I nervous? I'd wanted to get him in the mood for a year. He was here. We were officially sharing a room. I didn't plan to fall asleep anytime soon.

He held out a glass of champagne. I took it and drained half of it as I cast my eyes over him. He looked sharp in his blue and black outfit.

A corner of his mouth turned up. "You all right?"

"Me? I'm great. This is really nice."

He took a sip of his bubbly and stepped closer. "Are you sure?"

"I'm fine. Really."

"I mean sure about this. I thought this was what you wanted."

"It is. It is!" I took another sip. Oh my God. The glass was empty. I set it down. I'd already had a few drinks today, so this was about as relaxed as I was going to get. "Are *you* sure?"

Neil gave me a full-on smile then, his gray eyes twinkling. "I am."

"Can I ask you something?"

"Of course."

"Why did it take so long for you to be, um, interested?"

Mid-sip, he almost choked and set his glass down while he recovered. "Oh, Pepper, I've been interested since the moment I first saw you in that suite at Cocktailia. But you may be aware I'm a careful kind of guy—"

"I'm aware."

"I wasn't always that way. Not completely. You know how it is. Sometimes when you're a bartender, there are temptations ..."

No kidding. I was pretty sure I'd given in to more temptations than he'd ever even dreamed about.

"... and I've sown a wild oat or two. Had a couple of relationships that went nowhere. But I'm getting older ..."

Right. He was three years older than me, max.

"... and these days, I want more," he continued. "And I thought maybe, um—"

"Yes?" I was dying of curiosity.

"I thought maybe you just wanted me for my body."

A burst of laughter escaped me, and I clapped a hand over my mouth for a second as his eyebrows rose. Most guys would be thrilled to be wanted for their body. But not Neil.

"Of course I wanted you for your body," I told him. "But I had a wicked crush on you for all kinds of reasons that went way beyond the physical."

"You did?"

"I *do*. And everything about you makes it—something more. Your kindness. Your bravery. Your need to take care of everybody. That big, sexy brain of yours."

Now he laughed and stepped forward and slipped his arms around my waist. He leaned in for a deep, hot kiss that melted what was left of my mind. I clung to his neck, then sighed as he released me, still feeling the heat of his mouth, the tickle of his trim beard.

Neil topped off his glass and poured another one for me. "I feel bad about this weekend. This was supposed to be a romantic getaway."

"It will be." *As soon as I get another one of those kisses.* "Just —truncated."

"But I still want to make it up to you by taking you some-place absolutely magical."

"I'm listening." I took another sip of champagne.

"How would you feel if a job is involved?"

"Oh, no, not again!" I took a step back. "And I refuse to work for Mr. Mixy."

He grinned. "It's not Mr. Mixy. It's a friend of Mark's. But if you don't want to go—"

Mark, huh? Mark lived in London. Intriguing. "Where?"

He waved as if pushing the subject away. "Let's forget it. I don't want to make you work on our getaway. Mark says his friend needs us, and it might be for more than cocktails, since your name came up specifically. But we can do a simple weekend instead—in South Florida, maybe?"

His words were dismissive, but a smile played about his lips.

"WHERE?" I demanded.

He sipped his bubbly and stared at me, prolonging the suspense. "How would you like to go to Scotland?"

"Scotland? *Scotland?*" I couldn't help hopping up and down a couple of times, sloshing my drink. So I set it down and hippity-hopped a few more times. "Are you serious? Are you going to wear a kilt?"

Neil laughed. "Let's not get ahead of ourselves."

"Yeah, OK. Because there are a lot of things we need to do

before we progress to you in a kilt." I raised a flirtatious eyebrow at him. I wasn't nervous anymore. Neil was making my dreams come true.

"I'm not sure kilts are my style."

"They could be."

He set down his glass and stepped forward again. "I like your style. I like this." He traced my skin along the neckline of my little black dress, leaving a trail of tingles. His voice grew husky. "I like everything you wear. But I especially like buttons."

His fingers lingered over the top button. And then he popped it open.

I let out a little gasp. "I—I didn't know this about you. Why do you like buttons?"

He pressed his warm lips to my cheek. "Because you can open them as slowly as you want." He slid his mouth to my jaw before kissing his leisurely way up my neck. A hot thrill went through me as he murmured, "I like the anticipation."

"Yes," I breathed as his fingers slipped lower and loosed another button. "I noticed."

WHAT'S NEXT

Don't miss _Smoked by Scotch,_
Book 8 in the Bohemia Bartenders Mysteries, as Pepper
Revelle and her friends face silly celebrities, stone circles and a
sinister stalker during a gig that brings them to Scotland!

Want to get notified when the next book comes out?
Subscribe to my fun, occasional newsletter—and get a free
Bohemia Bartenders story—or follow me on BookBub or
Goodreads.

I also have a Facebook group where we hang out and chat
about life and books — please join us in Lucy's Lounge (answer
the questions to get in). And you can always find me at
LucyLakestone.com.

Read on for a look behind the scenes in the
acknowledgments and a cocktail recipe!

Acknowledgments

New Orleans on Easter weekend is a blast. The parades in this book are inspired by those I saw on a trip to the city, but any inconsistencies with reality are my own. As with the previous novels in the series, this one is set in a timeline parallel to our own, in which I did not introduce a pandemic. Thus are the glories of fiction.

The naval base in New Orleans is a real place, though I've taken liberties with its current status and condition. I was inspired by a few photos I took from the outside in the spring of 2023 and the interesting work of video bloggers who've toured the space. Even though the facility contains a theater and a gym, I've put the rooms near each other and added others at will in a layout of my own invention. And the condition of the base in my book may not reflect its state now. As I write this, its fate still hangs in limbo, though there are proposals for a complete redevelopment of the property.

I was also inspired by other real places in New Orleans. One is the delightful Music Box Village in the Bywater. It's really fun to go there and play with the musical installations. This structure inspired the one that met an unfortunate fate in this book.

The bejeweled cross obtained by Pepper's parents is inspired by a real piece once possessed by popes and then owned by several others, including daredevil Evel Knievel.

The real estate scam in Texas that Neil mentions is based

on a real case. I heard about it on the *FBI Retired Case File Review* podcast, in which Jerri Williams interviewed retired agent Richard Velasquez, author of *Texcot: Dreams, Lies and Fraud.*

I got a little of the flavor of New Orleans' criminal past—and the near-death of jazz—in Gary Krist's *Empire of Sin: A Story of Sex, Jazz, Murder, and the Battle for Modern New Orleans.*

Another great book that blends New Orleans history with cocktails is *Cure: New Orleans Drinks and How To Mix 'Em* by Neal Bodenheimer—proprietor of the wonderful NOLA bar Cure and others—and Emily Timberlake.

Mahalo to Jeff and Annene for their hospitality at Latitude 29 in New Orleans.

Cheers to Jeanne for another great adventure, chasing Easter parades around the French Quarter.

Thanks to my friend Tim Elliott for insight into firefighting practices. Any errors in my characters' strategy are my own.

Much love to the Harbaugh Literary Salon—Pam, Cathy, Kimberly, Annette and Billy. Thanks to Alethea Kontis for occasional writerly escapes from the daily grind. I appreciate the support and motivation of The Office writers. And a shout-out to my friends in Florida Star Fiction Writers who are boon companions on this journey.

For friendship and insightful feedback, I owe gratitude to Maria Geraci. And I am deeply grateful to Holly Martin for her wonderful editor's eye and steadfast support.

Special thanks to Karen, whose friendship has meant so much in the past year, and to Cathy T., who always checks in. You know how they say you find out who your friends are when times get hard? I treasure you.

To George: Thanks for being my travel buddy, best bartender, and everything.

And thank you for reading these mysteries and joining the Bohemia Bartenders and company on their adventures. They've become my dear friends, and I hope they are yours, too.

A MINT OF SPRING

One of my favorite New Orleans cocktails is the Bourbon Milk Punch (sometimes made as a Brandy Milk Punch). It's kind of like a boozy milk shake; in fact, some bars serve it frozen. I thought it would be fun to create a variation made with rye whiskey, given the title of this book. And to get a pretty pale green color in celebration of Easter along with a pleasant  flavor twist, I decided mint should be involved.

Well, the mint rich simple syrup (rich = double the sugar) I made was not quite green enough or minty enough for the cocktail, so I caved and used crème de menthe instead. Neil, of course, makes his own crème de menthe with fresh peppermint leaves, vodka, and simple syrup (sugar and water).

If you're virtuous, you can make your own crème de menthe, if you have a few days. The vodka and mint leaves have to hang out together for a while before you add the simple syrup and more mint. It's possible to get a nice green color with a homemade liqueur, though it's more likely to be a paler color. I won't judge you for adding food coloring.

I took the easy route and used a bright green store-bought version for this cocktail. A very small amount will give you both minty flavor and an ethereal pastel green color evocative of spring. It's a sweet addition to an already sweet cocktail. This is definitely a dessert drink.

Of course, you can make a traditional Milk Punch with rye *or* bourbon without the mint. Either way, it will be delicious. The milk smooths the corners of any zippy rye you might use, so if you want to judge the true character of your rye, may I suggest a Sazerac?

2 ounces rye whiskey
1/4 ounce crème de menthe
3 ounces whole milk
3/4 ounce simple syrup*
1/4 teaspoon vanilla extract
Garnish: nutmeg, freshly grated, and a sprig of mint

Measure whiskey, crème de menthe, whole milk, simple syrup and vanilla extract into a shaker with ice and shake until very well chilled. Strain into a rocks glass or other charming vessel. Grate a sprinkling of nutmeg over the top and garnish with a sprig of mint.

*SIMPLE SYRUP

This basic ingredient appears in many cocktail recipes, including the one above. You can use white sugar or make it more interesting with raw cane sugar or demerara sugar. And there are endless variations (including mint simple syrup) if you want to play.

Heat 1 cup of water and 1 cup of sugar in a saucepan over medium heat, stirring until the sugar is dissolved. Remove from heat. Store the cooled syrup in a glass jar with a secure lid for up to a month in the refrigerator.

BOOKS BY LUCY LAKESTONE

BOHEMIA BARTENDERS MYSTERIES

These funny mysteries star Pepper Revelle and a team of mixologists who travel to colorful events where life is a cocktail of fun — until it's shaken into madcap mayhem ... and murder.

RISKY WHISKEY

BAFFLED BY BITTERS - *story free to subscribers*

WRECKED BY RUM

VEXED BY VODKA

JIGGERED BY GIN

BEGUILED BY BOURBON

SHOCKED BY CHAMPAGNE

WHY OH RYE?

BOHEMIA BARTENDERS COCKTAIL COLORING BOOK

The **BOHEMIA BEACH** Series

Award-winning hot contemporary romance

In a beautiful small city on Florida's east coast, artists meet, create, laugh and love. Where restless hearts are fueled by secrets and imagination, romance is impossible to resist. Welcome to the seductive tropical escape that's home to drama, humor and lots of heat – Bohemia Beach.

BOHEMIA BEACH

BOHEMIA LIGHT

BOHEMIA BLUES

BOHEMIA HEAT

BOHEMIA NIGHTS

BACK TO BOHEMIA - *story free to subscribers*

BOHEMIA BELLS

BOHEMIA CHILLS

Bohemia Beach Series Boxed Sets:

Books 1-3 | Books 4-7

The **STORM SEEKERS** Series

Writing as Chris Kridler

FUNNEL VISION

TORNADO PINBALL

ZAP BANG

Storm Seekers Series Boxed Set: Books 1-3

About the Author

Lucy Lakestone is an award-winning author who lives on Florida's east central coast, among the towns that serve as an inspiration for the hot romances of her Bohemia Beach Series and the jumping-off point for the Bohemia Bartenders Mysteries. She's been a journalist, photographer, editor and video producer but prefers living in her imagination, where the moon is full and the cocktails are divine.

She also writes storm-chasing adventures as Chris Kridler, and in her spare time, she chases tornadoes.

Learn more at LucyLakestone.com

facebook.com/lucylakestone

instagram.com/mslucylakestone

amazon.com/Lucy-Lakestone

bookbub.com/authors/lucy-lakestone

goodreads.com/lucylakestone

pinterest.com/lucylakestone

youtube.com/@lucylakestone

threads.net/@mslucylakestone